UMBRA'S WINTER

Umbra's Winter

Fey & Fate
Book 2

ANDREA STANET

Dragonlight Press

Book design by Andrea Stanet
Cover art line drawing by Alla Rusyn

Dedicated to

My mom

and to the memories of

Marie Montrose
and
Susan Stanet

Acknowlegements

Many, many, many thanks to Bryan Walko for help with beta-reading and editing, and to my husband, Michael for being the best sounding board and for helping me wrangle all of the different threads in my mind into a coherent whole.

And thank you to everyone who has supported Dragonlight and the Fey & Fate universe. We could not have gotten here without you!

Contents

Prologue

I know how to count all the way to twenty, and I tick off the number of moonrises since I last found a meal big enough to fill my belly. Three. My tummy squeezes, and it hurts. The alley behind the food smells draws me in, and I rush to the giant, garbage bin, a dim light flickering over a closed door.

My body shakes. When I look at my hands, now covered in red, yellow, and green slime, the colors of my skin flicker between black, brown, tan, blue, white, red, and back again. The fingers become thick, then shrink to baby sized, then grow again until they're Mami's hands.

I miss Mami. She'll come find me and give me hugs and kisses until I giggle. Where is she? If only I had listened to the boy. He said to stay put next to the stream while he climbed a tree to pick the fruit at the top. *Hermano?* Brother? But high up among the leaves, he didn't see the boar. Its nose snuffled in the dirt. Piglets sniffed around behind her. Mami always said stay away from any animal with babies. Nothing presented more danger than a mother protecting her young.

Hide.

On quiet, bare feet I backed away from the water. Feet the color of night with tiny pink toenails, dirt caked underneath. One tree's wide trunk caught my attention. It looked strong. A good hiding place. It sparkled, as if the tree smiled, inviting me in. The knot on its side was just big enough for me to climb in.

The knot became a tunnel with a far-off bright light. Curious, I followed it to the end and climbed out. The forest flared. It hurt my eyes. All the trees gleamed, like the smiley one. Now it was too much. I searched for the stream.

It had disappeared. I spun again to return to the direction I came from. The tree with the knot... where did it go? I screamed, "Mami!" and suddenly, I found myself in the dark alley again, shaking and changing uncontrollably now. The knot in my stomach squeezing, more painful than ever.

Sliding the garbage open, I plunged my hand inside and pulled out some long, wet strings. A mushroom caught in the tangles. Whatever these things were, I had eaten them before and knew they wouldn't harm me. I shoved the handful into my mouth chomping and snuffling like that boar with her babies.

I didn't notice the man until he trapped me, too close to escape. And there was nowhere to run anyway. Dogs growled in the distance on the other side of the fence closing off the alley. They began to fight, snarling and barking and snapping. I couldn't see them, but they were close. Even if I could climb it and escape, I'd become their supper.

My eyes flicked to the door. Would anyone hear me behind it, and if they did, would they help?

"You hungry, little rabbit?" The scary man came closer and bent to my level on one knee. "Donny's got something for you." His hands rubbed together, and I thought he might be hungry as I was, or those dogs were, but not for food. I stepped away.

One of the dogs yelped, and my head swiveled toward the sound. I flinched. Then the man spoke and touched my hair. My breath sawed in and out of my body like when I ran for a long time. Words came from his mouth, but I couldn't understand anymore. My body shivered and shifted...

Like a miracle, the door opened. Loud music made me crouch and grab my ears. Another man came out, wiping his hands on a white cloth hanging around his waist. I couldn't see any other part of him with the light blazing behind him like the gods from one of Mami's stories. He said something to the first man, who growled—like the dogs. But he stood and left.

Relief shook me harder. The second man came closer, whispering, "Shh...shhh... you're okay now."

Chapter 1

Rebus's voice changed to Dúl's. "Shhh... Umbra, it's okay." Strong, familiar arms tightened around me, rubbing circles along my back. "You're fine, love. Just a dream."

A moan escaped my lips, and I realized I must have woken him. Again. The dreams came more often now since I had started drinking an herbal concoction before going to sleep to help me retrieve my memories.

"The same dream or something new?" Dúl pulled me closer and cradled me to his chest, lips butterfly soft against my temple.

I cleared my throat of its morning gunk. "Some new details. An older boy in the dream. I don't remember what he looked like, but I think he was my brother or something. He left me alone for a minute, and a wild boar frightened me into hiding in some tree that took me to the Summer Court. And our accents sounded Spanish."

"That narrows things down considerably. Did you dream of Donny again?"

"Yeah, and Rebus. That night. Plus, one other

different thing. Before I crossed into the Dreaming, I got a glimpse of my skin. You know before all the shifting took over. It was very dark, like ebony. I think that's my natural skin tone." It was a few shades darker than I normally wore, but not by much.

"Works for me, love." Dúl hooked a finger under my chin and planted a soft kiss on my lips. It didn't remain gentle for long as we both pushed the bad dreams aside and fell into a much more satisfying place.

~*~

Later, I traced my fingers along the contours of Dúl's shoulders as he bent over the black concave glass in his lap. Seated between my legs, he leaned back against me. His bare back rose and fell against my chest. He sighed. I slid my hands down his arms and then hugged him. His bed-messy hair tickled my cheek.

After spending these past weeks waking up in the Dreaming next to the King of the Shadow Court, I knew that sigh. It wasn't the contented one he made after we'd untangled our sweaty, sated bodies from each other. Nope, this was not a happy sound.

"Problem?"

"Yes. I don't know. Perhaps. I can't fathom what she is up to."

An image moved across the glass of an old woman with crinkly, white hair streaming down her back. She stood straight and strong. A complex web of lines crisscrossed her face. I didn't understand what he saw, but then again, Nemesis wasn't my sister. Dúl knew her almost as well as he knew himself.

"She's talking to a nasty, hairy spider. I'd find that weird if it weren't for the fact that you spend plenty of time talking to ravens. What are you picking up that has you so worried?"

Dúl didn't answer for several seconds while he watched. His sister stroked her bottom lip and smirked, clearly amused or pleased at the report she heard. "She's smiling."

"Umm...okay. That's weird why?"

He turned his head to frown at me, his forehead slightly wrinkled. I tried to caress the stress away from his brow.

"No, love. My sister never smiles. Not even as a child. She's not behaving like herself. First, she wouldn't speak with me when I went to her lands. And now, she looks like someone about to eat the world for breakfast."

My thumb found his bottom lip, and I forced my mind away from how badly I wanted to kiss him. "Well, you said yourself, she might have been angry that you went to see Athena, right?"

"Merc, love, Nemesis is always angry about something. Nothing has ever stopped her from speaking with Orion or me. Not even our relationships with Athena. We may hate each other on the surface, but beneath the petty fighting, we are still siblings. Why do you think we haven't killed each other yet?" A smile that bloomed on his face, so sad that my own eyes prickled.

"I'm sorry, *mi amor*." Her refusal to talk to him had hurt him more than he had let on until now. "Something is obviously, wrong. I can look into it for you."

"No. You've got your hands full from what I hear." Now his grin became lopsided. The expression always made my insides melt, and I regretted that I needed to leave his bed to head to work in the Waking.

"Ugh. Please don't remind me of what you got me into. I have a meeting this morning with the senior ops. That's always fun. I think they're worse than their underlings."

I gazed out the huge glass balcony doors overlooking the Shadowland horizon. It amazed me that I had any sense of the time of day. The balcony railing shimmered with a thin layer of frost. The oaks and maple trees had shed most of their brightly colored leaves. The heavens were always the same purple and blazing orange of sunset, with hues and constellations changing only slightly according to the time of year.

Dúl's bed faced the balcony so that when he woke, he could see the sky. To the left of the bed, a huge chest of drawers stood next to the exit leading to the rest of the castle. My own suite of rooms, in another wing of the castle, gathered dust.

When we first met, Dúl pretended to be the King's liaison in order to get close to me. He hired me for a rescue mission that ended up uncovering a massive move by the vampire nation against the fey courts.

Once he revealed his true title and status, he offered me the job of a lifetime.

One day I had been a mercenary, specializing in saving changeling kids—human/fey hybrids—from the clutches of vampire drug dealers synthesizing designer drugs using fey blood. The next day, Dúl ritually transferred some of his shadow powers to me and named me the head of his surveillance/security network, the Shadows. The title granted me all kinds of power in the court and a cushy job in the Waking. Everything should have been perfect.

Between us, things *were* perfect. I had never been happier, certainly not with my drug-addicted ex, Paris. But the vampire threat still hung over our heads, Dúl was worried about his sister's suspicious behavior, and then there was my job.

I'm the boss, and if I do say so, damned good at what I do. But my staff hadn't read that memo yet— the Anton situation all over again.

Anton was a fullblood from the Dawn Court who was part of my team when we rescued Morgan— Dúl's second-in-command, technically his fiancée— from the vamps. He didn't trust my leadership. To be fair, I hadn't either. He refused to follow my plan. His alternative went badly, and he paid the price for both our mistakes with his life.

Now, I needed to get my Shadows in line before something big came up. Dúl and I both felt it. Some- thing big—a more dangerous threat than the vampires —threatened the fey. Whether Nemesis was making a play to control the Dreaming or if the vampires were increasing the stakes, I needed to be sure the Shadow Court was prepared and defended.

"I warned you in the beginning, the Shadows have always been unruly," Dúl said and waved a hand over the scrying glass to clear the image. "If they become too troublesome—"

"No, I've got it. If you get involved, I'll just look weak. In fact, I have to get to the office. But I hate to leave you so upset." Now that his lap was clear, my leg swung around, and I straddled him. Nothing but thin underwear separated our skin. The bed tempted us both back between the sheets.

I couldn't help but to wrap my arms around his neck and kiss him deeply. He perked up almost instantly, and I groaned. "You could order me to stay, you know. *Your majesty.*" I nibbled his earlobe and reveled in the sensation of stubble against my cheek.

In response, he gripped my ass with both hands and squeezed us closer, with a moan of his own. "As much as I would love to..." He paused, bent me backward, and brought my left nipple into his mouth, right through my black tank, teasing with his tongue, making me writhe against him. My nails dug into his shoulders until he broke contact. "Unfortunately, we both have pressing responsibilities today."

In sync, we brought our foreheads together and sighed, as if we shared one mind. Ever since he infused me with his power, we had an uncanny sense of each other. Inklings of when the other was happy or hurting, even when we were separated.

God, I love him.

His face lit up as if he heard me, and I sensed he had the same thought about me.

"I know. Okay, no more teasing. But seriously, are you sure you're okay about the whole situation with Nemesis?"

"Fine, love. Either she's working through something that's causing her not to act like herself, or she's plotting a coup of the Dreaming. If the former, I'll give her space and hopefully, she'll snap out of it. If the latter..."

He didn't have to say it. The only choice would be for the siblings to eliminate the threat, even if it came from their sister.

We got dressed. I took my time partly because I know he enjoyed watching me, but also because I liked watching him just as much. Today, charcoal pin-striped trousers covered black boxer briefs, draping beautifully over the curve of his rear. A gray and black tie secured the collar of a black shirt that hugged his lean muscle in the most appealing way.

I dressed up more often now from my former uniform of black pants and a black tank top. Today, my usual caramel skin tone accompanied long, kinky coils pulled back into a ponytail. I wore black wool leggings, a heather-gray cable knit tunic, and knee-high boots. Dúl's gleaming leer suggested he approved.

Dúl came over and fingered a lock of my brown

curls, one of my features he enjoyed the most. His other arm slipped around my waist. "Your place or mine tonight?"

I rented a one-bedroom apartment in Yorktown that I hardly used, but I liked having it just the same. "Why don't we stay at my place? The change of scenery might be good for you. Get your mind off things for a while."

"Good idea. Send a message when you're ready."

By message, he meant to summon a raven, which I could now do with a mere thought thanks to him.

I nodded and kissed his full lips, losing myself in their softness and warmth.

"I love you, Umbra."

My birth name on his tongue sent a shiver through me. "I love you too. See you tonight."

When I neared the portal near the balcony doors, he said, "And love?" I turned to see what he wanted. "Watch out for those Shadows." As the room faded, his crooked grin disappeared last.

Edge of Winter

"He watches, your highness." The disembodied voice hissed from the darkness.

From the castle gate, the Queen gazed into the snow-covered forest around her. All was silent except for the occasional howl of a wolf pack on the hunt.

"Yes, *Lemooria*. His shadow floats over the land, undetected. Or so he thinks. The Shadow Lord will learn that soon enough that he isn't the only one who can command the darkness."

Pity. Of the others, Dúl had been the only one to show true promise and vision. The only one capable of the ruthlessness and focus necessary to achieve his ambitions.

The others allowed emotions and blood ties to bind them. Not the Master of Shadows. At least not until Umbra distracted him.

"And what of the other complication, highness? When will you reveal the truth to Merc?"

"Patience. Umbra has a role to play too."

A sizeable role at that.

The shifter with no memory—would the truth hurt

them and their relationship with the Shadow King? Love doesn't always survive when secrets are revealed.

The Queen couldn't suppress a smile that revealed sharp fangs. The fallout from her scheme would be delicious.

Aftermath

A few weeks ago...

Near a pier along the Jersey Shore, a black luxury sedan pulled up facing south next to an identical car facing north. Both engines quieted. The rear window of the southbound vehicle slid down as the driver's window of the northbound car did the same. Two men, both in dark shades and baseball caps, spoke to each other, neither turning to look at the other. At nearly 1:00 AM, plenty of people still roamed the boardwalk, even in these winter months.

Southbound said, "It's confirmed. Don is out. The Hudson Valley family is in chaos. It's like those numb-skulls can't wipe their own asses without step-by-step instructions."

"Pop told him not to screw around with those vampires."

"Word is he gave them up. Your father says he got what he deserved. But that shifter..."

"That shifter has been a problem for our business for years, losing us money even before the vamps." Northbound took a drag on a silver vape pen and blew out a cloud of smoke. The air smelled of marijuana. "So, what does he want me to do?"

"We can't have a power vacuum in any of our territories."

"I have my own business here."

"Then send someone. But I would have expected you to want to avenge your little brother."

Northbound laughed. "And start a war with the vampires? Nah. No thanks."

Southbound paused. His car started up. "Not with the vamps. Go yourself or send someone. Don't matter. But someone needs to put things in order up there." His window rose. The tint completely obscured the driver. The car continued on its path.

"Fuck." Northbound rapped on the privacy screen and then closed his own window as they rolled away from the pier.

~*~

Paris stared at the wall after Merc left, ignoring the bills they had scattered around the room. He wasn't even in the mood to go get high. None of this was worth a damn—not Merc, not the drugs, none of it. Why had he tried so hard to have a decent life anyway? What made him believe he could work at RavCorp? He should have just given up long ago.

Back when *she* abandoned him.

Naori was born in the Dawn Court. As soon as she reached adulthood in the Dreaming, she emigrated to the Waking and became an FBI agent. "I would have done well in the Shadow Court," she used to tell Paris. "But they were almost as annoying as the Dawn Fey."

"Can you take me there, Mama?" six-year-old Paris would ask as he snapped peas into a bowl. "I want to see the Dreaming."

"Perhaps someday. Your father..."

Was not welcome there. He'd been to the Dreaming, of course. Paris had heard the story dozens of times. Once upon a time, a lovely fey met a charming human soldier stationed in South Korea who wandered into the Dreaming.

In the beginning, Naori's parents were hospitable but didn't approve once her acquaintance with the human resembled something more. They forbade the two to see each other. The human had no option but to return to the Waking. Naori returned with him against their wishes.

She thought they might forgive her after a few human years after their grandchild was born. Paris was in preschool when she tried to take him home to meet her family.

Servants bowed deeply when they greeted their former mistress and her changeling son at the door.

A scowling fey appeared and shooed the servants away. He glared at Paris's mother before scolding her. "You dare to return here with this creature and don't even bow to show the proper respect?" Was this his grandfather?

It was the only time Paris ever saw his mother bow to anyone. "*Abeoji*, this is my son. I thought—"

"You thought you could bring this half-breed here and raise him as one of us? I said that human was beneath you." Cruelty rolled off the man in waves.

Paris whimpered and tucked himself behind his mother. He didn't know his father's parents either. He'd been so excited to finally be able to say he had a grandfather like the other children at school. Pain ripped through his young chest. Only many years later would he recognize it as the breaking of his young heart.

Naori straightened and shielded him behind her. "He is your blood, Father."

"He is tainted. If you insist on keeping him here, he can make himself useful with the servants."

"Father!" She took a deep breath. The hand she had on Paris balled into a fist. "Where is Mother?"

"She will not come out to speak with you unless you come alone and beg her forgiveness."

Naori fell silent, then turned to lift Paris onto her hip. "I'm sorry, my love. This was a mistake." They left and trudged back to the portal. Back to the Waking. Paris never asked about the Dreaming or his fey family again.

His mother changed after that day. Paris didn't realize it at the time, but now looking back, that was when things started to go wrong with his mother. It never helped that his father would come home, grease stained and crabby after long days fixing cars. As his mother became more distant, his father drank and shouted more.

One night when Paris was in the fourth grade, he heard them fighting.

"I don't need this, Thomas! I gave up a good life for you. I work my ass off, and all I get in return is a drunken, stinking, weakling!"

You have me, Mama. You have a son.

"You're full of shit, Naori! You hated the Dreaming. Your father is a tyrant. But be my guest. If you think it's so much better there, get the fuck out!"

Paris's heart stopped as he remembered his grandfather's words. "Servants... Come back alone." *No, Mama! Don't listen to him.*

One day, she did. The bitch left him. Ashamed, he concocted a story of her dying from a drug overdose.

Now, Merc left him... Well, he'd show them. He'd get back at the fey and at Merc too. Paris would show them that he was no one to cast aside. Not without consequences.

Chapter 2

After the portal landed me in RavCorp's Manhattan office garage, I detoured to the corner café. With my large orange-and-white cup, I rode the elevator to the top floor of the lower West Side building made mostly of glass. At the surveillance and security corporation owned by the Shadow Court in the Waking, my office had a cozy sofa, warm lighting, and photos of ravens on the walls. Instead of heading there like I wanted to, I went straight to the second-floor conference room.

Dozens of fullblood fey gathered around a long rectangular table. The building and all its rooms could grow or shrink like Dúl's office had the first time I'd been here. It was like working in the TARDIS. The chair at the head waited for me along with a large cardboard box on the tabletop. I fake smiled at the Shadow Senior Operatives—SO's or operatives for short—and sauntered to my seat. They all stood, waiting.

I sipped my coffee before sitting, flaunting my ties to the human world, and surreptitiously checked the chair for any sign that it was an illusion. Someone had pranked me a few days ago with a non-existent chair.

"What's in the box?" I slurped, eyeing the sides and top of the object.

Of course everyone feigned ignorance, looking at their neighbor. Finally, one of the bigger SO's, a redhead named Tynan cleared his throat and spoke up. At least one of this group had some balls.

"Mistr...Chief, it was waiting here when all of us arrived. We have no idea what's in there. Perhaps a gift from his majesty?" His voice dripped with honey, but al least he corrected himself to my preferred title.

"Hmm...I somehow doubt that."

I held my composure although inside I was burning up. The juvenile pranks, always in a public forum, pissed me off. Short of firing them all, I didn't know what to do about it.

Running to Dúl made me look weak and reinforced their ideas that I hadn't earned the position. Flipping out was behavior as immature as theirs. Unfortunately, they had closed ranks, so I couldn't isolate one or two troublemakers. I suspected at least one—the only one who had spoken up, his implied challenge delivered and received, loud and clear.

How could I play this? Not opening the box implied fear while opening it would certainly lead to some type of humiliation. At least they didn't catch me off guard. This time.

After one more sip to steel myself, I set my cup down, propped one foot on the chair and withdrew my dagger from my boot. Old habits. Carefully, I slit the seal.

In an instant, a swarm of ravens flooded out of the box, as if a portal to a raven dimension opened at the bottom. More birds than could fit in ten boxes filled the room, circling my head, cawing wildly.

At first, I ducked and covered my head, purely on instinct. Then I remembered that I didn't have to be afraid of ravens. I was the freaking Chief of Shadows!

"Quiet!"

The birds, as one body, found places to land. It amused me to see that some landed on the heads of the SO's.

I pointed to one of the ravens at the front of the sizeable flock. "You. Why are you here? I didn't summon you."

It hopped forward and squawked at me. *Called. Emergency signal. Trapped until you free us.*

"I see. My apologies. Someone thought it would be funny to pull you all away from your work. You may return to what you were doing."

The raven dipped its head in a birdie bow, cawed, and took flight back into the box. The rest followed. A few black feathers on the table left the only sign they had been there.

The operatives stood and stared, open-mouthed. Only one—Tynan—smiled. I sat and took another sip of coffee to control my voice before speaking. I was fuming but would be damned if I would give them the satisfaction of showing it.

"I believe you all have reports to deliver. Let's get this over with. I have a busy schedule today."

After the meeting ended, I returned to my office, shut the door, and plopped down on the couch. I then picked up a thick pillow and screamed until I was out of breath.

~*~

A little while later, stretched out on my office sofa, I contemplated the punishments I would rain down on my staff's heads. Someone tapped lightly at the door and entered before I could invite them in. I didn't need to look up to know who it was. I covered my face with the pillow.

"Oh. Poor Merc. Are the mean fey bullying you again?" Morgan's tone was mocking, and a month ago, I would have thought she was just being a bitch. Well, she was, but not as bitchy as she had been. It was kind of a default for her. At least now it was less of a personal attack.

Morgan had been much worse when I rescued her from the vampires, holding a grudge against me for something I had done as a child, which I hadn't even remembered. She was slowly getting over it. We weren't friends but found that we could work together for the good of the company and the court.

"Not in the mood for your sarcasm, Morgan. Is there something you wanted?"

"No, I simply expected that if you are going to act like a petulant child, that would be the appropriate way to address you." Footsteps thumped across the carpet toward my desk opposite me. The wheels of my desk chair rolled for a moment, and then the springs on the chair creaked. *Sure. Just make yourself comfortable.*

I lifted the pillow, glanced over, then regretted it. Dressed to kill as usual, she had on a black three-quarter-length pencil skirt with a deep slit in the front and a matching Victorian-style jacket that accentuated her tiny waist. A lacy black blouse under the jacket, both open to reveal generous cleavage, added a vintage, goth vibe.

The blouse made me pause. It was frillier, softer than I'd ever seen her wear. I pushed the thought aside. "You're calling me a child when those guys are the ones playing stupid pranks. Maybe you have your definitions mixed up."

"You're the only one I see sulking. Licking your wounds. If you think they don't see it as clearly as I do, you are sadly mistaken."

The words crossed the space between us and hit their mark. I gritted my teeth and silently cursed her for probably being right. "I was just calming myself down. I'll handle it."

Morgan crossed her legs and leaned back, perfectly manicured nails tapping her chin. I wanted to rip the lace-up boots—probably designer—off her feet.

"I'm certain you will. My guess is you're planning all manner of nasty revenge. What will you do? Make them run up and down the stairs until they fall over in exhaustion? Have them submit ten-thousand-word reports on the dangers of interfering with the ravens?

Perhaps you can fire them all and build the Shadow Network from scratch."

None of those sounded like bad ideas to me. I had been thinking more along the lines of tarring and feathering with molting from the main aviary on the building's roof.

"So, what, you think I should just be the bigger person and let them keep coming at me?"

She smiled then—a tiny bend of the lips that I still wasn't used to seeing. "Of course not. Merc..." Morgan got up, pushed the chair next to the sofa, and sat again, leaning in toward me.

I pushed myself upright and fixed my hair and sweater.

"Umbra, on a mission and if you came across your objective sitting out in the open, what would you think?"

"I'd think, *trap*." I had been in that situation when I first went looking for her. We thought she had been abducted by the Dawn King, Orion. When I got to the site where Morgan was allegedly being held, I found no guards, and the path to the building looked clear. Instead, booby-traps dissolved everything they hit into water.

"Of course, you would. Because the easy route often leads to more trouble than it's worth. Nothing worthwhile comes easily."

I hated that she made sense, and I hated myself for the warm feeling that filled me at her choosing to advise me. She could have just left me flailing around trying to figure out how to make these fey and changelings respect me as their leader.

"So, you think I should just ride it out? Pay my dues and they'll eventually stop?" Genuine curiosity smoothed the edge from my words.

Morgan laughed. "Oh no. They can keep this up ad infinitum. You have to gain their respect. Punishment won't work, however. Not for you."

"Why not?" My voice rose an octave.

"Dear child, I rule by fear because that's what works for me. But I've had many ages to build a reputation for being cruel and heartless."

"You're not—"

"Finish that sentence, and I will rip your tongue out through your ear. I am absolutely what the court thinks I am when I need to be. They need not know otherwise. You, however, are not intimidating."

I considered feeling insulted, but her point was more interesting. Still, I muttered, "I can intimidate when I want to."

A glare shut me up, nicely illustrating what she had just said.

"They don't know what to make of you, Merc. For all their rowdiness, the Shadows are like a family. You're their favorite brother's new girlfriend who's displaced the 'ex' they've grown used to, even fond of. By appearance, you only have your position because of your relationship with the King, and for all they know, you care nothing for them or the court at large. You have to show them you've earned your place here and that you're here for the entire court, not just your lover. Punishing them won't accomplish that."

The woman made sense. "So how do I prove myself to them?" It rankled that I should even have to.

"That I can't answer. Take heart. They're testing to see what you're made of. Some of the Shadows do believe in you."

My unsettling dream returned to me, and I told Morgan about the memory of Rebus finding me. "I guess if he managed to win me over when I was living like a wild beast, anything is possible."

"You became part of *their* family. How did he and Natalie accomplish that?"

I considered. "Relentlessness." A chuckle escaped me. "Always there, especially whenever I tried to bolt, but not in my face. Just visible. Nat was a comforting presence that I kind of gravitated to after a while. Rebus would have one eye on me while he worked on his projects. Eventually I got curious. As soon as he saw that opening, he started to teach me, and I was hooked."

"Well, it seems like you have the beginnings of an answer. What I can tell you is this—

work for the respect of the few whose allegiance you almost have, and the rest will follow suit in time."

I lay back down and absorbed her wisdom. After a moment, I turned my head toward her. "I feel like I'm on a shrink's couch."

"Don't get used to it." She slid out of the chair and sashayed toward the door. "The only reason I'm here is that all these pranks are making a terrible mess. There are bird droppings on the conference table."

I covered my mouth with one hand to stifle a laugh. She frowned and rolled her eyes.

"Thanks for the help, Morgan."

Without another word, she left and shut the door behind her.

Chapter 3

I followed Morgan's advice. For a few days, I watched for any sign of trustworthiness in my staff and formed a plan. I'd choose a squad for an easy mission and let those few get to know me. A little. Then maybe the word would spread that I know what I'm doing.

And when I don't, I'm an expert at winging it.

Then a better idea came to me. I called a mass meeting in the auditorium on the building's ground level. Every Shadow working for RavCorp was expected to attend, including those traveling out of the country and those in the Dreaming. It only crossed my mind that this could fail epically when I stepped up to the podium and saw all the blank expressions waiting for me to say something brilliant.

I'd settle for something not stupid. "Good afternoon. Those of you who came from a long way off, I appreciate your punctuality. I'll keep this brief as I know everyone is busy."

No reaction so far. The room was dead silent. I gripped the podium with both hands and cleared my throat. "I called you all here because I want to make an announcement."

"You're quitting?" a random voice shouted from the audience. A wave of laughter rolled through them. Suddenly the blank stares became expressions of hope.

My heart sank, but I plastered on a fake smile and scanned the room. One or two Shadows waited patiently, neither laughing nor sneering. I briefly held the gazes of those few.

"Not today, but if you show yourself, I promise if I ever do leave, you'll be the first to know." I kept my tone light and willed my skin not to flush with color. Sometimes being a shapeshifter is more than a blessing.

There were some chuckles and a couple of "Ooohs."

When they settled down, I said, "As you know, the vampire lab up north is still functional. Since freeing Morgan was our primary mission last time, we didn't destroy the building. It's been quiet up until now—biding their time, regrouping I expect. But we've gotten reports of some minor activity in the last two days.

"By the end of next week, I'm going to hand pick a squad of elite individuals who I think have what it takes to face the vampires. Anyone interested can see my assistant. I'll contact those eligible.

"However, understand this. While the place isn't exactly crawling with vamps now, they are no less dangerous in small numbers. Only the best—meaning, among other things, those who can follow orders—will be considered.

"Once we take down the facility, the next order of business will be to destroy the head vampire and remove that threat once and for all. Any questions?"

A couple of the Shadows seemed to consider. I noticed Tynan, the fullblood from the raven incident, studying me closely. If I wasn't misreading, he looked interested. *Good to know.*

When no one raised a hand or spoke out, I ended the meeting. It had gone better than I expected. No rotten fruit. No pig's blood raining down from the rafters. All I had to do was wait to see if anyone took the bait.

Over the next few days, I made sure to be more visible in the office. That was to hide the times I shifted into other forms so I could walk, camouflaged, among my Shadows and observe them.

One day, I roamed the halls of RavCorp as a plump, older gentleman, stooped and balding, who never seemed to be in quite the right place. I learned about a changeling named Cari—a champion kickboxer who lived in Connecticut.

Another time, a particularly blustery afternoon, I posed as a homeless woman seeking warmth between the inner and outer glass doors of the building. Under layers of threadbare coats and a raggedy blanket, I dozed against a shopping cart full of bags, newspaper, cardboard, and spare clothes. I had to hope that no one noticed the good condition of clothing. At one point, a raven messenger had to tell the security guards not to call the police.

That exercise provided lots of useful intel on my Shadows. For spies, they could be really damned unobservant.

Another potential squad member crossed my path. Maurizio, better known as Riz, defended me against a couple of his friends who mocked my ability to lead a team against the vampires.

He was the only one who glanced at my homeless woman disguise more than once.

The final surprise came when I was heading to the Dreaming on a Friday evening. With her coat on, my assistant, Danica, rapped at my office door.

"One of the SO's is requesting to see you, Chief. I told him to come back Monday, but he insists it will only take a minute."

"Yeah, sure." I bent over my laptop and started the shutdown sequence. When I heard the door open, I said, without looking up, "I'm meeting the King, so I suggest we make this fast."

"Fine by me, Chief."

A six-foot-three body of solid, lean muscle filled the doorway.

I stood up to my current 5'8" just for the sake of making myself feel better. "Oh. Hi. What can I do for you? Tynan, right? If you're planning to prank me again, I meant what I said about the King."

"No. I'm here to submit my name for your team." His

accent sounded slightly Irish or Scottish—I couldn't tell the difference.

"Um...I'm a little shocked. Why would you want to go on this kind of mission with me? I thought the consensus was that I don't deserve my position. 'Idiot' is the word I think I've heard most often."

"You've never heard it come out of my mouth."

"Right. You just laughed and let me open a box of pissed off birds."

He smirked then and reached up to scratch the red stubble of one cheek. "True, but my...colleagues have come up with some funny..." He must have realized I wasn't smiling, because he changed course. "Your handlin' of the ravens impressed me. The others yapped about it for days. No one expected you could talk to them."

After watching him with his eyes staring at his beat-up Chuck Taylors, I invited him in to sit.

I took the seat across from him and held his gaze. "I can do a number of things no one expects."

"You mean like shifting into ridiculous forms to spy on your staff?" He grinned like a cat who had just brought its master a decapitated mouse.

"Hmm...glad to know someone paid attention. What gave me away?"

"Nothin' really. The disguises were spot on. Let's say I have a psychic sense about people. The day with the birds, I knew that you knew it was a trick. I was laughing just as much at them as you. You didn't disappoint. In fact, you've handled the hazing better than most would."

"Yeah, well, I was trained by one of the best. Anyway, a psychic. That could come in handy. How's your stealth?"

"I'm insulted you'd even ask."

A glare from me made him more forthcoming. "I have excellent sneaking skills, and I'm a better than decent fighter."

My gut told me this fey could be trusted, and there was no sense in trying to bluff him if he was psychic. Still, I wasn't going to make a snap decision. "All right. I'll look over your files this weekend and let you know on Monday."

His smile stretched his face to reveal a gap between his two front teeth, and little crinkles around his gray eyes.

"Thanks, Chief. For what it's worth, I think you're just what this crew needs. I'm looking forward to working with you." He extended his hand.

I stood, shook it, and watched him leave. If the others accepted my offer, my squad would be complete.

~*~

That night, Dúl and I stayed in my suite at the castle. His sister had refused another of his messages. He was stressed.

We snuggled near a blazing fire, and my fingers played in his wavy hair. "It's looking like we'll have to hit the Fantine building again if we want to find out more on that Chevalier guy and what they're really up to. Once we get our hands on him, we can figure out what's happening with Nemesis. Are you sure you don't want me to—"

"No! No, please stay far away from her. She doesn't tolerate strangers under the best conditions. I'm may receive your head in a box if she catches you."

"But I'm not a stranger." I ran my fingers up his inner thigh. "I'm her little brother's chosen one. You'd think she'd *want* to meet me." Pushing him down to the lush blankets beneath us, I straddled him. I trailed kisses down his throat, down his chest. My fingers teased his belly, moving below the belt.

Any tension we were holding onto melted away as we came together in a tangle of arms and legs.

Saturday morning, we popped into the office for a few hours. He lounged on my sofa while I checked my email. "Hey, look at this."

He circled behind the desk. Images stared out at us of the three Shadows I had chosen. I had sent Najat, RavCorp's tech genius and the fourth member of my squad, their names before I left the office last night.

"Najat sent me their files. Recognize anyone?"

"The dark-haired one with the mustache. Maurizio. I hear he's quite the flirt. I don't know the Asian girl—a changeling, I believe? And, ah, I see you've selected Tynan. Excellent choice. He's the one who did the initial surveillance on you before we met."

"Stalker. Please tell me you don't still have someone tailing me."

"Do ravens count?" He grinned.

I whacked his arm and read the rest of Najat's message. She had been trying to hack the systems of Fantine International—dummy corporation of the vampires—since the day after we retrieved Morgan. It appeared they didn't conduct any of their business electronically.

If I can't find it digitally, it doesn't exist. If there is anything to find, she wrote, *it was done the old-fashioned way.*

"She sent this just a little while ago. Do you think she's here? I'd like to talk to her about Fantine for a sec."

He shrugged, went to open the door, and gestured me out with a nod of his head. "Let's go see. I'd like her to check on something myself."

~*~

When Dúl reached the door, he knocked twice and swung it open. I could see where Morgan learned her bad habit. I had just finished that thought when I barreled into his back. He had stopped short.

"What are you doing?" I started around him and froze. "Oh my God." The words blurted past my lips before I could stop them.

Najat was on top of her desk in a...compromising position. She shrieked and hurried to pull her skirt down, fix her glasses, and button her blouse all at once. The poor woman was so flustered, she looked like she might faint.

Morgan, on the other hand, was calm as a lake on a clear, summer day. She turned to face Dúl—I might as well have been a fly on the wall—and arched one eyebrow, daring him to say something. "Don't you knock?"

"We did knock. Obviously, you were too preoccupied to hear it." His black eyes glinted, and a muscle ticked at the side of his jaw. "If you're going to cheat, you could have the decency to be more discreet about it."

Cheat?

Morgan's expression was wicked. She smiled out of the corner of her mouth. "Like you are?"

"I am the *King*. I can't have you undermining—"

"Please. You're just upset that something is going on in the court that you had no idea about." There seemed to be some non-verbal subtext beneath their words, but it was hard to tell if they were genuinely angry, sniping at each other out of habit, or if some other emotions were at play.

Poor Najat looked like she wanted to crawl into the nearest volcano. "D-did you want something, Sire? Or Merc? Can I help you?" Her eyes added a silent, *please*.

"Um, yeah, I wanted to ask about..." I was kidding myself. Carrying on like nothing happened wasn't going to make this situation any less awkward. To be honest, I was having a hard time wrapping my mind around Morgan in any kind of tender relationship with anyone. The fact that she and Najat had such different personalities made it even more incredible.

Dúl spoke up. "Najat, Merc, would you give us the room, please? I believe Morgan and I have a matter to discuss." He turned my way. "Love, I'll only be a moment."

Najat grabbed her laptop and hustled past me. Since I had apparently been dismissed, I followed her out and slammed the door. By the time she and I reached my office, the shouting had started.

Even with the door shut and five rooms between us, we could hear them raging at each other.

"Why do you care who I sleep with? I didn't say a word when you moved Merc into the castle!"

"Of course I care! I understand why you would hide treason from the court, but why wouldn't you tell me?"

"Treason? Are you serious? Neither of us wanted this marriage... Oh, you thought I did, didn't you? Sorry to deflate that kingdom-sized ego of yours!"

"It's not about my ego! If my brother had found out before I did, you know what he could have done with the information! How could you not trust me after everything we've been through?"

"Trust? This has nothing to do with trust. Nearly my entire life revolves around you and this court! Can I not have something private for myself?"

Around and around they went. Najat couldn't look at me and sat staring at her wringing hands.

"Hey." I tapped her on the shoulder, and she straightened before looking me in the eye. "I couldn't care less who you sleep with if it means anything. If you two are happy, that's all that matters."

A tiny smile crept onto her face. "We are. We've been together a long time. Honestly, we never expected anyone to be here on a Saturday, certainly not the King. Before he met you, he rarely left his office when he was here."

"Oh." What could I say to that? Was all this drama my fault? My brain was purposefully avoiding the biggest question in the room, and although she didn't say it, I knew Najat was wondering the same thing I was—why was he overreacting like this?

I changed the subject. "So, regarding the Fantine mission..."

For the next hour, we sat together on the couch discussing the task ahead and the prospective crew members. Najat seemed optimistic that they would accept the offers.

Finally, a door banged down the hall. A moment later, it boomed again, and then there was silence. I expected Dúl to burst into the room at any moment.

Long minutes ticked by. Najat eventually folded her hands in her lap. "I think that's everything, Merc. If there's nothing else, I should be going. I'll have updated reports on the compound Monday morning, if that's all right."

"Yeah, sure. See you Monday."

She left.

Sensing Dúl's hurt and swirling emotional state, I resisted the temptation to stop by his office and returned to my apartment.

Once he cooled off, he found me there. "If I offer to lock myself in a stockade for a week, could you possibly forgive me? I've never quite understood the purpose of a stockade, but it seems appropriately uncomfortable and degrading." He shifted his weight from one foot to the other, hands held behind his back, reminding me of a schoolboy from an old movie.

"That would be the purpose of a stockade. You understand fine." I kept a stern expression since he seemed to expect me to be angry. But he was beating himself up enough. I didn't need to.

"I could order some court members to throw fruit."

"Or you could cut the drama, and we can talk about how you're going to think several times before dismissing me like you did. But I'll give you a pass this time."

Dúl came in, and I made some cocoa. We sat on the plush carpet between the sofa and glass coffee table, heads huddled together.

"I can't apologize enough for my behavior earlier. I was so taken aback. Morgan and I have known each other our entire lives, and I never imagined there was anything I didn't know about her or vice versa. As much as I'm loathe to admit it, her lack of confidence in me hurt."

"Understandable." It was like his bestie suddenly stopped telling him her deepest secrets. That never worked out well in high school movies. I paused, trying to decide if I wanted to ask the question that had been nagging at me. Did I really want the answer? "Was she right? Did you think she was pining after you all this time?" I had no desire to learn my boyfriend was pissy that his fiancé wasn't jealous of our relationship.

He turned the question over in his mind for a minute. "Yes. I believed—correctly—that there was some level of jealousy once my feelings for you became clear to those around me. My error was in the reason for her hostility. While I was able to openly express my desire for someone other than my betrothed, she did not have the same freedom. Barbaric and sexist as it is, as king, I'm almost expected to stray, but if she does, it's considered treason. Do you know she and Najat have been together for years? I'm amazed she never slipped up before now."

"Considering recent situations, a mistake like that makes sense. I think everyone is probably a bit 'off' right now. Call me crazy, but if neither of you wants this marriage, why not change it? Try talking to your brother or your sisters? Maybe now is a good time to revisit the issue, if not for your own sake, then at least for Morgan and Najat's. Why should they suffer because of your sibling feud?"

"I have actually been thinking about how to sway him to let us out of the arrangement, but you've met him."

They were both equally stubborn in their animosity toward each other, but I wasn't about to point that out. Instead, I snuggled closer to him and nestled into the crook of his shoulder. "You'll work things out. In the meantime..." He didn't need any more prompting to shift and bring his lips to mine.

In the morning, I insisted that Dúl smooth things over with Morgan. There was also some court business he needed to attend to that I preferred to avoid, so I spent the rest of the weekend in Poughkeepsie with my adopted parents, Rebus and Nat.

They had never formally adopted me. How could they? I had appeared one night from nowhere. They forged ID and papers when I needed to go to school and whatnot, but the courts were something to be avoided. They were my family nonetheless. The technicalities never mattered to any of us.

When they asked about Dúl, wondering why I wasn't with him, I told them the bare bones story of his fight with Morgan without giving too much detail. It wasn't my business to spill. They didn't pry. My family was good like that.

While I watched him tinker, I picked Rebus's brain about how to handle a crew, the vampires, and the Winter Queen. I learned a lot about management. Rebus explicitly forbidding me to go anywhere near the Winter Court made a lot more sense now than it had back when the Queen tried to recruit me.

The entire time, unspoken questions lingered and festered in my mind. All the drama about relationships and families brought me back to the boy I'd seen in my dream. Did I have a brother out there somewhere?

If I hadn't gotten lost, would we have been as tight as the Dawn soldiers Tania and her deceased twin, Anton, had been? Or would he have been a jerk to me like Dúl and Orion were toward each other?

Would I ever figure out what happened to the family I had been born into? A small voice in the back of my mind shouted warnings, that I might be better off not knowing.

Chapter 4

Eager to get the mission underway, I sent messages via raven couriers to Cari, Riz, and Tynan on Sunday. By late Monday morning, they had all responded.

They all accepted.

For a moment, glee filled me at having something go easily for a change, and I pumped my fist in the air before walking toward my office. Then I realized I couldn't share the news with either of the people I wanted to. Morgan had "borrowed" Najat for the morning, and when they returned around midday, Morgan carried on with work as if nothing awkward had happened on Friday. She made herself scarce all afternoon. It was hard not to take the clear avoidance personally.

Dúl was AWOL. I sensed through our energetic connection that he was safe, if agitated, so his well-being wasn't a concern. Still, I wondered why he was ghosting me. I forced my curiosity to the recesses of my mind and settled in to work.

First, I called my new team to a meeting to welcome them and go over some expectations. We listened to the updated reports on the lab from Najat and then finally boarded a plane for Canada. And all before five o'clock.

On the plane, Najat monitored two laptops and a tablet, lost in her own techy world. The others all sat together, joking around and relaxing. I should have been over there with them, getting to know them, and more importantly, letting them get to know me. That was the whole point in dragging along four people to do something I would have much preferred to handle alone.

Instead, I stared out the window into the darkness trying to silence my thoughts, particularly about Dúl. One unforeseen benefit of leading a team—I had to focus. Jeopardizing my own skin was one thing, but I wouldn't risk others. In a way, they were already saving my butt.

After we landed, we got into a black van. While Najat drove to the site, I addressed the Shadows. "Okay people, you've already been briefed about the vampires, but I wanted to reiterate a couple of things. Najat's intel says about a dozen vamps are working in the facility. It looks like they might be clearing the place out, so we have two aims.

"First, snag any files, computer equipment...anything we can transport that might help us locate Serg Chevalier. Second, destroy anyone and anything left in the place."

They responded with nods and grunts of understanding.

"Now keep in mind, it's night, so they'll be stronger than if we hit them during the day. That will give us the element of surprise—they'd never expect us to do something so—"

"Stupid?" Tynan grinned broadly. He must have plucked the word right from my mind because it was what I had been about to say. The others laughed and seemed genuinely pumped about the plan. "It's brilliant. And ballsy. This will be epic."

I had to smile back at him. "Exactly. Remember, if there's no clear shot at the eyes, you have to destroy the bodies beyond repair. This won't be easy, but after reading your files, I have no doubt you can all handle whatever is ahead. Questions?"

"Is there a more specific plan, Chief? Or do we go in the front door and start shooting?" Cari said.

"As much as I would love to do just that, it won't accomplish our objective. We'll split into two teams. The finer details will have to wait until we get there and scope out exactly where they are inside. And drop the 'Chief' for now. Just call me Merc. Or 'hey you.' Whatever. I'm more or less one of you now. Of course, with final say over strategy and a little added responsibility if things go wrong."

We hid the van in the woods about a quarter mile from the compound. I was having déjà vu about the last time I'd been here. Except then, it had been broad daylight. I started to second guess myself.

Four of us, dressed in black fatigues, began our trek to the edge of the forest. We wore earbuds to stay in touch with Najat, figuring there were so few vamps onsite, no one would be monitoring the channels. If trouble found her, she had an escape rune, as did each of the rest of us.

Tynan and I also had neoprene packs that crossed our chests diagonally and molded to our backs. Inside these bags were tiny yet powerful explosives.

I had no intention of losing any member of my team. Not again.

We skulked between the trees. I crept a few paces ahead, watching and listening for any movement. There were the usual scritchings and scrabblings of nocturnal animals moving about, but otherwise, the early night was still.

Footsteps from behind sped up until Tynan was at my side. "You called it right, you know." He kept his voice at a whisper.

I remembered Tania and how she was so chatty when we staked the place out, pun intended, last time. I had reached out to her a few times since then with no reply. I couldn't exactly blame her if she didn't want to talk to the person responsible for her twin's death. "What?"

"I sensed your uncertainty of whether you were doing the right thing moving in after dark. I'm sayin' it's a good move."

"You reading my mind or something? Because if you are, you'll have to stop that." Embarrassing thoughts of nakedness and toilets and Dúl popped into my head. The more I tried to shut them down, the worse they got. Suddenly, I was happy for the lack of light.

"Nothing like that. Just a sense of your mental state that came to me. I can read your thoughts if you want me to, but it takes effort, so I save that trick for interrogations."

"Good to know. And thanks. I mean for the vote of confidence."

We continued in silence until we reached the edge of the trees. I let out a soft whistle to signal a halt. The gates were locked. Two tractor trailers lined up in front of the building.

"Najat, talk to me."

"The drones and infrared pick up three on the west side of the first floor, three to the east, and the rest are on the first sub-level. Looks to be five or six. I can't see any farther down than that. The heat signatures all look similar, so I don't think you'll find any surprises. Still, be careful, Merc."

"Will do. Thanks." I turned to my Shadows—my team—and sent up a mental prayer for their safety. "Okay, Cari, Riz, take the ground level starting at the east and working back toward the main entrance. Quick and quiet as possible. Whatever you can carry easily. If you have questions or need eyes, stay in contact with Najat. Ty and I will deal with the basement. Clear?" Cari and Riz nodded.

"One last thing. You might hear giggling when you get close to the vamps. We haven't figured out where it comes from yet. It's annoying as hell, but don't let it distract you."

They frowned but nodded.

I turned to Tynan. "We good?"

"Yes, Merc. And you can call me Ty, by the way." The wiseass grinned at me.

I shook my head. With a hand gesture, I signaled everyone forward.

The front hall stank of old excrement, rotting meat, and mildew. Were they just now clearing away the humans, changelings, and vampires who had been killed during the raid to rescue Morgan? The bodies were gone from the main hall, but dried blood and gore coated every surface.

The east team split off from us and jogged to the right, systematically checking offices. Tynan and I hung behind. From the back of my waistband, I withdrew my shadow dagger. The memory of Dúl giving me the weapon surfaced. A pang of longing for him shot through me that I had to shake off.

Beside me, Tynan crouched down, setting bolts into a mini crossbow as he advanced. That caught me off guard. Where had he been stashing that thing? He turned his head, pointed to his eyes, and flashed a smile. I understood his strategy—he'd shoot them in the eyes. I guessed the bolt tips were probably poisoned to cause blindness even if he missed a kill shot.

We reached the beginning of the main vestibule. The two glass doors that used to be here were still blown open. Beyond the threshold, to the east was a set of steel double doors. To the west, the shorter part of the building's L shape extended beyond the front entrance toward the abandoned guard shed.

I held up a hand in the universal "stop" gesture. We hugged the left wall. I peeked around the corner. A short distance down the hall, light shone under one office door that muffled the vamps' voices.

I leaned back and whispered the information to Tynan. He nodded. We hurried past the open glass sliders and around to the wall where the door was. With weapons readied, we started down that pitch dark path. After a couple of steps, I stopped.

From my jacket pocket, I pulled out a small loupe, similar to the one Rebus used when he was making his enchanted gadgets. This was one of those devices.

I held it up to my eye and scanned the walls, floors, and ceiling for any signs of traps. The path seemed clear.

Nudging Tynan back a couple of steps, I whispered, "Can you sense anything from them?"

He nodded. "No clue we're here."

Perfect.

I went up to the door, gripped the knob, and slowly, tested to see if it was locked. It wasn't, and I pushed it just enough that the cylinder didn't click. Score one for the Shadows.

Moving back toward my partner, I concentrated on what Dúl showed me when he explained the powers he gave me. I imagined myself growing dim, almost as if I were simply changing my skin color during a shift.

In addition to adopting a dark camouflage, I started to feel lighter. Transparent.

I knew I wasn't fully invisible because I had tried it in front of a full-length mirror. But when I looked down at my hand, all I saw was a dark, hazy form.

Behind me, Tynan mumbled a curse. Holding up one hand to silence him, with the other, I eased the door open a few inches then listened. The vamps didn't speak. From the types of thuds inside, it sounded like they were packing boxes. I tiptoed forward. If I squeezed in through the opening, all they would see was a bodiless shadow against the wall.

I moved to slip through the open space.

Inside the office, a bookshelf to my left and a file cabinet to my right were being cleaned out by two of the enemy. The third was typing away on a tablet that was propped up on a padded keyboard stand.

"Ah ah ah," the giggling voice chimed in a singsong. I had nicknamed it Psycho Kiddie and kind of wished it was a real kid that I could smack.

The two vamps who were standing turned toward me and froze.

Tynan burst through the entrance and fired off two quick shots at the vampire nearest to him. A second later, as the other two watched their partner drop in a mess of black gunk streaming from his eyes and mouth, I lunged at the vamp closest to me. Two quick jabs to the eyes, and he was done.

Giggles filled the air as if the source enjoyed seeing the vampires get slaughtered.

The last vampire barely had time to register what happened. Still, before I could shift focus to target him, he leapt over the desk and was in my face. His palms slammed into my chest. I flew backwards and hit the wall. The shadow silhouette came off me like a silk robe sliding from my body.

Tynan stopped reloading the crossbow and rushed at the vampire's midsection. The mammoth vampire, who had at least six inches on Ty, reacted like he was nothing more than a bug flying into a windshield.

The vamp snatched a handful of Ty's clothing and bared his fangs, drawing Tynan toward his mouth.

With a roar, I pushed off from the wall, every nerve along the back of my body screaming. Weapon in hand, I stabbed into the vamp's neck before he could sink his teeth into my partner. The shadow dagger was enchanted to cause pain and blindness.

The brute dropped Tynan. With a garbled scream in some language I didn't understand, he clawed his eyes.

Ty whisked a blade from a sheath tied to his thigh and finished the vampire off. When he was dead, the laughter stopped. But I wondered who else in the building might have heard it.

We threw files, papers, and the tablet into the box, which our enemy had conveniently started for us.

As our hands flew to complete the task, I checked in with the others. "Najat?"

"All good. You still have a few downstairs, but the first level is clean."

"Cari? Riz?"

"Check. Vamps down. Riz is hurt. The room we found looks like a bookkeeper's office."

"Sweet. How bad is Riz?"

He answered for himself. "Dislocations in my wrist and elbow. Nothing fatal."

"All right. Do the best you can and then stay put. Najat, get in here and connect with them. Ty and I are heading downstairs."

"Copy that, Merc," she said, and we cut the chatter.

We finished packing up our box. Ty reloaded the crossbow, and then we made our way back to the junction where this hall met the main one. We left the package we carried near an office closest to the front entrance. Then we backtracked to the steel doors.

Even without much light, I knew these doors would be dented and charred. I would have liked to avoid this room, but it led directly down to the basement levels, and that was where we needed to go. Plus, a task in there required my personal attention. The room would be locked from the inside and the interior destroyed, courtesy of a dawn soldier's grenade.

I took point. Ty was right on my heels.

The center of the doors bulged and twisted outward. The lock was snapped. After a few good, hard tugs, they unjammed and flew open. Inside, the room still held a sulfuric odor that settled into the walls and floor tiles. Shrapnel from the grenade shredded the paint all around the space. Everything was blackened as if a layer of soot settled over each visible surface.

I wished we could go through this building with a fine-toothed comb, but it was too risky with the half dozen vamps on the lower level. Besides, it seemed to make the most sense to see what they considered top priority to destroy.

In the middle of the room, Anton's remains lay on their side, burnt and motionless. We should take him out of here for a proper burial, or whatever the Dawn Court did to pay last respects to their fallen warriors. I owed him at least that much. He had been gravely injured and then saved us by blowing up the room to slow down the vampires who tried to prevent us from reaching Morgan.

We had to check out the downstairs. I knew this, but my body refused to move.

The room became stuffy, the air hard to pull in, as if my lungs were rejecting it. Memories of Anton and Tania's final goodbye flooded back to me. I could have prevented this scene if I had been less stubborn.

I had to let go of the thoughts of how my error in judgment caused Anton's death.

Finally, focusing on one small task, I withdrew a headlamp from my pants pocket. Next, I turned to Tynan. "Can you help me move him, please?"

He folded up the crossbow and stashed it in his jacket.

Silently, we settled Anton's remains near the door. About three hundred points along the back of my body where I had hit the wall, not to mention two hand-sized sore spots in my chest, stung when I lifted the big fey's remains. The pain helped keep me in the present moment and out of the past. After Tynan put on a headlamp of his own, I started toward the stairs leading down.

His hand on my arm stopped me. "One sec. Are you okay? Need a minute?"

"I'm fine. You?"

"Good, but I didn't just come across someone whose death I feel responsible for."

I sighed. "Look, Jiminy Cricket, you have an awesome talent, but if we're going to work together, you're gonna have to dial it back. If you can't help what you sense, at least keep it to yourself. When I need to share, I'll let you know. Clear?"

"Sure. You're the boss."

Great. Now I had offended him. There was more I wanted to explain. I'm not even sure why because, really, I didn't owe him an explanation. But he had been decent to me, and honestly, I liked him. We'd talk later.

Poking my head through the opening, lamp off, I listened for signs of life in the darkness. Hints of voices echoed toward us in the distance.

"Hey, we won't get the drop on these guys again. I think that giggling voice is warning them."

"Got it under control." A distinct chill colored his voice now.

I let it go, turned on my lamp, and went down the stairs.

There were two procedure rooms on this level that

could be seen from observation areas upstairs. But I had never seen the other offices down here.

Sure enough, the voices were coming from another direction than the surgical areas. And I had hoped we could get out of this without having to fight six more bloodsuckers. That wasn't happening.

A quick scan of our surroundings gave me all the information I needed about the layout down here. My ears did the rest. Clicking my light off, I motioned for Ty to do the same and then shifted into stealth mode, changing the color of my skin to deep black. Ninja-face, as I liked to call it.

Just before we headed toward the lit offices, the idea came to me that we should check the shorter hallway for unoccupied offices first. I reversed direction.

The operating rooms were pristine and abandoned. Across from the closest one, an office had an empty desk with wires hanging off the edge to the floor. The ransacked drawers of a file cabinet gaped in one corner of the room. They had already been here.

All the way at the end of the hall, next to the far hospital setup, a door was closed. I padded over to that one. It was locked. Fortunately, locks were a specialty of mine. I clicked on my lamp.

Strangely, this door wasn't made of any high-grade steel. It was just a plain slab of finished wood with a knob. We could kick our way in if we wanted to. Maybe it was nothing more than a fancy supply closet.

On one hand, if someone wanted to hide something valuable, it might be a good trick to put it in the last place anyone else would expect. Hide it in plain sight. On the other hand, the door might just look weak to lure in nosy people like me. Both possibilities seemed equally possible.

"Tynan, come here." He moved closer. "What do you make of this thing: disguised to look easy or trap?"

He considered for a few seconds. "Er...feels like both."

Of course. Just what I would have done, especially if I expected that the place might be compromised at any point. Hide the object where no one would think to look, but in case they did check, set a booby trap to destroy it and them.

"We have to get in there, but my guess is that it might blow the whole place."

"Well, we were going to do that anyway," he said, sounding lost in thought, as if he wanted in as much as I did. "But what about the stuff those guys are trying to get down the other end of the building?"

"If we're right—and my gut says we are—whatever is in this room will be much more important than a bunch of files. The problem is if it blows, we'll be stuck down here." And so much for reclaiming Anton's corpse. It was a small comfort to know he'd want us to complete the job no matter what.

"Understood. There are always the runes."

"If we have time to use them. Plus, we might blow the trap and not get the what we came for. I'm only telling you this because it's extremely risky and there might not be a payoff. I can give you enough time to get out before opening this."

I thought I might have offended him again, but he didn't sound it when he answered. "Thanks. I'll stay if it's all the same to you."

I had promised myself I wouldn't lose any of my squad. But Ty was no child. He was a grown fey who could make his own choices. "All right, stay. I might need help carrying out whatever it is anyway."

He chuckled. "I'm here to serve, Chief. So, what's your plan to get us past that door?"

~*~

As badly as I wanted to know what was in that room, I couldn't forget that there were still vamps on the long side of the building. Ty and I crept along the hall where they were working and stealthily set charges onto the walls. If we couldn't have the files, neither would they.

I was relieved that Psycho Kiddie hadn't sounded another gleeful warning like before. Maybe we hadn't gotten close enough for Giggles to detect us. Or maybe it wanted us to destroy the place. It certainly seemed to enjoy chaos and destruction.

Once our bombs were set, we returned to what I thought of as the special closet. How could we open it? And where was the trap if there was one?

"Ty, reach into the little front pouch on my pack. There should be a thin coil of wire."

Another invention of Rebus's, this wasn't exactly

foolproof, but it was better than nothing. Tynan handed it to me a second later.

"You'll want to stand back a little. Maybe keep an ear on those guys. Tell me if they sound like they're finishing over there."

He didn't ask any questions and moved as told. Maybe he could sense I was in my element now. Adrenaline coursed through me as I pulled out a length of wire about as long as my forearm. Taking the free end with one hand, I switched my lamp back on and got down on my belly, being careful not to touch the door with any part of my body.

Shining the light along the bottom of the door, I carefully poked the end of the wire underneath. A sigh of relief escaped when it slid under easily. I fed it through a couple of feet. "Seek," I whispered and held the end of the spool. It grew warm in my hands and began to glow purple. The wire took over and slithered deeper in.

It didn't go far, so the room seemed to be about the size of a closet.

The wire tugged to the right, paused, then pulled left. I let out more line. But the wire changed its mind.

The spool retracted some of the slack. Then the tip peeked back toward me and worked its way up the seam between wall and door, stopping at the knob. I sat up to follow its progress. Again, the spool glowed brighter for a moment.

Up and across the top seam, down the left side

hinges. When it finished its inspection, the spool wound itself up again.

Shielding my lamp with my hand, I rose to my feet and gestured Tynan over to me. "We've got two traps —one on the knob and one inside."

"That's a neat gadget."

"My dad—adopted dad—made it. I think we should take the hinges off if we can do it quietly. They don't look too rusty."

"Or we could cut through the door." He hesitated for a moment, seeming to gather his courage, and then gave the center of the panel a light tap. "Nothing but wood."

"Um... and what do you suggest we use to cut it?"

He grinned. "You're not the only one with cool doodads."

I nearly laughed at the word "doodads." He reached inside his jacket and pulled out what can only be described as a poor imitation of Doctor Who's sonic screwdriver. I stifled another chuckle. "What is that exactly?"

Teeth still showing with amusement, he said, "Laser, of course. What did you think it was?"

I had a feeling he suspected what I had thought. Using the laser as I kept watch, he cut a four-foot-tall rectangle into the door. By necessity, it was narrow. I was the only one who could fit, so I had to enter alone.

"Keep your light off. I'll be out fast as I can."

His response was a look that said, "Duh."

I turned my back and prepared to shift. My skin

tingled and rippled, the muscles softening like taffy. Everything pulled in on itself, and I shrank. I went from a 5'8" fully grown adult to a 4'11" middle-schooler.

I hated really small forms. They made my body feel tight, claustrophobic. I forced the thoughts from my mind and ducked into the room.

There was no way Ty would have fit in here with me, even small as I was. It really was a supply closet. Or used to be one. Packets of alcohol prep pads, a few stray rolls of gauze, and band aids littered the floor. To my right, a narrow shelf held a few boxes of syringes and a few bottles of something I couldn't pronounce.

To my left on a similar shelf stood a single, thick, leather-bound book. Journal? Some kind of spell grimoire? I had heard of those, but never thought they existed in real life. Why would anyone booby trap a book? Whatever the reason, I needed to figure out how to disable it.

Think, Merc. Think!

As far as I knew, although they used it sometimes, vampires weren't big on magic—that was more of an issue when dealing with fey, so I guessed that the device was probably mechanical in some way. Maybe a toggle or pressure switch.

The book stood straight up, not leaning against anything, so that suggested some kind of balancing support in the middle. And when I pulled the book off the support, I'd likely pull the safety pin. But what would be the result? I pulled out my trap detector again.

This time, I poked the wire against the bottom of the book. It wriggled under the book from the spine toward the open edge. A third of the way through, it stopped and heated the spool.

As I was puzzling this problem out, Ty tapped on the door. "You might hurry it up. Sounds like they're moving."

Not exactly a simple thing here.

Just then I heard, "Shit!" and Ty's head poked through the opening. The rest of his body was trying to follow.

"What are you doing?" I hissed.

"Scoot over. They're coming."

Before I could tell him there was no way in hell he'd fit in here, I was mashed up against the shelf with the book. His body slid against mine as he really and truly squished into the space. He was hunching over my miniature form forcing his leg in when he jostled me.

I bumped the book. *Damn it!*

Just as I braced myself for an explosion, the wall opened to the left. I fell forward. My face hit the floor, breaking the headlamp with a muffled crunch. Ty's foot dug into my thigh as he finally got his leg in. At the sound of voices coming closer, we both froze.

The voices moved away, as if they had turned the corner. Then footsteps clomped up the stairs. They were gone.

"Goddamnit, Ty. Let me up! And give me some

light." I felt my nose for blood, but there was none. My forehead hurt. A lump was already forming. Ty gripped my arm, found my hand, and pressed his lamp into it.

I shone it around. "What the hell..."

Still crouching and squeezing in, he shifted closer to me. "Holy shit."

"This wasn't on any of Najat's blueprints."

A short foyer led into a simple and secret office. "It looks like we just hit paydirt, Ty."

Chapter 5

The office was nothing special—a plain, pressed wood desk and computer chair that could have come from any Staples. No computer, phone, or wires. A single, short file cabinet sat to one side of the desk, with a big ledger book on top. A layer of dust had settled into the room.

"We don't have time to go through this stuff, but the way it was hidden, I'm sure we need it."

Tynan nodded agreement. "How will we get everything out?"

I thought for a few seconds. "The portal runes. They're set to go directly back to my office."

"Good idea." He reached into his jacket, but I stopped him. Portal runes weren't mass produced, so we had to be conservative.

"No, you keep yours. I worked solo for a long time without shadow portals. Nice to have, but I'm fine without it."

He looked like he might argue, but he shut his mouth, walked around behind the desk, and searched it. Together, we piled the ledger and files we found in the desk drawers on top of the small cabinet.

I took the stone from my pocket, placed it on top of the pile, and moved back a few paces. Then I spoke the words I had been taught. "*Oyé akit.*" *Take us home.*

A dark ball of swirling shadow encapsulated the rune stone. It grew larger and larger, until it swallowed the pile. A moment later, the whole thing disappeared.

I checked in with the rest of the squad. "Najat, position."

"We are at the tree line past the guard house. Cari and Riz are with me."

"Sweet. Give us two minutes, and then light this bitch up."

"But—"

"One hundred twenty seconds. We're coming out. Where are our friends?"

There was a pause, and then she said, "Er...they are... loading the trucks in front of the building. They're blocking your exit." Her voice dropped, and I could envision her shoulders slumping.

"Not a problem. See you in a minute." To Ty, I said, "We have a problem."

We wriggled out of the closet, I shifted back to normal size, and we worked our way up to the main floor. There was a front office before the entrance. We paused by the empty room to peek outside. All five vampires were loading boxes and file cabinets into the trucks along with wooden crates that I assumed were the remaining batches of FeyX—the drug they had been working on.

"I want them in here when the charges go off, but then we might get stuck. I'm not using the portal until I know the others are safe."

Ty shrugged. "We draw them in then."

Slow grins bloomed on both our faces. He quickly loaded his crossbow, and then casually picked up the box we had left, setting the weapon on top. I pulled up an image in my mind of two throwing daggers. They appeared in my hands, shadows swirling within them. I led the way. We strolled to a spot in front of the glass doors.

"Hey!" When one of the vampires turned at the sound of my voice, I taunted, "Didn't I kick your ass a couple weeks ago? Hard to tell. All you bloodsuckers look alike!"

They roared and rushed into the building. I crouched into a fighting stance while Ty set the box on the floor. He stayed bent over, reaching for his weapon.

My daggers found their marks as the first one charged in. The second vampire fell to a crossbow bolt. The signature giggling started, and the other four vamps streamed through the doors.

Before they reached us, barely audible over the stupid psychotic laughter, three pops sounded in rapid succession. The last one in line smacked the back of his neck as if an insect had chomped on him. All three vampires arched their backs as dark shadows enveloped their heads, like hoods, blinding them. They fell forward, one at a time. I didn't know what happened and didn't care.

"Thiry five seconds!" Najat's voice filtered into my ear.

I knew the vamps would recover in a second. Inside my back pocket, I pulled another tiny gadget. "Restrain," I said to it, and threw it into the heap of vamps. A net of sticky, gossamer threads burst out of it and settled over them. A holdover from Rebus's days in the Winter Court that he passed on to me.

"Go! Go!" I waved wildly toward the door as I shouted to Ty. He snatched up the box and ran. I followed, legs pumping, muscles screaming, lungs on fire. Tynan was ahead and passed the gate.

The squad was ahead. Blood rushed through my ears. I couldn't hear anything outside myself. Najat gesticulated like a madwoman, her eyes bulging. Before I could get clear of the gate, a series of explosions set the night on fire. A shock wave hit my back. Then I was flying.

I smacked into the fence. Instinctively, my arms wrapped around my head, and I curled into a ball, waiting for the rain of debris to stop, praying nothing too big crushed me.

When the explosions stopped, I pushed up onto my hands and knees. My ears rang, head swam. Something might have hit me in the back of the head. It was pounding. And then my team was there beside me, Najat and Ty kneeling on either side.

Cari stood in front of me. Next to her, Riz held a sniper rifle.

"That-that was you back then?" I hoped I wasn't shouting.

He shrugged and smiled in a lopsided way. I thought of home and really wanted to be back there. "Epic shooting, dude. Thanks."

They helped me up. With no further trouble, we reached the van and used the runes to return to Rav-Corp. Despite what I was sure was a concussion, and my failure to retrieve Anton's remains, I counted our first mission together as a smashing success.

~*~

Back at my office, I reclined on the couch with an ice pack held to the back of my head. My hair was loose and extra fluffy because braids made the headache worse. Riz and Cari stood whispering together for a few seconds before he sidled over to me. "Chief... uh, Merc... we wondered—would you be interested in celebrating with us? Cari and I were going to head back to court, maybe some wine, some food... We could bring it here. You don't look like you should move too much."

Unable to cover my shock at being included, I quickly recovered with a smile. "That sounds awesome, but since we're here, maybe we should celebrate Waking style."

That meant ordering a couple of pizzas and picking up a twelve pack of Sam Adams.

Once everyone had a bottle, I lifted mine. I had to

keep my voice down because my head pounded just from the act of breathing. "A toast to an excellently executed first mission together. You guys were great. Thanks, congrats, and *salud*." I must have conked my head harder than I realized. "I mean cheers!"

Everyone clapped and drank. I set my bottle on the floor after my first sip. I hated beer. They, however, seemed to enjoy it. Ty, Riz, and Cari joked and shared their respective experiences. Najat sat at my desk, clacking away with a smile.

The files and papers we collected were in a pile in the center of the room.

The door flew open. Everyone froze. All talking cut off as everyone gaped.

"Merc! Are you all right? What—" Dúl stopped short when he saw that he had an audience. He cleared his throat and continued, calmer. "Are you okay?"

With a sigh, I pushed myself upright. "Guys, thanks again. Be here first thing in the morning, and we'll figure out what we've got."

They packed up the pizza boxes, gathered the empty bottles, and hurried out. Najat shut her laptop. Her eyes seemed to be avoiding Dúl's at all costs. I couldn't blame her.

Once they left, I glared at him. "First of all, you really need to learn to knock. As long as I'm Chief of Shadows, this is my office. If respecting my space is a problem, fire me." As soon as the words left my mouth, I knew they were way too harsh. The drumbeat in my skull, the delayed stress of the mission, and his prolonged absence beforehand crashed in on me all at once.

He cocked an eyebrow but said nothing.

"Second, you don't get to disappear without a word and then act all freaked out because I'm out doing my job." I hadn't meant to shout. The throb in my head warned me to take it easy.

His eyes were wide in what I assumed was shock at being spoken to this way. But then his expression softened. "I suppose I deserve that."

"Yeah, well..."

He glanced around the office as if he didn't know what to do with himself. I wasn't going to make it easy for him, so I didn't offer him a seat next to me. He settled for putting his hands into the pockets of his indigo jeans.

"I had some things to look into, which I believe it best not to discuss until I have better information. I thought you were safe with your parents. At least until tonight. What were you thinking going off on that kind of mission without telling anyone?"

"Telling *who*? *You* were MIA. And am I not the one in charge of the Shadows? Do I really need to clear every action with you?" I clenched my hands in my lap.

Dúl groaned and pinched the bridge of his nose. "No, but if there had been a problem, and you needed some sort of reinforcement, it would have been good to let someone know your plans."

He had a point, but I wasn't quite ready to admit it. "Well, you and Morgan were off doing whatever you were each doing, and I couldn't sit around with my thumbs up my ass until you decided to be reachable, so..."

He came and sat next to me, taking one of my hands from my lap.

"Umbra, my lack of communication wasn't meant to shut you out. I apologize for leaving you without a means of reaching me short of being in grave danger." His lopsided grin as he held my gaze mellowed my heart. He caressed my face and then gently plunged his fingers into my hair. I winced.

"I'm sorry, love. I am unaccustomed to considering anyone else's feelings when I act. Morgan is used to it, so I tend to just go off. I'll do better in the future."

"You plan to do this a lot?" I smiled back at him until a stab of pain hit the back of my head. "I'm sorry too. As much as I love your hands in my hair, you're killing me right now."

He picked up the discarded ice pack, moved so he cradled me, and held the pack against my head. Relief flooded through me as we continued our 'make up' chat. Before the night ended, we went home together.

Chevalier

Inside a log cabin that sat atop a massive underground bunker in Quebec, Serg Chevalier listened to the soldier's panting report. His hand squeezed his iPhone. He pushed his round, brown-tinted shades up onto the bridge of his straight nose. The tints were dark enough to camouflage the red rims of his eyes, but light enough to see his black pupils.

"Everything, sir. It's all ash. Nothing we could do to stop it."

The tittering giggle of the *Lemooria*, the parasitic spirit that infected all vampires, surrounded him, relishing his rage and pain. According to the soldier, no one had survived last night's blast in St. Catherine's. The lab, the subjects, and all the staff, save a few soldiers who had been outside on guard or transport duties, were all gone.

"Salvage what you can, then whoever is left, join me here as soon as possible." The more his irritation increased, the more his French accent muddled Chevalier's words to his underlings. But none would dare ask for clarification.

He ended the call and crossed the rustic room to stand in front of the stone fireplace. Chevalier had a good idea who was responsible for this—that shifter/fey/whatever-she-was. The one who the addict was dating. She'd left a cutesy note when she delivered that idiot Donny, tortured and bloody, to the VampX lab in Poughkeepsie. Chevalier hadn't been amused. He hadn't even considered turning Donny. That was how angry he had been. Too disgusted to keep the changeling around as a servant even with the prospect of his eternal torture. Chevalier merely tossed Donny to his underlings to feed from.

The addict had given up Merc's name with little prodding. Chevalier guessed it was because of the way Paris had been shamed and unceremoniously dumped before Merc shacked up with the Shadow King.

Chevalier moved to his right and sat in the log-framed club chair near the small fire and listened for the spirits' voices. The *Lemooria* had only revealed themselves to him when they considered him worthy to deserve the truth about the vampires' nature. The *spirits* drove the vampires to feed on blood. The more the bloodlust disturbed the vampire, the tastier the treat for the spirits.

Some vampires became addicts, sinking into a pit of despair in their never-ending quest for an escape from their own self-loathing. Others embraced their fate, relishing depravity and sadism. Chevalier was this last breed and at just over 200 years old was one of the oldest in the nation.

He recalled his turning, barely into his adulthood, just after the Battle of Waterloo. A member of the Young Guard, he had been injured and captured by his sire. Over the course of the longest night in Chevalier's long memory, the sire fed, taunted, defiled, and tortured until the guard deliriously begged for the release of death. And then came the offer.

"You wish to die, little soldier. But I can heal you, if only to continue your pain indefinitely. Or I can transform you into one like me and end your pain. Which will you choose?"

He chose to end one pain in exchange for a different type of torment, at least until he understood that he and his brethren were at the top of the food chain. There was no reason to feel anything for the human, fey, or changeling animals. As abominably as they treated each other, how was his behavior toward them any worse? They were strictly pawns—meaningless until he gave their lives purpose.

How dare that meddlesome shifter tamper with this natural order?

You can certainly teach her some lessons. Make her pay for her interference.

"Yes, and I know exactly what to do—slowly reap compensation for every loss I've suffered. Retribution will start with the changeling addict."

This could also show good faith to our partners. They would be pleased to see you taking a more active role in furthering their plans.

"*Oui.* Then they take control of the Dreaming and

help us to conquer the Waking. The inferior beings will service the vampire nation, and it will be a beautiful thing."

Chevalier knew exactly how to inflict the most suffering upon the shifter for crossing him. Physical pain only scratched the surface of the punishment he envisioned. He grinned broadly as he tapped the number on his cell.

Chapter 6

It wasn't the romantic reunion it might have been because I spent a good portion of the night in the Dreaming with healers tending to my injuries. Dúl had to carry me because when I wasn't having dizzy spells, I couldn't see straight. Good thing I had left the beer alone.

Even with their care, I had trouble sleeping, so it was no problem for me to go back to the office in the morning before my meeting with the Shadow Squad. The information we brought back from the lab nagged at my mind. What could be important enough to lock away in a booby-trapped secret office but expendable enough to keep at a remote location? If I were in charge, I'd want the most important stuff close by.

Dúl made up for his absence threefold, never leaving my side and catering to my every need. We found the file cabinet, box, and papers the others had brought out. By the time the squad arrived, Dúl and I had purged the filing cabinet and at least glanced through everything else. When they filtered into my office, he and I perched on the edge of my desk, leaned back, and crossed our ankles. We moved in sync without even trying.

He was dressed in a black, pleated skirt over chunky knee-high boots and a navy, long-sleeve tee that hugged the contours of his chest and arms. Knowing that we would spend several hours sitting on the floor surrounded by dusty papers, I kept it casual. Baggy, black cargo pants and a cropped black tank with a cropped, pink zip-up seemed appropriate.

I still couldn't deal with my usual braids, so Dúl gently swept my hair into a messy bun.

Terrible communication skills, but at least he could do hair if we ever have a daughter. Unfortunately, the weight was still too painful, so I nixed hair altogether.

Where had that thought about a daughter come from? I had never seriously considered having children. When my ex- boyfriend Paris and I had been together, so much time and energy went into his needs that the issue never entered my mind. Plus, with my dangerous line of work, kids never seemed realistic.

But now, even with Dúl's "entanglement," I let myself wonder if having a family with him was possible someday. Did I want that? Did he? As a king, he'd probably be expected to have children with his wife, who could still end up being Morgan. Maybe that was just a human thing. I refused to let my thoughts wander down that rabbit hole.

The rest, though, was not unpleasant to consider. While the notion of kids wasn't a top priority, there was a nice little spot in the back of my mental landscape—a cute cabin with a picket fence and a cat sitting on top of it—where the idea could live.

As the squad settled in, Tynan stood near the closed door, Najat scooted behind my desk, and Riz and Cari lounged on opposite sides of the sofa, their knees meeting in the middle. Ty spoke for the group. "So, what have we got? State secrets of the vampire nation? A roadmap to their leader?"

"All that was in the file cabinet was a big, leather-bound journal. Unfortunately, it's in some language neither we nor Google have ever seen. Najat, I'm going to surrender this to your brilliance."

"It all looks like bookkeeping. Now I see why Najat couldn't find much on their systems. They kept the most incriminating records manually. Phones are all burners. But there is a list of addresses matched up to phone numbers that should be useful."

I pointed to the box Ty and I had saved. "In here we have some journals and maybe formulas. Hard to tell because they seem to be written in some kind of cipher."

"I can take that, Merc." Riz reached forward, a dark curl falling over his forehead.

"You're a codebreaker?"

He smirked. "No, but one of the members of the Milan unit is the best I've ever seen."

When he stood, I handed the books to him, and he left. Cari offered to have some of her unit go over the phone logs to see if they detected any patterns. Najat took her computer and the leather journal with her to her own office.

Tynan lingered behind. "How's the head, Chief? Still giving you a bit of pain?"

"Merc is in good hands." Dúl's hand eased behind me and circled my hip.

I held back a smile, but Tynan, clearly not too bright in the morning, offered his king a lopsided one. "Of course, your highness. Just checking. I'm sure the rest of the operatives will be relieved to hear they're healing well after showing such bravery and concern for the team."

Dúl's glare was charged enough to disintegrate Ty, so I figured I'd better intervene. "All good, Tynan. Thanks. And I didn't do anything you wouldn't have done yourselves."

"Mayhap, but I believe my telling will be much more fun than yours."

I laughed. "Whatever. I'll hold a big briefing once we know something more concrete. Now, if you don't mind, I do need to rest." My head throbbed again.

Almost too quick for me to see, the corners of Ty's lips drooped a fraction, and the crinkles across his forehead deepened. But then his features smoothed out, and he was his snarky self again. Funny how I could pick up on the subtle change so easily in someone I barely knew.

With a dramatic bow, he backed toward the door. "As you wish, Chief." Before leaving for good, he bowed to Dúl. "Your majesty."

Dúl muttered something under his breath that I chose not to ask about.

~*~

By the next day, the pain in my head had faded to a dull ache, and the dizziness went away. I showed up to work in what I now thought of as 'field gear,' black jeans, black tank, and a new navy pea coat with extra pockets sewn into the inner lining. If I needed a new coat, might as well upgrade, I figured.

My two long braids were also back.

I called the SO's together for a meeting, the non-locals connecting via scrying glasses or phones. Najat hadn't found anything, and the codebreaker in Italy was still hard at work according to Riz.

But Cari had some news to report. More accurately, Tynan had pointed something out to Cari's crew in addition to what they were already seeing on their own.

She explained, "We weren't really looking for anything specific, just whatever seemed to form a pattern. So, we started looking at the cell phone pings. They clustered around areas where there were confirmed VampX labs. No surprise there.

"But one of those areas has shown recent activity even though that lab was very recently destroyed." She gave Ty a nod.

I perked up at that from my seat at the head of the table. She had sent me a message that hinted something might be worth checking out—hence the field gear—but I did't realize it would be the Poughkeepsie lab, active again.

The thought of my old enemy, Donny, who I left for dead at the hands of the vampires he betrayed, sent a wave of heat through me. That fire was chilled only by the thought of Paris, who played *me* dirty by working with Donny.

"Show me the addresses," I said, a knot slowly forming in my throat. It shouldn't come as any big revelation that he might still be involved with the vampires. He's an addict, and the way things ended between us was admittedly ugly. Still, my heart sank when I saw my former address on the list.

I swallowed. "I'll handle this myself. Keep me posted of anything else that comes up."

"Want some company, boss?" Ty, who I now noticed was dressed in black fatigues and an olive, hooded tee shirt, gave off an aura of all business. He stood, as if I was going to have company whether I wanted it or not.

A sarcastic comment sprang to my lips, but I paused. The message he was sending was subtle yet powerful. He was ready to follow me and making no secret of it. Appreciating the gesture, I swallowed my knee-jerk snark. "I've got this, thanks. Some personal business isn't as finished as I thought. However..."

We shared a car up to Poughkeepsie and then split up. He headed out to the lab, while I paid a visit to Paris.

Chapter 7

A sense of dread settled in my gut as I staked out the entrance of my former residence and waited for Paris to go home. While I could have used my new abilities to wrap the shadows around me, concealing me from all but those who looked very carefully, I resorted to my second nature and shifted.

Today, I became a little old woman, wrapped in scarves, shawls, and a shabby wool coat. I pretended to wait at the bus stop in a long skirt. My ankle boots were too short to cover a little patch of leg. Only saggy nylons protected that spot. My poor legs froze. If anyone noticed how many buses passed me by, they didn't bother me. The sun sank behind the buildings stabbing me with a pang of longing for a cozy fire instead of the raw wind.

Finally, Paris showed up.

He staggered toward the building, thankfully alone, and pulled out his key to the outer vestibule. Once he was inside, I counted to sixty before following. Not that it would have made any difference—I still had my own set of keys to the building and the apartment.

Upstairs, I listened at the door. No sounds came from within. In his state, he probably crashed before making it to the bedroom. Disappointed in him that he hadn't thought to change the locks, I let myself in. It would have been one of my first priorities if our situations were reversed.

As expected, Paris sprawled on the sofa in his boxers. Beer bottles, assorted fast-food wrappers and bags, and dirty dishes covered every available surface in the room. My dude desperately needed to open a window or buy an air freshener. It smelled of mold and unwashed laundry.

What surprised me was the childlike giggle, so faint I questioned whether I really heard it or if my sub-conscious was just screwing with me.

It wasn't.

His body remained stock still, but his eyes popped open. A dim lamp on a side table highlighted the red rims around his eyes. *You dumb ass.*

The vampire nation was either slumming, or I got someone's attention.

A slow smile unveiling newly grown fangs wasn't necessary to tell me what he'd been up to since our last meeting. "He said you'd be around sooner or later."

"Who did?" My mouth went dry. I knew what he was going to say but needed the confirmation.

"Chevalier. He says he'll be seeing you soon."

"Aw, Paris. No."

"Like you give a shit. You saw how messed up I was,

but you just kicked me to the curb anyway. Dropped me like a bad habit when I needed you most." He sat upright, moving faster than ever. Than before being turned into the enemy. Unused to his new power, he nearly propelled himself off the couch.

"Don't try to blame me for your stupid choices."

"Choices?" He laughed, a sarcastic sound that filled me with anything but good humor. "You want to hear about my *choices*, Merc? I was picked up from one of the X houses and brought to the big boss a little while after you blew up the lab.

"He made me watch while his crew chowed down on Donny. Then they tortured me. Three days wanting information on *you*. And you know what?" He rose, slowly, from the sofa. "I told him everything. Because fuck you, Merc. Fuck. You."

The giggling surrounded him again, slightly louder than before. Lost in his rant, he didn't respond to the sound. His gruesome chuckle mixed with it. My skin crawled.

I began to back away. If I stayed here, there were only two choices—kill Paris, or let him kill me. I didn't think I could do either.

He stalked toward me, every movement predatory. His eyes gleamed black contrasting the crimson rims. "Even after I spilled my guts, almost literally, he made me beg for death. And then, instead, this is what he gave me. Never ending hunger. And all because of you." Paris lunged from his seat.

I dove to the side. He crashed into the small dining table near the window.

The door was about ten feet behind me and shut. No escape that way. "Paris, I never meant for any of that to blow back on you, but if you were on Big Daddy vamp's radar, that was because you got in bed with Donny to begin with. That wasn't my fault."

Paris's leg muscles bunched again. He leapt at me with a roar. Ready this time, I ducked under his arms and raced toward the bedroom.

Catching my braids, he threw me backward. I sailed onto the table, crushing it. My head exploded with pain. Adrenaline forced me to move—rolling away from a foot aimed at my jaw. Again, he used too much force and slipped, tangling himself in the debris. He cried out as he landed in a split, his balls narrowly missing a jutting piece of wood.

I was in no shape to fight him with these enhanced abilities. Plan C—run.

Snatching up the table leg nearest me, I hurled it at the window and then skittered toward the same.

Half a second after the leg crashed through the glass, I followed and slammed against the rail of the fire escape. Paris reached the window with eerie speed. I flung myself over the rail and hung there.

Suspended four stories up, I willed my back to shape and stretch. I didn't have time for a full change. I prayed I didn't need one.

Between the slats of the fire escape, I saw Paris leaning out the window to see if I had hit the ground.

"Where are you, you stuck up bitch?" He climbed onto the platform.

"There you are." Paris crouched and started to pry my fingers from the rail. "I can't wait to see you, your family, and those fullblood fucks all go up in flames." There was a feral growl in his voice. This wasn't Paris anymore. Focused on making me fall, he didn't notice the shift taking place.

"Bye, bitch." He stood and lifted his foot to stomp on my hands.

I let go. My newly formed wings wouldn't carry my body's weight upwards, but they allowed me to glide to the ground, unharmed. I disappeared into the night.

If Paris had told the truth about giving all my secrets to the vampires, I needed to warn my family. My feet flew over the pavement as I half ran, half glided, through back alleys and deserted streets, the two blocks toward Rebus's bar.

~*~

Since it was the middle of the week, The Bar was dead. Only a few hardcore customers nursed drinks and chatted with Rebus. Nat was somewhere in the back when I rushed across the dim room.

The jukebox in the corner was off in favor of a small flat screen television above it. A couple of guys watched replays of some football game from a round table close to the TV.

Rebus glanced up from cleaning glasses. "Hey! If it isn't my favorite spy master." He whispered the last part although no one was paying attention.

"Hey, Reeb. Where's Nat?"

"Went upstairs a little early. Had a headache, and it's not exactly jumping in here. What's up?"

"I need to talk to you both."

He called Nat upstairs and while we waited for her to come down, I pulled him by the arm toward the back office. Rebus was behind the desk, and I sat across from him when she joined us there, out of the patrons' hearing range.

I told them what happened with Paris. "And now that we just blew Chevalier's facility sky-high, he might come after you guys as payback."

"That little shit!" Nat rarely cursed, but it warmed me inside when she did.

Rebus didn't need any coaxing onto the Paris-bashing train. "I always said he was no good."

"I know, guys. I should have taken him down, but..." I hated to admit that Paris still had a hold on my emotions.

Nat leaned down to hug me and stroke my hair. "Of course, sweetie. Years of history don't erase themselves overnight. That's why you should have let *us* deal with him."

I gave a weak laugh. "Thanks, but I owe him. Big time. I should be the one to finish things with him. In the meantime, what are we going to do about Serg Chevalier?"

Rebus shrugged and seemed surprised I was even asking. "We'll do what we've always done. You and I have screwed up people's plans plenty of times.

The Bar is warded and secure against vamps, fey, and changelings. So is the apartment. Chevalier, Paris... Let 'em come."

I wasn't reassured, but what options were there? He couldn't abandon his business to hide out in the Dreaming like I wanted him to. "All right. But I'm going to station a couple of Shadows to watch the place anyway. Extra backup can't hurt."

"Sure thing, babe," Rebus said. "We'll be fine. Now why don't you sit down and tell us how the job's going?"

I did and later spent the night in their apartment, unable to shake the sense of dread that something bad would happen as soon as I let them out of my sight.

~*~

The next morning, I was up before the sun. I left my parents a note and then borrowed a few blades, restraints, and a sedative. Rebus wouldn't miss them.

Paris may have thought I ran off, shocked and scared about his new status as a vamp, but all he succeeded in doing was to piss me off.

The first rays of sun were brightening the sky by the time I reached the building. Since I broke his living room window last night, he would have to be sleeping in the bedroom unless he wanted an evil sunburn. One thing Donny told me before his timely demise was that vampires could go out during the day, but they couldn't exactly hang out in direct sunlight, especially without eye-protection.

The streets were quiet this early, but I found an

alley to shift in. I liked the wings last night, so I took the time to embrace the sensation of them stretching into shape, little pinpoints pricking my skin as each feather sprouted. Meanwhile, I shrank as small as I could to reduce my weight. Silent as an owl, I flew up to the broken window and stepped inside, careful to avoid any broken glass.

The muscles along my spine flexed, and the wings folded. It was like being some kind of dark angel. Tip-toeing, I crept toward the bedroom.

Paris sprawled across the bed, still clothed. I knew that position. He must have taken a hit of VampX, or maybe he had upgraded to FeyX by now, and passed out cold. Good.

I pulled a wooden cylinder from my pocket and fit a small dart into the opening at one end, aimed, and blew. The dart lodged in his neck. He never budged. The sedative dose was small and wouldn't last long.

Working fast, I restrained his hands behind his back with a set of Rebus's magical cuffs. While he snoozed, I took down the curtains from all the windows, filling the apartment with light. It wouldn't do more than irritate him initially, but that was good enough for me.

I waited.

As I watched him sleeping so peacefully, I stewed. Soon, I lost patience and stalked over to the bed. Drawing my knee in, I kicked out and slammed my heel into the side of Paris's face. That woke him up.

He yelped and struggled against the bonds. "What the fuck?" With his hands behind his back, he toppled off the bed, conveniently into a nice bright patch of sunlight streaming across the rug. He screamed. I pounced.

After rolling him to his back, I planted a knee on his sternum. "Here's how this is going to work. I went easy on you because of our past, but clearly that was a mistake, you backstabbing shit. You're going to tell me where to find this Chevalier asshole, or I will destroy you piece by fucking piece. Nod if you understand."

He was still groggy from the drugs in his system but signaled that he heard me.

There wasn't exactly a handbook on how to handle an addict ex who would rip my throat out in a heartbeat. This was the quickest and most practical route to the information I needed without acquiring any bonus piercings, courtesy of his new fangs. It seemed fair enough to me.

Paris moaned. "Sun...face is burning...Let me up, stupid bitch!"

"Whatever. Where is he?" I grew bigger and heavier and leaned into my knee until I heard his joints crunching and resisting.

I let him wheeze curses for a few dozen seconds and then eased up. "Answer me!"

It was pitiful and pathetic how quickly he gave in. I'm no professional torturer, so I can only imagine how easy it was for Chevalier to get my whole life story out of Paris.

Chevalier was in Quebec. I'd deal with him soon enough.

I told myself that I had to end Paris because if I didn't, he'd come at me again with a vengeance.

My hand rested on the shadow dagger in its sheath at my hip. I gripped the hilt and gazed down at my ex-lover. Not too long ago, I was planning a life with him. But he had betrayed me in so many ways I didn't know where to start counting.

I kneeled next to him. The dark red around his eyes radiated down his cheeks, his skin cracking and peeling. Yet he stared back at me, defiant. I wanted to destroy him, but somewhere behind the evil that now inhabited him, was a man—as flawed as he was—who I once loved. I couldn't do it.

Standing, I sheathed the knife. "You deserve to die for everything you've done to me. But I'll spare you for now. Enjoy your tanning session."

I kicked him across the jaw again. Showing mercy would probably come back to bite me in the ass, but maybe luck would be on my side. Maybe since he was a new vampire, the sun would actually do enough damage to kill him. Or if not, maybe Paris would be scared off.

Before I left, I gave him another double-dose of the sedative, cut his clothes from his body, and repositioned him in the sunlight. It wouldn't kill him. But it sure would make him feel like hell.

Now we were almost even.

Chapter 8

Before heading back to the City, I called the office, too wound up to wait until I got there to share the information I'd learned with Dúl. He was still at the castle, so I called Najat instead and set her to finding Chevalier's location.

I detoured to my apartment to use the portal from there to my suite at the castle. From a casual viewpoint, it appeared to be a privacy screen with the shimmery image of the dusk sky in the Shadow Court embroidered into a black background.

When I stepped up to the screen, the image swirled until I was looking into a dark void. I stepped in. Quick as a blink, I was in my room at the castle. Too eager to bother searching for Dúl myself, I mentally summoned a raven.

A moment later one landed on my balcony rail. I let the raven in. He seemed to favor me and often came when I called.

"Feather, do you know where the King is?"

"Parlor."

"Thanks. Want a snack?"

He bobbed his head twice and followed me over to a tall dresser. A container with a sliding lid held dead crickets. He helped himself, and I went down the long, curving staircase made of stone.

A huge ballroom and formal dining room took up one side of the first floor. The ballroom led into a throne room, which had a separate entrance and was hardly ever used, at least not by Dúl.

Facing the immense double entrance doors from the stairs, the east side of the first floor had a more modern office toward the front of the castle where Morgan met with the Dreaming's residents to mediate their issues. Down the hall from her office was a cozy dining room, several parlors, and less formal sitting rooms. The back of the building also had kitchens and a hall that led to a rear extension and the grounds.

I poked my head into each of the parlors until I heard voices in the next room. My spine tensed as I opened the door. It would have been polite to knock, but I reasoned that this was technically communal space.

Opening the door quietly, I heard Dúl laughing and reminiscing about some encounter involving him and Morgan. They had their backs to the entrance. Morgan actually chuckled as he spoke. They stood in front of a very realistic painting of the Winter Queen. And there was a third person in the room.

The new woman had deep umber skin with a mass of dark red curls on one side of her head. The other side was shaved. She wore a tight green dress

—seasonally inappropriate at that—which clung to every millimeter of her perfect, hourglass curves. Her arm was linked with his.

I looked down at myself, dusty and disheveled, like someone who just came in from the field. Which I had. I didn't know who this woman was, but the urge to slink back to my room and at least splash some water on my face was strong.

Too late. He saw me and waved me over.

"Hey." I forced a smile on my face and crossed the room, stopping in front of him and the stranger. I didn't love that she was still hanging on him.

He turned but made no attempt to extract himself either. "Merc, love. Is everything all right? I didn't expect to see you until later. You look..." He frowned.

"Intense," Morgan cooed when he faltered. Great. Morgan noticed that I was flustered too.

The redhead grinned, like her long, lost best friend had just returned to her. Something was definitely off here that was beyond my current capacity to figure out.

"Everything is fine. Mostly. I looked for you at the office and wanted to discuss something. Seems to be a bad time, though. We can talk later." I hated that I felt stupid and out of place. I had to get away from this room.

"Nonsense." He came to me, wrapped his arms around my waist, and briefly nuzzled my neck. "This is actually perfect timing. There's someone I want you to meet. Over his shoulder, he said to Morgan, "We were done, right?"

"Yes, my lord. I'll take my leave." Morgan started to go.

"Actually, this concerns you too, Morgan." No way was I suffering this awkwardness alone.

The other woman sauntered over and took my face in both her hands, inspecting me before planting a kiss on my forehead. "Merc! It's so good to meet the person who's captured my big brother's heart! No offense, Morgan."

Morgan didn't dignify the comment.

"You're Athena?" If it were possible for me to will the floor to open up and swallow me, I would have.

This was possibly one of the top three worst ways to meet Dúl's sister for the first time. They looked nothing alike, but he'd talked about her enough that I should have realized who she was. She pulled me from her brother's grip and gave me a warm hug.

"It's... um, nice to meet you too," I muttered, trying to smooth down my hair.

The painting they had been looking at was over a long sofa. I pointed to the picture and sat. "That's Nemesis, right?"

Athena nodded. "Yes, an uncanny likeness, right down to the last wrinkle around her scowl." She scrunched her own nose, as if someone farted.

The portrait bothered me for some unknown reason. "It seems different somehow than when—" I stopped and avoided glancing toward Dúl, not wanting to let on that we had been watching Nemesis.

"Don't worry, he spies on everyone. One day, he's going to see something he doesn't want to."

He frowned at her, but I could tell he wasn't really annoyed. I was reminded of times when Rebus or Nat would get exasperated but never mad when I was a teenager. "There was something off about her when we were scrying, but I can't put my finger on exactly what. The picture just seems wrong somehow. Or maybe there is something up with her, like Dúl said."

"You could have seen an illusion," Morgan said, head tilted to one side as she considered the image. "If she wanted to block your scrying. A djanin could intercept with a realistic enough copy. Or there could be another shifter we don't know about impersonating her. No offense, Merc."

What could I say? Just because they had no record of any other full shape shifters didn't mean they didn't exist. "Djanin? I thought they were extinct or run out of the Dreaming or something." Rebus told me about them when I was young, but I remembered next to nothing—a "vanquished race" whatever that meant.

Dúl lifted an eyebrow and joined me on the sofa. "There are a few scattered around the Waking, but they would have no reason to attack us. We far outnumber them. It would be suicide."

"I'm pleased to hear you're finally being realistic about our nasty crone, Brother. There's no imposter or illusion. It's a power grab, of course. One can expect no less from Nemesis." Athena's lush lips twisted in a way that definitely did not flatter her otherwise smooth features.

"Oh-kay... Serg Chevalier still seems like our best path to a solid answer. We're getting close. I think as soon as Najat gets a bead on him, we should take him out before Paris has a chance to alert him. I left him immobilized, but that won't last long."

"Paris? As in your former... That's where you're coming from?" Dúl's brow furrowed, and he gave me a slow once over, pausing at the remnants of cuts and scrapes on my hands and face.

"Yes, him. I was following up on a lead from the phone log we found, and it brought me to him. He's been turned. After he tried to kill me—"

"Kill you?" Dúl's jaw tightened. "Of course. You went without backup. Again. Did you also wear a *Bite Me* t-shirt?"

"I made him tell me where to find Chevalier. Then I left him to roast in the sun. Everything was fine."

Morgan just shook her head, her back stiff. "All right. That's wonderful, but I don't see why you need me here."

"I-I just wanted your input." *And a buffer.*

She had been dealing with my responsibilities for a long time. It would be stupid to reject her insights for the sake of trying to prove something. Solving this puzzle and protecting the court would go much further in showing my value to the Shadows.

"Oh." Her posture relaxed a little. "Well, in that case, I agree. If you've got the opportunity to get rid of the threat, you should take it. Cut the head off the snake, so to speak. Send the vampires into chaos, which should make it easier to suss out who they're partnering with." She gave me the tiniest smile, and I appreciated the moral support.

"So, you intend to lead the assault? Again?" Dúl's irritation was palpable now, even without our link.

My mouth opened to respond. Nothing came out. How could he think I wouldn't be directly involved? None of this conversation was going according to plan.

Morgan stepped in. "Isn't that why you made Merc Shadow Master? Why wouldn't they do the job they were hired to do?"

Yeah! That!

"I hired them...I hired you, Merc, to lead. I thought you'd delegate more. Yet you insist on recklessly throwing yourself into danger."

"That's what I do. You knew that. You *wanted* that. No one ever said I would change and become a desk jockey."

His features pinched, and he seemed about to say something that would most likely lead to another argument. We were doing more of that lately. Not the flirty banter we shared before. Real fights. I was having *déjà vu*, and not in a good way.

Athena bailed us out. "If you two can postpone your relationship angst for a few moments, I need to return home. These cold temperatures in your court are intolerable."

Dúl rose to embrace his sister and kiss her on the cheek.

"I'll see myself to the portal." Athena waggled her fingers over her shoulder at me as she exited. "Lovely to meet you, Merc! Please stay alive. I look forward to getting to know you better soon!"

Once she was gone, Morgan picked up where we had left off. "The question for now is whether a strike team should prepare to ambush this vampire lord. Truthfully, Merc, you don't need to consult either of us. But since you have given us the courtesy, my advice is to follow your instincts.

"On that happy note, I will leave you two to your fight and inevitable make-up sex. One question, Merc. Will Najat be joining you as well?"

It was a testament to how I was growing used to Morgan's biting bluntness that I could answer without flinching. "Probably."

"Well then, I suppose I had better go say some goodbyes of my own."

By the time she was gone, I had taken some deep breaths and calmed my annoyance. I knew that Dúl was only worried about losing me. Still, I couldn't send others into a situation I wouldn't enter myself. He had to understand that.

"Look, if you don't think we should make the attack, we can discuss that, but I'm not going to fight with you about how to do my job. I've come back from plenty of scrapes without having anyone with me. I'll be fine."

"Yes, I've seen the injuries firsthand." He leaned in, closing the gap between us. "I can't lose you, Umbra." Our foreheads almost touched.

"Then don't try to stop me from doing what I need to do, and just keep taking such good care of me when I return." I smiled then. "How do you think I feel? You're a king, with plenty of enemies, not the least of which are your own siblings. You could be assassinated or something. I'm not asking you to give up your throne."

He gazed into my eyes, scorching my insides with his intensity. His fingers trailed butterfly soft over my cheek. "I would in a heartbeat if I could."

I claimed his lips with mine for a sweet moment. Then I reminded him, "I would never ask you to."

"All right, love. Not that I can stop you, but I think you're right about your plan. You'll take the same squad?" He nuzzled my neck.

"Yeah. It worked out well last time. Ty makes a great second-in-command, and at the end, Riz came in clutch."

"You mean Tynan and Maurizio?" His lips twisted in irritation again, which I found oddly adorable.

I kissed along his throat and straddled his thighs. "You know, we've already had one fight. If you're going to have a jealous fit about my team, that will be double the making up. I just happen to have some time until Najat contacts me."

I pulled back and watched him lick his lips. The glint in his eyes was wicked, just as I wanted.

"Yes, I am insanely jealous that they have the honor of protecting you. Meanwhile I am stuck in my office worrying. However, I'm fine with *saying* we fought about your male team members and skipping right to the reconciliation." His kiss stole my breath.

"Excellent plan."

Chapter 9

As it turned out, I didn't have much time to kill at all. Two hours later, I was stepping through a portal from my suite to my office. Dúl left for a fun-filled meeting with Orion and Athena. Nemesis's odd and suspicious behavior continued to stress him.

The team brought me up to speed on what intel they had gathered. Then we gave Najat the floor.

"It has been challenging to find Monsieur Chevalier up to now because he is quite careful to avoid leaving a digital trail. However, with Paris's cell phone and a general location, I have been able to trace Chevalier's cell. I have GPS coordinates."

She pressed a button on her keyboard and a 3D image streamed out of a tiny, dome-shaped object on the desk. "He is here. On the outside, it appears to be a simple log cabin in the forest, with a barn less than a hundred yards away. However, it has been reinforced with concrete, bullet-proof glass, and there is also a bunker underground. I would imagine he's made a good number of enemies, human and otherwise."

"Najat, you are incredible. I won't even ask how you learned all that, but it's amazing." I wanted to hug her.

"There's more. After the destruction of the Fantine facility, it seems he brought the remaining employees to this bunker. Several phone numbers from the log pinged to the general area. He's not alone."

"Has Paris tried to warn him yet?" I didn't know how long it would take him to free himself and heal enough to act, but I wouldn't bet my life or the lives of my team that it would be long.

"I have not seen anything from his phone yet."

"There's a small stroke of luck. But still, we're going to need to go in a little stronger than last time. Okay, Shadows, consult with Najat about numbers and then pull your squads together. We'll meet for a briefing in the conference room in 30 minutes."

I *could* delegate when I needed to.

Everyone filed out, all except for Tynan, who stayed with his hand on the doorknob.

"What's up, Ty?" I had thought about shifting as I had usually done before a job, but as he stood there, I changed my mind. If I was trying to gain their trust, constantly switching faces or bodies wouldn't help the cause.

"How are you feeling? The head and all?"

"Um, I'm okay. Seems better. Thanks for asking." Where was this going?

"That was pretty crazy back there. Putting yourself at such risk."

"What was crazy about it? I had to make sure

everyone got out, didn't I? Why don't you come in and sit down? I have a feeling there's more on your mind than my head injury."

He did, settling on one end of the sofa while I took the opposite side.

"I don't know if I would have done the same. Seven hells, I *know* I wouldn't have. The whole point of having leaders and footmen is for the footmen to bear the brunt of the danger."

"Yeah, sorry. Not that kind of leader."

"That's my point. You don't seem to grasp that your safety comes before ours. You call the shots from a distance. *You* have to make it back. Fallen Shadows can be replaced. But who can replace you?"

This from the guy who was recently pranking me. "This is a switch. You didn't seem so concerned when you were hazing me." A smile softened my words.

He watched me for a few seconds, incredulous. "That was an act, ya ninny. And not dangerous. All due respect, Chief, I've trailed ya for years. I know exactly what you're capable of, but I didn't want to let on to the others. Figured I'd help change their minds one at a time. I see you picked up on that strategy."

Still surprised at being called a ninny, I didn't know how to respond. I had totally forgotten that Dúl said Ty was my tail.

He was still talking. "Listen. I care about what happens to you. You're probably the best thing that's happened to this court in a long time. We need you in one piece. So, think about maybe not putting yourself out there so much."

I let out an amused huff. "Jeez, you sound just like him. Suddenly, all you guys seem to think I can't handle myself because I have a job title."

Leaning closer, he became more intense. "That's not it at all. For the King's part, he loves you and can't stand the idea of you getting hurt. Don't tell him I said this, but he doesn't always think things through. Offering you this position made you happy, takes care of your needs, and keeps you close. He didn't consider the downside.

"For my part, it's not just friendly concern. I have a bad sense about this Chevalier character. It's hard to explain, but there are...energies being aimed at you—coveting, curious but also pure hatred. Sadistic. Some creature—not sure if it's Chevalier or the one pulling his strings—isn't sane, and it particularly wants to see you suffer. This entity is holding back. Something is tying its hands for now. And it hates you even more for that. The whole thing is a jumble, and that scares me. Too many layers I can't pick apart."

That was sobering. How did I end up on so many radars? "I guess it makes sense he would hate me after what I did to his businesses. I all but directly challenged him with that Donny stunt. Probably not my smartest move."

"Right, but it's more than that. This feels very old, ancient. It's almost like different... Think of the energies I see as ribbons. Each being gives off its own ribbon. But what's reaching out toward you—which is strange in itself—are several wound together as one. I don't know what it means, but it's making me uneasy. You should stay far away from this vampire and let us take him down. Delegate." With that, he brightened a little, but I could still see the tension in the set of his jaw.

"I believe you, Tynan, and I appreciate you telling me all this. But let's say I don't go. How does that look to the Shadows? I'd be right back at square one. Pranks and chaos. Distrust and disrespect. You know I'm right."

Ty laced his fingers together as if he wanted to clobber something. He didn't—couldn't—argue.

"Look, I'm not going to take any stupid risks—"

"Like going to see your now-vampiric ex-boyfriend?"

I didn't bother to ask how he knew about my movements. If Dúl still had Ty tailing me, I reasoned that even the President had a secret service detail. It meant I was important.

A laugh burst out of me, and I couldn't keep my face straight.

"Ty, I can't just hide out here. It's not who I am. Anyway, if Chevalier wants me as badly as you think, he'd come for me here eventually. I'll just have to trust that you guys will have my back."

He stood to leave, clearly not thrilled with that answer. With his hands jammed into his pockets, he nodded and headed out.

"You can count on us, Chief. I'll make sure of it."

~*~

When I entered the conference room, two dozen faces followed my progress to the front and gave me their rapt attention as I stood behind the podium. A vibe of eagerness settled into the room. It was infectious. I couldn't have sat out this mission if I wanted to.

"Okay, Najat. You got numbers for me?"

"As far as I can tell, you're looking at about fifteen. But I'll have a better picture once we're there."

My conversation with Ty must have been weighing on my mind more than I thought because I made a snap decision. "Actually, I think I'd like you to sit this one out. Can you use the ravens or some other means to get in close?"

I had a moment to worry that she'd be offended at not being included, but instead, she breathed easier. And when she caught my eye, that confirmed it had been the right decision.

"Absolutely, Chief. You'll be covered either way."

"Awesome. Now—"

"One thing that may cause us some challenge, Chief."

I waited. It was still daytime.

"There's a fast-moving storm heading into the area, which not only will cause some issues with travel, but will also blot out any sunlight, although in the deep forest it may not matter."

Someone cleared their throat from behind Najat. "Chief?"

I was starting to feel like a school teacher. "Yes?"

It was Cari. "One of my group had an idea."

"Okay."

Cari's underling, who looked more changeling than fullblood, appeared to want to crawl under her seat. But she spoke up anyway. "Well, I have a cousin in the Summer Court. We heard how the shadow weapons did okay causing the blindness and all, and how the Dawn weapons were pretty useless. But the Summer Court's weapons are all fire-based. Wouldn't those maybe be more effective?"

I smiled at her. It was a good suggestion. "You're probably right, and if time were less of an issue, I'd send you to see what could be worked out with the Queen. However, you've given me an idea."

Everyone stared at me expectantly. "We've seen that human weapons have been effective. Anyone know how to work a flamethrower?"

Lost Summer

When the bird of paradise swooped in to sound the alarm, the Summer Queen was lounging in a hammock beside the hot spring behind her *manción's* west wing.

Someone was entering the court through the Night Lanes.

Many men, majesty. But not men. Do not understand.

The beautiful but simple creature did not have the intelligence to formulate more cohesive thoughts, unlike her brother's ravens or her hated sister's owls.

At once, Athena donned a gauzy wrap to cover her nakedness and sent the bird to alert her captain at arms. Then she headed to her quarters for attire more suited to battle.

Her suite of rooms was on the second floor of the estate's main house with a balcony that gave her a view for miles into the mountains and valleys of the Summerlands. Bypassing the first dressing room, lined with rows and rows of gowns and pretty things, she flung open the bamboo doors of the smaller wardrobe.

Silk linings infused with diamond dust for strength protected her skin and fit beneath leg greaves, arm gauntlets, and full armor shaped as large leaves. The suit of armor was green to provide cover among the rainforest climate surrounding Athena's home.

She was able to get most of the suit on by herself but was forced to call for an attendant to aid with tightening and attaining the perfect mold to her body so she could move unhindered.

Decco, one of her only male attendants, answered the delicate tinkle of the summoning bell. He would ride with her to meet the threat before the enemy crossed out of the Lanes.

When her garb was tied and secure, she turned to Decco. "What am I forgetting?"

"Helm, my lady?"

With a chuckle, she gathered her mahogany curls at the nape of her neck so he could settle the leaf helmet onto her head.

The final piece was her shield, a coming-of-age gift from her father. It reflected her enemies' deepest fears back at them so that they imagined they were under attack from the illusions. The shield also granted full protection from weapons or magic aimed at her.

"Are the guards waiting? My mount?" She breezed through the hall, down the stairs, and out to the stable where a majestic white unicorn was saddled and ready. It wasn't a real unicorn, of course. The real ones were endangered, even in the Dreamlands, and therefore off-limits, especially for battle purposes.

This mount was a white mare enchanted to appear as if a horn grew from its head. Just because it would be wrong to have the real thing didn't mean Athena had to deny herself of all the prettiness. Besides, the illusion might make an enemy think twice about facing off against unicorn magic.

As it stood, Moonbeam was fully armored and wore head protection. While she didn't have a horn, she could deliver a wicked head butt and lethal hoof kicks.

Athena mounted up and trotted to the *manción's* gates on the *funicorn*—her made-up word meaning false unicorn. The captain of the guard saluted, and her contingent of 25 leaf soldiers fell into place around her. They rode to the border of the Summerlands.

Waiting for them was a motley group of mythic creatures who were neither fey nor changeling nor even human. Upon closer inspection, most of them wore dark glasses. One of the contingent removed his wraparound shades and stepped forward. The red rimmed eyes explained much.

Raising herself up to her most commanding, Athena placed a hand on the short sword at her hip. "Who are you and why do you dare trespass upon my realm? Turn back and we will let you leave in peace. However, you *will not* advance farther." She brought the shield up, turning so the shining surface faced the vampires.

She was glad her dear brother had warned her that there was some threat attacking the Dreaming. Of course, Athena knew without a doubt that Nemesis was behind the whole thing. The megalomaniac would not rest until she had control over all the lands. Just because she was the oldest did not mean she was the smartest or the fairest or the most inspiring.

Those were the qualities that made a good leader. Athena called on them now, as the vampires had not moved to leave. The illusion of the Summer soldiers' numbers being five times what they were, should have sent the vampires scattering back into the portal. And where was the one commanding that portal?

"Guard at the ready!" Unsheathing her sword, she raised it over her head, preparing to give the signal to attack. Under his arm, her captain and consort gripped a long lance, its tip glowing orange. To her left, Decco held her standard high, the sunburst declaring her sovereignty in the Summerlands to all who could see it.

The enemy, in an unorganized fashion, brandished their own weapons—claws, fangs, and guns.

She bellowed, "Last chance, intruders! Go back where you came from!"

The vampire speaker, who had removed his glasses earlier, answered in a grizzled, hard voice. "Athena, daughter of the despot and usurper, Mephisto, we hereby reclaim these Summerlands for their rightful rulers! Or whatever."

Athena was still processing what he said when two things happened. First, the vampires charged and were met head-on by her forces. But she did not get the chance to engage in battle alongside her soldiers.

The second event was a mere pinprick under her

arm, at the vulnerable spot between plates of armor. In an instant, her mind began to whirl.

Decco was beside her. "My lady? Your highness?" The words were reverential, but the slow grin spreading across his face was anything but.

Before she lost consciousness, Athena swore that his face darkened and dissolved. As if

he were turning to smoke. Or shadow.

Shadow Descends to Night

Dúl slammed his office door, stormed to his desk, and in one furious motion, swept everything from it to the floor. Jeckyl and Hyde, his two ravens who perched on high branches in the aviary, woke, squawked, and flew out of sight. They had seen their master in a temper before.

This tendency to fly into rages was the reason he kept so little on his desk. He'd wrecked enough priceless items in his long lifetime to know the safe places to store them.

The mild destruction did little to curb his rage and frustration. He wished Umbra were here to provide a balm to his soul, not to mention the release of tension they often gifted him with. But right now, even the thought of his beloved could not cool his desire to rip someone's throat out.

Specifically, whoever had taken his youngest sister.

Dúl dropped into the chair behind the desk and pulled the bloodied message from an inner pocket of his suit coat. The message had been tied around the slit throat of one of Athena's birds of paradise. One of her soldiers had found the slain creature and rushed the note to the Shadow King.

It read:

In the distant past, you stole what was not yours to claim. The lands you call home will be returned to their rightful ruler, and retribution will be taken. Suffer the consequences of the father's sins.

Dúl was unsure what it all meant, but he had a strong and sickening feeling of who would have all the answers he needed—Nemesis.

He hadn't wanted to face the growing evidence that she was behind the Dreaming's vampire troubles. But Athena had made an excellent point when they last spoke. Nemesis had always been put out that their father chose Orion as sole sovereign, despite Nemesis being the eldest. Although he never fully accepted the position, she had always held a grudge, compounded by the fact that Athena claimed the warmer realms.

Still, something felt wrong. He brushed it off as sentimentality toward his older sister. He would love her even if she was behind trying to destroy the Dreaming as they all knew it. But emotion wouldn't stop him from taking her down.

Chapter 10

The wind buffeted the charter plane as it made its final approach to a private landing strip. At 4:30 in the afternoon, the cloud cover made it appear closer to nighttime. Disturbing as that was, I tried to focus on the positive. Two flamethrowers were on board with us.

As it turned out, the two cabins—side-by-side on the same property—were located in the Boreal Forest in northern Quebec, their backs to Hudson Bay.

Cameras were stashed among the trees and brush all around the place. There was no point in trying to disable them because that would alert them to our presence. Instead, we used the overcast weather to our advantage.

The gray skies gave us more darkness to hide in. The fullbloods and I all had varying abilities to camouflage ourselves in the shadows. We could sneak in as long as we moved slowly. The changelings, for the most part, found other ways to move through the landscape undetected. For all the undisciplined office behavior, their professionalism in the field impressed me.

I changed forms. My legs shortened and bent in ways unnatural to a human, while my arms also changed shape. Fur sprouted all over as my clothes absorbed and merged into my body. The skin, bones, and muscles of my face stretched and reformed into a snout. By the time I was done, I was a gray wolf, padding through the newly fallen snow.

Supports raised up the main cabin. A balcony wrapped around the entire house. Snow had already capped the pitched roof, and smoke wafted up out of a stone chimney. The front had a huge window, a fancy carved door, and a deep eave. A single lantern over the door lit the entrance.

A blackout shade was drawn over the window.

Between the two structures, a frozen stream flowed from the tree line and veered toward the second cabin and around its east side.

The smaller of the two buildings, what Najat had taken for a barn or shed, sat level to the ground. The basic design was similar to the first, except there was no balcony, just a simple porch under the front eave.

The windows on this cabin were smaller rectangles, and it seemed to have a room in the attic because another window broke up the blanket of snow. The cabin seemed empty with no fire burning and the windows all shuttered.

Once I was about fifty yards from the bigger lodge, I slowed and began to sniff for vamps from behind the cover of the trees. The only scents I detected came from that main dwelling.

As expected, several vampires surrounded the place, lying in wait. Giggles must have alerted them. As annoying as the gleeful voices were, they made for a good alarm system.

After getting the needed information, I retreated until I couldn't smell the vamps anymore and shifted back to a two-legged form in gray and white winter camo. My hair and face morphed into the form and colors of a matching balaclava. Two of my unit joined me, including one changeling with a flamethrower strapped to his back.

We converged on Chevalier's place. Three five-person squads descended from the sides and back of the property. I approached from the front with a Shadow on either side of me. Tynan insisted.

The new snow muffled our cautious steps. A faint rustle sounded to my right. I whispered, "Stop," into my communication bud and listened.

As if approaching from a far distance, the giggling started off faint and amplified in a matter of seconds. At the same time, as if it had been some kind of weird kid-army battle cry, at least ten camouflaged vampires attacked.

One lunged at my midsection. I dove and slid past him. He overbalanced as I rolled to my back, willing two throwing daggers made of shadow into my hands. He turned to press the advantage of me being on the ground, and my daggers flew. One struck his eye—the poison enough to blind him completely. The other went wide.

I bounded to my feet and ducked under his flailing arms. With the shadow dagger now in hand, I stabbed him through the other eye to finish the job. Black ichor seeped from the wound to stain the snow.

My two companions engaged with another vampire, hand-to-hand. He was choking the Shadow, Eddie, with the flamethrower. Eddie's partner, Lara, latched onto the vampire's back and was trying to wrench his head around. But there was no sun, and the vamps were at their strongest. I rushed over to help.

Before I could reach them, Eddie withdrew a key ring from his pocket. He jabbed one of the vampire's eyes, which was enough to free himself. He dropped to the ground, gasping and clutching his throat. Lara followed up with a blade to the vamp's other eye. I went to help Eddie.

My Shadows were holding their own against the vamps, but I still wasn't liking the outcome. As far as I could tell, at least two of the first team were down. Time for reinforcements.

The rest of the team waited in the trees for my signal. I whistled a short, piercing blast to call them into the fight.

All the while, the stupid laughter grated on my every nerve ending.

"Can you get that thing up and running?" I asked Eddie. There was no need. He was already settling it in the crook of his arms.

"Where do you want it, Chief?"

Wooden stairs switchbacked up to the balcony, but

my way to them was blocked. "Clear me a path to the front door."

"You got it, Merc." At that his eyes bugged out of his head for a second, as he seemed to realize what he had called me.

Amused, I said, "It's fine, just get me inside."

He pulled the trigger, and a stream of orange, yellow, and red burst forward 50 feet. Everyone in its path, vampire and Shadow alike, threw themselves to the sides to avoid the blast. Eddie advanced until my path was, in fact, open.

"Nice job, Ed. If you survive today, I'll make sure you get a bonus." I winked, sent him to provide backup to some of the others, and bounded up the stairs, two at a time.

When I reached the top, the door was cracked. Swiping a handful of snow from the balcony rail, I formed a large, hard snowball, and threw it as hard as I could at the opening.

Nothing happened, but I heard something fall over inside. I approached the entrance.

Positioned at the hinge side of the door, I peeked in. When no one was visible, I kicked the door wide before flattening myself against the wall.

Nothing happened.

I crept in.

Normally, a cozy room is inviting. This one gave off a creepy vibe, a too-perfectness that screamed *stay away* even as it beckoned. A massive stone fireplace was opposite the door, the stones arranged in the triangular shape of a roof. Gigantic logs bordered the stone, creating a miniature version of the cabin's exterior view.

Next to the fireplace, I saw part of a dining table. A wall obscured the rest. I assumed the kitchen was behind it.

Directly in front of me, stairs led up to a loft with a king-sized bed against the railing. Big antlers and a stuffed deer head decorated the walls. Besides the fire, hanging hurricane lanterns provided dim light.

There were two small, plaid couches on opposite sides of a table made of a big slab of tree trunk.

Closer to the fire, rocking in a chair and facing me, was the hippest hipster I had ever seen in my life.

His ankles were crossed, legs extended in their tight skinny jeans cuffed up at the bottom over Converse sneakers. A deep V-neck t-shirt with an ankh logo was under a leather jacket with the sleeves pushed up. And of course, no hipster would be caught without a man bun and a beard.

He had on sunglasses, like most of his kind, but they were only lightly tinted brown with wire rims. Just enough to conceal his eyelids.

"Jeez, are you going to break out some Starbucks next? Herbal tea and scones?"

He smiled benignly as that invisible presence seemed to laugh at my sarcasm. Or was it mocking me?

"I have to ask. Where is that giggling coming from? It has to be the most annoying sound I've ever heard."

"That? Oh, it is just the *Lemooria*. No consequence to you. Why don't you sit?" Chevalier's French accent lengthened his I sounds to E's.

"I'll stand. There's no need to pretend this is more civil than it really is."

"And you Americans call the French rude." His grin was predatory.

"Whatever. Here's the deal. We've got you out-numbered and surrounded. I'd bet my forces have all but obliterated yours by now. I'd like you to answer some questions. If you cooperate, I may not feel the need to torch this lovely cabin."

"Very arrogant. She showed that with the crude changeling, leaving him to be found like that."

"Who are you talking to?" And was he talking about me? "And if you're referring to Donny, I was trying to be nice. Thought you'd appreciate the gift. After all, he did rat you out."

Chevalier cocked his head as if hearing something I could not. "'E was unimportant. 'Owever, if you would like me to return the favor..."

From behind the wall, Paris appeared, looking like a refugee from a horror flick. His skin blackened and peeling, he grinned showing teeth too white in con-trast to his burnt skin. A sledgehammer hung by his side, and I didn't want to ponder what he planned to do to me.

To say I was caught off guard would be the under-statement of the year. "H-how?"

"Night Lanes. Leading my employers through, I

learned the hard way that you never go in without a weapon. Although, this was unnecessary with the new guide navigating." Paris's voice sounded raspy, as if he made up for a lifetime of non-smoking in the past few hours. "I couldn't even be mad about being replaced. Dude's got skills. And it looks like I might have a use for this after all."

Chevalier rose from his seat. "Well, I will leave you two to catch up. I have other business to attend to. Eh, Merc, you had some questions. Here is one for you. While you are here being defeated, who is in the Dreaming protecting your fey?" With a chuckle, he strolled toward the kitchen.

I lunged after him. Paris's hammer, swung like a baseball bat, stopped me short. He missed my ribs by millimeters.

Now I had no choice. I either had to kill him, quickly, or I wasn't getting out of here alive.

The head of the hammer smacked against his palm as he approached me. The giggling, even farther off now, reminded me of what he had become despite the fact that I couldn't see the red rims of his lids.

"Najat," I said, not taking my eyes off Paris. He had taken a step closer. "Alert the courts. Repeat, alert the courts. Something might be going down, and they need to be on guard." *Hell, I might be going down in a second.*

Paris's breath rattled in his lungs. He must have been on the verge of death when he woke and escaped. Why couldn't he have just died in that apartment? I still didn't know if I could put our history aside long enough to take him out.

"It won't help, you know. It's already too late for you to save your precious courts. Things have been in motion for a long time, and you can't stop them." Closer.

Could I talk him down? "What things, Paris?" I backed away. We were locked in a perverse dance that had to end in one of our deaths.

"Like I'd tell you. And you can't torture it out of me this time." He laughed, a harsh, sound that was nothing like the one I remembered from so long ago. "Anyway, you won't be around for the surprise." *Whack.* "The siblings are done, and they won't even know what hit them until it's too late."

The mention of the siblings—of Dúl—tipped my nostalgia meter far away from the side of sparing Paris's life. There was no longer a choice to be made. Even if I could sacrifice my own life, I would never sacrifice Dúl's.

With a mere thought, shadow weapons formed in my hands—a throwing dagger in my left and a long sword extended from my right.

Another step closer, another step back. Almost in swinging range again.

"Neat trick. What? New powers were your payment for fucking the king?"

"Nah, did that for free. Finally, someone who doesn't stink of vampire filth."

He telegraphed the direction the next swing was

coming from, and I dodged to the side. At the same time, I flung the dagger sidearm. The angle was off. I missed him by a mile.

But it was enough to make him duck out of the way too. We circled each other, knowing each other's fighting styles and techniques.

With my sword in the right hand, I held my left a little away from my body and willed another throwing blade to appear.

The misdirection worked. As he prepared to dodge another projectile, I slashed with the sword at Paris's arm. The razor-sharp blade relieved him of hand and hammer in one swipe. He screamed and charged at me.

In another fluid motion, I rammed the sword into his chest. Two jabs with the throwing dagger, and his eyes were gone. Sometimes, the quickest way was best.

I didn't—couldn't—linger to watch the body shrivel up. I'd have nightmares about that last expression on his face, mouth contorted in a rage-filled scream.

Running toward the kitchen, I knew I was too late. Chevalier had escaped. We'd search for him once the fighting was over, but my gut said he was gone. Maybe he thought he got his revenge for the two labs by making me kill Paris. But he was dead wrong. All he had succeeded in doing was to piss me off and make this personal. I'd make sure we met again.

Chapter 11

I got the call about the Summer Queen while en route home. Deep down, I sensed Dúl's anguish and ached to be there with him, to comfort him. But what could I do? Even though I had no siblings, I understood that nothing would really soothe his hurts until his sister was safe. But I'd do whatever I could if the damned plane would just move faster.

As soon as I got off the elevator at the penthouse floor, I rushed to his office. The room was messier than I had ever seen it, and he was slumped in his chair, brooding in the dark. Only a single small light near the door allowed me to see him at all.

I crossed the room in a flash and pulled him to me. "*¿Lo siento, mi amor. Qué necesitas?* Whatever you need, I'm here."

His arms wrapped around my waist, and his head nestled against my belly. He sighed. I hugged him, kissed his raven hair, willed every ounce of love and sympathy I had into him.

He didn't seem inclined to talk, so I held him for

several minutes. Finally, he lifted his head, met my gaze, and cleared his throat.

"Thank you, Umbra. I needed that. As much as I would love to spend the rest of eternity shielded by your arms from this horror, Orion will unfortunately be here soon to discuss... options."

I sat on the desk and crossed my ankles.

He rested his head in my lap, his fingers tracing patterns along the outside of my hip. Another deep exhale spoke volumes about his thoughts on the "options" his brother would propose. "Love, were you aware you lapsed into Spanish just now?"

"Oh? No. I wasn't aware..." My shoulders tensed. Discomfort wormed through me, which I wanted to examine about as much as I wanted to explore bulimia as a weight loss method. "Anyway, what's on the table so far? Someone should examine the note. In the Waking, forensic teams can find people with traces of DNA left on objects." Why was I human-splaining?

He glanced at me. "Your deflections are usually smoother than that, love." At my glare, he smiled wistfully and ran a finger across my bottom lip. "All right, we won't discuss it. In the Dreaming, those with fey blood also leave signatures, echoes of themselves. A team of Shadows is looking into it but have found nothing so far."

"Okay, what about enemies? Who would—"

"Later, love. When Orion gets here. We'll spend more than enough time hashing out every possibility multiple times, I'm sure. For now, I just want to breathe you in."

So, we waited for the Dawn King. My unease grew.

Orion arrived minutes later.

Despite the cold weather, he showed up in long cargo shorts, hiking boots, and a Baja hoodie hand-woven in blues and sea greens. His blond hair hung loose, framing his bronze face and hanging around his shoulders. I hadn't noticed last time I saw him that his roots were brown, and in some areas, it looked like dreadlocks might be forming. He might have been a surfer going to a beach bonfire rather than a king deciding whether to attack one sister in hopes of re-covering the other.

The brothers greeted each other with chilly nods. No handshakes, certainly no hugs. Even speaking each other's names seemed hard for them. Dúl turned toward the conference room. Orion's guard rearranged themselves to flank him through the *treacherous* halls of RavCorp.

Inappropriate as it was, given the reason for their visit, I experienced a jolt of happiness when I saw which of his guards came with him.

"Tania! I didn't expect to see you." I hadn't spoken to the one person I knew in the Dawn court since we rescued Morgan.

She flinched and allowed the barest curve of her lips to show. The expression read less as pleasure and more as constipation at seeing me again. "I've been given a promotion." Her Caribbean lilt sounded stiff.

"After Anton's death, one of the other guards moved up to be Lord Orion's lieutenant, and I was offered the open post."

"That's fantastic! Congratulations, although I wish it had been under different circumstances."

The faint smile faltered. Not surprising. She had to be remembering her twin's sacrifice and death during our mission together. I knew she didn't exactly hold a grudge, but she held me responsible. Maybe I was wrong about the grudge.

I noticed after a moment that the two kings were eying us with grim frowns. Feeling my face flush, I stepped back toward Dúl. At her lord's side, Tania looked straight ahead.

Morgan had appeared without me seeing her and ushered us off to the smaller of the conference rooms.

The kings sat at either end of the oval conference table. Orion's people stood behind him, Morgan sat to Dúl's left, and I took a seat at his right. Dúl then produced the note that was recovered from Athena's court.

When Orion saw the blood on it, he gasped and gripped the edges of the table. It was a testament to how crushed the brothers were that Dúl didn't use the reaction as an opportunity to deliver a nasty dig.

"Not her blood, brother. One of her messenger birds'. Its throat was slit, likely to prevent it from raising an alarm." He went quiet for a moment before mumbling, "You know how noisy those blasted things can be."

"True." Orion said. After a few seconds of pinching the bridge of his nose, he held a hand forward for the note. His eyes shone. I passed it to him.

After reading it, he looked across at his brother. "*'Sins of the father?'* That sounds a lot like Nemesis."

"Agreed." Dúl steepled his fingers as he gazed across the table. No expression altered his features to expose his thoughts. My only hint of his angst was the bond we shared, and even that wasn't giving me much to go on.

So, this is Dúl in full king mode. It was a little sexy but somewhat unsettling at the same time.

"Given the treasonous circumstances, we have no choice but to apprehend and imprison her. I am prep—"

"Apprehend? You couldn't even make it past the castle doors to pay a friendly visit." Orion smirked. "You told us how off-kilter her behavior has been. There's nothing to say she wouldn't flat out attack you on sight if you went back."

Dúl checked his temper. "Last time, I went there alone. I am proposing...both armies to storm her lands until she is subdued." He rubbed a hand over his face, and this was the first crack to show in his armor. "While I have no desire to go to war with our sister, she's given us little choice."

"You can't be serious, Dúl." Orion leaned forward, hands placed flat on the table in front of him. "That would be exactly what she wants. It weakens us all, and then she could use the vampires to secure the rest of the Dreaming when our numbers are thinned in our respective lands. War would be madness."

"And what is our other alternative? You know she won't kill Athena outright. She's all but given us a schedule for the torture she intends to inflict."

Once again, I didn't have siblings, but this sounded much too extreme for my mind to process. It never sat right with me that Nemesis might be the culprit behind the vamps' movements. But Dúl had been more and more certain that it was her, so I assumed I was missing a piece of the puzzle.

Now I wasn't so sure that either of the brothers was seeing the full picture. Something had to be done, but full out war? I hated to say it, but I agreed with Orion.

"How can you even consider attacking your sister without solid proof it was her? It's all circumstantial. In the human world, if this were a court case, it would be thrown out..."

A glower from Dúl snapped my mouth shut. Even Morgan, composed and frowny as ever, wore a new expression: shock. Weren't we brainstorming? If I wasn't supposed to voice an opinion, why was I here?

Then I looked down the table at Orion and his soldiers. If smugness came out of slot machines, I had just hit the big Cha-Ching. All except Tania, who closed her eyes and shook her head. *Damn.*

I didn't know what they were so happy about. Not like they had thought of it. I started to sputter, trying to quickly think of a way to recover.

Dúl's lips pressed into a thin line, and I gave up. Clearly, I had done enough damage.

Orion, however, jumped right in to piggyback on my misspoken ideas. "Your Shadow *Master* makes a compelling point. Not about the humans. Obviously, they are beyond irrelevant. But before we engage in an act that will hurt us all, perhaps we should investigate further. You should be able to get someone in covertly. It's your specialty, isn't it?"

My reasons for disliking Orion flooded back. The emphasis he put on the word "master" made me want to punch him. He was goading Dúl for kicks. Between the two of them, it was a wonder there was any Dreaming at all.

"It's *my* specialty," I blurted. In for a penny, in for a pound or whatever the stupid saying was. "*I* can get in." Maybe by throwing myself on my proverbial sword, Dúl would forgive the mortal sin of disagreeing with him in front of his most hated enemy.

If Orion's wider grin didn't tell me that this was exactly the wrong thing to say, Morgan's death grip on her pen and Dúl's sudden paleness did.

All this political posturing was over my head. On one hand, I wanted to shut up before I got exiled to the Dawn Court. But on the other hand, I had never been one to keep my opinions to myself, so why was it coming as such a surprise now?

"No." Dúl's sudden statement into the thick silence jarred everyone. "However, I will take your suggestion under advisement." He stood, his fingertips resting on the conference table. "Once we have a viable plan in place, Brother, we will contact you. Until then, Morgan will see you out. Merc? A moment?"

He stalked out of the room. To the casual observer, he was cool and collected. But I wasn't the casual observer. I had memorized every movement of Dúl's, and right now, if he were any stiffer, he would have been made of hardening concrete.

I followed like a scolded puppy, which pissed me off. Too bad his office wasn't soundproofed. This was going to be a doozy.

Chapter 12

Dúl stopped by the door while I charged into the dimly lit room. Before he could get the upper hand, I went on the offensive. "Okay, what do you want to fight about first? How I dared to disagree with you in front of the oh-so-horrible Dawn King? Or shall we go toe-to-toe about how you don't want to let me do my job?"

Sometimes the best defense is a good offense. This was not one of those times.

The aviary was still quiet. When I turned to face him, he was gripping the knob and shaking. His image blurred and darkened, like he struggled not to dissolve and disappear into a shadow. The anger vibrating through him reminded me of the Flash when he tried to conceal his face.

When he finally spoke, his words were slow and strained. "You have no idea what you've done."

Puffing my chest, I stood my ground. "I'm sorry! I didn't intend to embarrass you in front of your brother, but if you expect me to agree with everything you say, you've got the wrong person!"

"Embarrass?" His pupils had dilated so much, his eyes looked pure black. "I don't give two shits about what my brother or his underlings think. You have completely undermined my plans, and now I am forced into a less than advantageous position."

Something wasn't adding up. "What are you talking about? Weren't you the one about to start a *war* with your sister without even confirming her guilt?"

Dúl took a few deep breaths, fingers steepled around the bridge of his nose, and lightly banged his head against the door a few times. "Morgan warned me to confide in you. We've ruled together so long, I'm accustomed to her anticipating my movements and playing along."

"Well maybe you should have only had Morgan in there with you and left me out of it!"

When he removed his hands from his face, a mask of weariness lay over his features. "No, that's not what I was implying. I should have shared my intention regarding Orion. But try to understand, kings don't generally explain themselves to anyone. I should have known better than to expect you to go along quietly."

Now that he was under control, he crossed the room and sat behind the desk, leaving me standing.

"Sit." He waved at the chair opposite him.

I did. "What the hell happened in there?"

He scrutinized me until I wanted to squirm and say something snarky. But I was still mad and wouldn't let him intimidate me.

"What do you make of my dear brother?"

Odd opening, but I went with it. "Kind of a jerk. Thinks he's better than everyone."

"The same could be said of all four of us. What else?"

"I remember from talking to his soldiers that he's pretty in-your-face. Doesn't approve of sneaking and spying. I personally thought it was kind of dumb."

"Quite. And he loves to disagree with me. I would have eventually suggested a covert mission, and he would have circled back to the idea of an attack, just to contradict me. And if we then declared war on Nemesis?"

"I don't know—he probably would have insisted on storming the castle head on."

"Yes. He would have insisted on a frontal attack. Many of his people would have been killed. And while the Winter Court was distracted by him, I could have sent someone quietly in to find out what is really going on with my sister."

It made a twisted kind of sense, but at the same time, it horrified me. "You'd sacrifice all those lives for the sake of a distraction?"

"Merc, when—and I do mean when, not if—when we declare full war with the Dawn Court, would it be better for their numbers to be thinned ahead of time? Or do we risk more of our own people by fighting him at his full strength?"

Well damn. It was ruthless, but I couldn't argue that his first responsibility was to the Shadow Court. And he was right. The only reason they were having sit-downs was because of the external threat. Sooner or later, they'd find some other reason to go back to inflicting what damage they could on each other.

There was a lot to be said in favor of being an only child.

"All right. I think it sucks, but I understand. Why didn't you just tell me?"

Dúl shrugged, more his usual self. "As I said, I'm un-accustomed to consulting with anyone. I won't make the same mistake again. Now, about our second order of business."

"Don't even think about telling me I can't do it. Seriously, you can't keep trying to stop me from doing what you brought me here to do. How do you think it would look to the rest of the Shadows? Most of them don't respect me as it is."

"Are you done?" He arched an eyebrow. I nodded. "Had my plan gone as intended, you would have been the one to complete the task. I believe you'll need to press your father for more information. Tell him it's a matter of your own life and death. My issue is that you again backed me into a corner in front of my brother."

Because he wasn't making sense yet, I waved my hand, encouraging him to continue.

"I couldn't keep you from doing this now without looking fearful, weak—unkingly—to the other courts. And denying you the mission would, as you say, make you look incapable as well. The difference is that now you will be doing this with many eyes on you instead of under cover of a distraction."

"Okay, good point, but I can handle it."

"You don't understand, Merc. No one moves through the Winter Court undetected."

"Come on—"

"No one. Do you know the scrying mirror I've been using to watch Nemesis?"

After I nodded, he continued. "That mirror is a poor imitation of one my sister has. When each of us came of age, we were given an artifact by our father. Usually an enchanted item he had won in battle. Nemesis received the mirror. With it, she can literally see everything, everywhere in her realm."

"That must be awkward for honeymooners in her court." I flashed my teeth and waggled my eyebrows to lighten the mood, but he was having none of it.

"More awkward for anyone trying to sneak into her lands." His mouth twisted to one side as he shot a pointed look at me.

In the aviary, Dúl's two ravens flapped up to the branches and perched near the glass where they could see into the office. They must have sensed it was safe to return now that the tension had eased.

"You know, you make Nemesis sound like such a whack job—cruel and paranoid. But if she's that bad why does anyone stay in her court? They can't all be too terrified to leave."

"No, for the most part her people worship the ground she walks on. They also report any odd goings-on to her guard. The Winter Court will be by far the hardest place you ever infiltrate. Being my lover might have saved you from the worst punishment if you got caught in the past. That may work against you now.

"Do you understand why I am anxious about you taking this on?"

I rose and slowly went around the empty desk to nestle myself into his lap. *"Si, amor."* This was the second time a Spanish endearment had popped out. It unnerved me, but it flowed as if it was the most natural thing for me to say. I went with it and stroked his cheek. "I do understand. But at the same time, you need to show a little more faith in me. You're not the only one who was a little embarrassed in front of the Dawn contingent."

His hand caressed up my thigh and around to my rear. "Yes, I see that now. I apologize for that. And since this is a mission of utmost importance, you're honestly the only one I can entrust it to." Burning touches trailed up my back. "But I don't have to like it."

"Dúl, I swear, I will find out what Nemesis is up to and get Athena back. And I will return to you safely. I promise."

I eyed his lips and leaned my head against his, my heart rate speeding up. Dúl sighed. With longing, I envisioned him lifting me up and easing me onto the desk. He groaned, as if to let me know he was thinking the same.

A flutter of movement behind him startled me. It was just the ravens floating out of sight.

Dúl hugged me to him. "Love, you have no idea how badly I want you right now."

"Oh, I think I have an excellent idea. You're not alone. But..."

"But."

"I know." I still kissed him then, long and deep. After I pulled away, I wrapped my arms around his neck, relishing his scent and his warmth. "I'm going to head to Rebus's and then I'll be back. You'll feel better if I have backup in the Winter Court. Does that sound reasonable?"

He kind of grunted as disappointed in the timing as I was.

I whispered into his ear. "Promise me that when this is over, we can christen that desk."

I felt his cheek shift in a smile. "Come back to me safely, and I'll do anything you want. That's a promise."

Chapter 13

The Bar in the middle of the day was a different universe than on a weekend night. The lights were brighter, while when business was booming, they were dimmed. All was quiet, but I could hear Rebus on the phone in the back office, probably placing orders.

I walked back to find him, making some noise so I didn't startle him. I listened for Nat, but she was either out or upstairs in their apartment. That was lucky. I would have loved to see her, but Rebus might be more open if it were just the two of us.

When I poked my head into the office, he glanced up, smiled, and waved me in, holding up a finger to signal he'd be done in a minute. I stood by the desk, playing with some of the knick-knacks he had there —some of his former gadgets that no longer worked or that had been upgraded. Even though I now had access to an arsenal of weapons and gadgets, I still loved how Rebus tailor made his inventions to each particular need.

It was the difference between a hand-crafted quilt

from a fair and a mass-produced job you could get in any department store.

When he ended his call, Rebus came around the desk to give me a bear hug. We were both standing about 5'8" since I had reverted to my usual, casual self for this visit. I had snagged one of Dúl's cable knit sweaters that hung past my hips and wore it over blue jeans and ankle boots.

"Hey, sweetheart." Rebus planted a kiss on my cheek before releasing me. "Haven't seen much of you lately. How's my favorite spy master doing? We haven't had any real chance to talk since you started the job."

"Yeah, it's been a little hectic. If you hook me up with a cocoa, I'll tell you all the juicy tidbits about the Shadow Court that aren't classified."

"Deal."

Instead of going out to the bar, we veered into the small kitchen in back. I had spent many afternoons at the little table up against the wall, doing homework after school or grabbing meals while the happy hour crowds imbibed liquid sustenance. Along the far wall was a stove and grill where Nat prepared the finger foods for the bar's patrons.

Rebus grabbed a small pot, cocoa mix, and a couple of mugs from a cabinet to the left of the stove. He poured milk into the pot and began to heat it. "Okay, kiddo. Cocoa is in the works. Spill. Tell me all about life as the chief Shadow."

I started with the pranking and then eased into

the troubles we were still having with the vampires. I made sure to warn him to be on alert in case they decided to retaliate against me.

"Do you have any idea what the deal is with the giggling? And Chevalier seemed to be talking to someone I couldn't hear. I would have assumed he was just nuts, but I've heard the laughter."

"Ah, yes. That. I did some digging on their origins, and indeed I learned a few interesting things."

I leaned forward. Anything that could help us at this point was welcome.

"So, the most surprising thing I learned was that they were originally creatures of the Dreaming."

My jaw dropped. "What? How is that even possible? They're so...unnatural."

"Yup. There were these spirits—the Lemooria—sort of parasites that were run out of the Dreaming in the days before the siblings ascended. By their father, in fact. These parasites found a way to latch onto human hosts and the vampire nation was born. They're living beings possessed by the spirits who slowly drive them deeper into madness."

I was still trying to process the whole "run out of the Dreaming" piece. I wondered if the changelings ever considered the possibility of having other long-lost kinfolk. I mean, for me, that could be anyone because I didn't know who my peeps were, but for others... The idea took hold although I couldn't put my finger on why.

"Were there other races kicked into the Waking?

Why would they force creatures out of their world, anyway? I mean, jeez, it's big enough. Couldn't they live and let live? the older generation fey sound like assholes. Moreso than the fullbloods of the current generation at any rate."

"Yeah, well, that was all even before my time, so I can't say. Remember, I lived in the Winter Court. Before the siblings took over from their father, there were no courts. Just one big fey realm that they had a problem sharing with others."

"Wow. I wonder if Dúl remembers anything about that time. He would have been really young, but I'll ask. He might not have made a connection, but it might be relevant. Speaking of..."

Rebus had been stirring cocoa into the warm milk and now paused to glance at me over his shoulder. "I don't like the sound of that. I'm thinking you're going to start poking again into those places I don't want to go."

His expression tore a hole in my heart. "I know, Reeb. I'm sorry. I wouldn't keep pushing if I didn't really need to know." I shared the recent details of Dúl scrying on his sister, the brothers' suspicion that Nemesis was making a play for the Dreaming, and the attack on the Summer Court.

"It's getting critical, Rebus, and what you just said about the vampires suddenly makes a lot more sense. What if there were other races that wouldn't mind a little bit of revenge against the fey? Nemesis could have a whole army just with the promise of being able to reclaim their homes."

Rebus brought the two steaming mugs to the table and placed one in front of me. He blew across the top of his, not responding for several seconds. "Tell me again what you saw in the scrying mirror."

I explained that Dúl's main point of confusion was that she had smiled while conversing with a spider. Rebus's eyebrows lifted at that.

"Huh. That is odd." He didn't elaborate and went quiet again for another minute or two. "Okay, you're obviously planning to try to get into the Winter Court to see what's what. I will tell you right up front, you most likely won't make it past the surrounding woods. However, there might be a way."

What it boiled down to was my only chance of avoiding detection would have to be infiltrating without backup. Dúl would probably not go for that. Putting that problem aside, Rebus gave me a rundown of things to watch for.

"The smiling is something to be concerned about. It's been a long time, and she could have mellowed. But her brother would know if she had."

"Maybe she has a consort..."

His look said I was so far off base, I wasn't even on the same field anymore.

"Nemesis has had multiple consorts over the years. Didn't make any difference."

"So, what did she do if she found something funny or if something made her happy?"

"When she was amused, she would let out a sort of huff. That was the closest thing to a laugh I ever heard. And her big sign of satisfaction with anything —happiness is a foreign concept to her—would be a single nod of her head."

"Okay, so I should look for those tells?"

"Not necessarily."

I thought for a moment and sipped my cocoa. It had cooled and was probably sludgy on the bottom. Somehow Rebus and I slipped back into mentor-student mode.

"Well... we've been working under the premise that something is off with Nemesis but it's definitely her. What if it isn't her at all? If someone were impersonating her, they'd have studied her behaviors. Didn't seem to pick up on the smiling thing if that's the case. It doesn't make sense though, Rebus."

"Why's that?" He finished off his drink and stared into the mug, thoughtful.

"How would someone do that? They'd have to do a wicked spell, or they'd have to be—"

He peered into my eyes. "Go on, say it. They'd have to be you. Or like you. Is that so much of a stretch? I mean *you* exist. Why wouldn't there be others?"

When he put it that way, it made sense, although I didn't want to consider the implications too deeply. I hoped it wasn't another shifter, if only for my own sake. The note left after Athena's abduction and the new information about the vampires clamored in my brain for more attention that I couldn't give right now.

"Okay... let's say however it happened, that the Nemesis currently in the Winter Court is an imposter, and they've got her behavior down cold. I need something to verify one way or another."

"Right. You'd need the most closely guarded secret in the Winter Court. One of the reasons it's so hard to get out of her guard once you've reached a certain level is that she can't have her secret get out. Usually, the only way out is death."

What on earth, or rather, what in the Dreaming could be that dire?

Rebus took the empty mugs and put them in the deep sink. He washed them both, dried them, and put them back in the cabinets. Still, he didn't speak.

Finally, he returned to the table. "You have to understand how it is in the Winter Court. Nemesis controls every aspect of everyone's lives. In exchange, she makes sure everyone is cared for completely. No one wants for anything, unless you count little things like privacy and autonomy. It's a tradeoff most of the fey in her court are willing to make.

"They treat her like a goddess.

"As a result, she has an image to uphold. Order, perfection...nothing can ever be amiss with her. The story goes that when she was a child...

Stag Hunt

Outside the door to the throne room, Nemesis smoothed her tunic and riding pants while mentally reviewing the arguments she would present to her father. Court had finished moments ago, and she'd watched until the last of his subjects exited. Only Father's advisor, Olu, would be present, and he always advocated on her behalf.

"As your only heir, sire, she must be prepared to lead in every situation," he would say.

Father typically grunted, neither disagreeing nor agreeing.

She pushed open the heavy double doors, rolled her shoulders back, and strode down the center aisle toward the golden throne. "Father, I have a request." She didn't let his eyeroll or sigh deter her. "I want to join the hunt. My riding teacher says my skills are exemplary, and my illusions can help to confuse the animal once it is found."

"Magical trickery for a hunt? Preposterous. No, go and attend to your studies, or perhaps your mother could use your assistance."

Nemesis ground her teeth, nodded stiffly, and walked out with her chin lifted. She'd hoped she wouldn't need her secondary plan. Undeterred, she walked calmly to the infirmary. At this time of day, the elder healer tended to Nemesis's mother as the early stages of her pregnancy made her quite ill. The other two traveled to the villages surrounding the castle tending to serious ailments beyond the locals' capabilities.

The room stood unoccupied, two bare beds side by side. In the corner of the room, a massive desk held vials, odd contraptions, and scrolls.

Some time ago, when Father injured himself on another hunt, Nemesis sneaked in while the healers worked on him. Too busy to worry about ejecting her, they answered her questions. Perhaps they thought the princess was interested in their vocation. Nemesis was simply curious. One could never have enough information.

There was an herbal tincture that they fed to the king to numb his pain and help him to sleep through the worst of their ministrations. She found the brown bottle now, stuffed it into her pocket, and turned right when she exited the infirmary—toward the stables.

For the briefest moment, she paused. The stable hand, Lon, was not much older or larger than herself. How much of the tincture would put him to sleep? Would too much harm him? Kill him?

No matter. If he died, which Nemesis doubted, it would be instructive for next time she needed to remove someone from her path. She poured half the bottle's contents into a cup and filled it with nectar from the kitchens along her way.

When Lon saw her approach, his eyes lit up as they always did. "Princess, what are you doing here?"

"I had hoped to join the hunt today, but Father refused me. Again. I thought you and I might spend some time together, but..." Nemesis shrugged and offered Lon the cup.

Grinning, he accepted it and chugged the contents. And dropped like a sack of flour two blinks of the eye later. She dragged him behind a bale of hay, took his clothing pausing for a moment to study his naked physique, and swapped her garb with his. Waving one hand before her face, she cast a glamour over her features. As long as she didn't speak, Father would be none the wiser.

The hounds nearly presented a problem. Her scent coupled with Lon's face confused them. But they knew her and went on with their business.

The hunt proceeded. To Nemesis, It was more boring than expected after hearing all the tales over dinners of rousing chases and near-death encounters with magical boars or stags with treacherous antlers that could gut a fey. This was just a lot of drunken riding in circles.

Her father missed a shot, and she took her time climbing down from her mount to retrieve his arrow. Unhurried, she searched through the brush for the king's special golden fletching, which now blended in with dead leaves and colors on the ground.

When she finally found it and pulled it from the soil, she heard rustling. The princess stood. She turned. A noble's arrow pointed in her direction, mistaking her for an animal. A moment later, pain shot through her shoulder as she was knocked backward. Her head smacked into a tree, and everything went black.

~*~

Rebus said, "They often enchanted their weapons since they were taking down magical creatures. The wound would never healed properly, despite the king having access to the best medics in the realm.

"Fast forward to when she took her throne. She decided right from the beginning that she didn't want any of her subjects to know, so measures are always taken to hide the fact that she doesn't have full use of the arm.

"Watch her movements in front of others. She'll always hold her staff in her right hand close to her body. She doesn't shake hands with anyone or allow anyone to kiss either hand. If she has to take something, it is always with the left. Those are the signs to watch for. If this Winter Queen uses her right arm, especially out in public, she's not the real deal."

I thought hard about what I had seen in Dúl's scrying mirror that day, but I couldn't remember what she had been doing with her hands. It was a start. Dúl had probably been so distressed about the whole situation when she rejected his visit, he most likely hadn't thought about her movements either.

"All right, I can work with that. Now, talk to me about how I can get into the court without anyone noticing. Dúl's not going to like me going in solo. I may have to leave out that little detail."

"I'm not crazy about it either, but it's the only way I can think of. Otherwise, you and any team will likely be killed on sight."

"All right. Let's not have that." I assumed I would have to impersonate one of the Winter soldiers. As I soon learned, I needed to mimic something else entirely.

There weren't but so many animals that lived in the arctic segment of the Waking; even fewer that lived in the Dreaming. My transformation had to be into something that would move around freely, wouldn't be subject to hunting, and would be large enough that I could manage the shift.

"Nemesis has a particular fondness, or respect might be a better word, for certain creatures: spiders, owls, and Tundra wolves. In the Dreaming, the Tundra wolves evolved to be able to take on human forms."

"What, you mean like werewolves?" I laughed.

"Where do you think the werewolves in the Waking came from?"

Dawn Attack

Orion woke and slipped from his bed like a ghost. Melodia, his queen and consort since before he had taken the throne, stirred, purred like a contented cat, and turned over to resume her slumber. Watching her satisfied stretches and peaceful smile as she dozed boosted his ego like nothing else. Part of him wanted to go back and curl his big body against her petite one, to gaze in wonder at her caramel skin contrasted against his own golden tan. He could almost feel the silk of her long black hair, fanned out behind her on her pillow.

A larger impulse, the same sense of disquiet that had driven him out of bed and into the dawn chill, prevented him from acting on that pleasant desire.

Bare chested and in loose shorts, he shut the balcony's glass doors and leaned against the glass bricks that formed the balustrade and the entire castle. Orion took in the vista of the beach. The sun was in its usual position, perched on the horizon, lighting the sky in shades of pink and gold.

What was it that had woken him? Certainly nothing

tangible, and this frustrated him. Extra forces now patrolled the borders to the Summerlands in case the vampires decided to attack from there. How unexpected to be more worried about that side of the realm and not the Shadowland borders. Strange times in the Dreaming, indeed.

Off in the distance, a loud boom made Orion's head shoot up. He scanned the surface of the water more carefully. Had something happened to the underwater detention units? A brief calculation reassured him that no one would be down there now. In truth, they were rarely used. The last prisoner had been Dúl's shifter.

He refused to refer to them as a changeling. If his brother's young lover was fey, Orion was a puffer fish. Whatever their heritage, they brought with them the hope of tempering Dúl's chaotic nature. Perhaps there could be peace between the two courts yet. Some day.

He also had to admit, he admired Merc's spunk. With better influences, they would have made a strong Dawn soldier. He felt more confident than he had expressed about their chances of getting to the bottom of the courts' troubles.

A second loud noise sent a shudder through the entire castle. In the bedroom, Melodia sat up and rubbed her eyes. Orion poked his head inside to let her know he was nearby.

There was a flurry of quick raps at the door.

"Enter!" Only one person ever knocked in that way.

A barrage of jumbled words preceded the tiny fey

who could have been mistaken for a child, yet she was nearly as old as the Dawn King. "My lord! One of the sea eagles delivered this, and then it just keeled over and started foaming from its mouth. The court—"

"Not here, Chesnae. Outside." He bowed to his queen, briefly, regretting the alarmed expression that marred her lovely features. "Apologies, my love."

Once outside, he held his hand out to the petite attendant. "What do you have there?"

Chesnae handed him a rolled and yellowed piece of parchment. Before he could open it, she said, "Look! The sky!"

Over the western horizon, a red ball rose up high overhead and then arced down, growing larger as it approached the balcony. Thoughts flitted through Orion's head. *Someone is using Athena's arsenal against us...Melodia!*

As he pivoted to run to his queen's aid, to shield her before the gigantic fireball reduced the castle to molten sand, Chesnae blocked his path. Her malicious grin confused him just as the needle prick in his chest did. "What—?"

Orion's vision blurred. But first he saw Chesnae's face darken and dissolve into a formless phantom.

It was her childlike voice that whispered, "If you're curious, the note simply said you always were the most trusting fool of the bunch."

Chapter 14

I hung around until Nat returned. After updating her on work and the day-to day stuff, she asked the "mom" questions—was I remembering to hydrate and eat? And she reminded me to rest once in a while. Fortified, I headed back to the City . My head spun from all the information I had received in just a couple of short hours. No wonder Rebus had always spared me—it was a lot to process.

When I reached RavCorp, there was a definite vibe of somber frustration in the air. I peeked in on Najat, but she hadn't found anything to help us with the journal. The other Shadows were busy following up on leads to find Chevalier, who had dropped off the grid again.

Checking on all these little details, while tedious and discouraging, also provided a needed distraction from my immediate problem. I had promised Dúl not to take off on missions alone anymore, so I couldn't go through with my plan yet. I also couldn't lie to him.

Our last few fights had happened because of taking the path of least resistance by withholding information. So even though I knew he was going to give me a hard time, I felt like I had to tell Dúl the truth—that taking any backup with me would be a certain death sentence for two exceptional Shadows and might also compromise my cover.

I ran into Morgan during my search for him. "How are things here?"

"Just as chaotic as when you left. That was quite a position you landed us in. I gather all ruffled feathers have been smoothed?"

"Yeah—I didn't know. I wasn't trying to mess things up."

"Not to worry, young one. Things will right themselves eventually. They always do. Did you obtain the information you needed from your...mentor?"

That was her less-than-subtle way of finding out what to call Rebus since everyone knew he wasn't my birth father. He and Nat had never "legally" adopted me—I showed up one day out of thin air—so he wasn't, technically. While I always called them by their names, I never got offended if someone called them my parents. They were the closest thing I had to parents, and they cared for me as such.

I realized that Dúl referred to Rebus as my father before. It seemed like the wrong time to hash out the specifics, especially not with Morgan, so I left the issue alone.

"Yeah, I got some interesting background on the vampires and some insight about the Winter Queen. I should be able to get some better answers soon. Have you seen Dúl?"

One brow arched, probably because I was about the only person in the building who ever called him by name. "The king is in his brooding chamber probably preening one of his birds."

I opened my mouth to defend him, but she cut me off.

"No matter your feelings for him, Merc, you will never be able to call him the most proactive of rulers. It is just a fact of life with him. No need to take offense."

I could still sense her resentment toward him, but it felt less personal and more about being overworked. Instead of responding, I nodded and continued to his office.

He was doing exactly what she said. The smile that tried to creep onto my face had to be suppressed.

"Hey."

Dúl glanced up, a raven—smaller than Jekyll or Hyde—perched on his finger as he stroked the top of its head with the other hand. "Any luck?"

I sat across from him, not wanting to disturb his bonding time with the bird who eyed me as if I had better know my place where the king was concerned. "Um...yes and no."

No reaction. He just continued to pet the bird. I told him what Rebus said, none of which seemed to surprise him. I skirted around the issue of me going to the Winter Court alone until I couldn't avoid it any longer.

"I wondered how long it would take you to get there," he said, his voice cool and aloof. "At least you told me the truth. I thought you might actually lie about it, which I wouldn't have held against you, by the way."

This was going in a direction I hadn't expected. "You're not upset? Won't order me not to go?"

"Oh, I am absolutely furious. I knew this would be the outcome, and there's nothing I can do to change it without creating other problems for us both."

Finally, he got up from his chair and returned the raven to the aviary.

"All right, so if we know we can't avoid this, help me out. Do you remember anything else at all from your scrying that seemed off about Nemesis? Maybe you saw something that just didn't register at the time."

We rehashed everything, but in the end, there were no new details. I wanted to linger, but the longer I took to figure out the Nemesis puzzle, the longer Athena, the Dawn Court, and the Shadow Court were in jeopardy. I said a quick goodbye and started for the door. I would use a portal to get as far as the border and then sneak through from there.

Before I let the door close, I poked my head back in. "One last little thing, *amor*?"

Dúl had returned to staring into the aviary. Morgan wasn't off base about the brooding. He turned toward me, eyes hopeful that maybe I would change my mind.

"You're the king. And there are problems going on all around you. The tension among the Shadows is thick as pea soup. You don't have to sit up here alone, fretting."

"I'm not—"

"Yes, you are. But so are they. The point is that you should be with them. You know—being supportive. Proactive."

He smirked. "You've been talking to Morgan. I liked it better when you were enemies."

I grinned back at him. "I love you. Go take care of your people, and I'll see you soon."

Hopefully, I'd be able to keep my promise.

Chapter 15

Surprisingly, my journey through the Night Lanes was uneventful. Nothing attacked or even tried to scare me. It was as if all the creepy crawlies took the night off. That wasn't likely, so I figured I wasn't giving off a vibe of fear. There were too many unanswered questions swirling through my gray matter.

Exiting a little ways from the Shadow Court side of the border, I put my plan into action, tucking any equipment I might need later into pouches, pockets, and ponytails.

Before I left, Dúl gave me a tiny ice sculpture that Nemesis had given him to mark the anniversary of the formation of the courts. Apparently, she always gave him a gift as sort of a gag since she knew he resented the situation. I withdrew it now and placed it on the ground nearby.

My face rippled and bubbled until my jaw distended. Fangs grew, and finally it was that of a wolf. Complete with a wolf's sense of smell.

Dúl's sculpture was of a raven in flight and en-

chanted to never melt. I used it now to pick up Nemesis's scent, easily distinguishable to me from his.

Nemesis smelled of crisp pine sap, and ironically, a hint of maple. From everything I had heard about the Winter Queen, there was nothing sweet about her. Except maybe that she sometimes tried to make her little brother smile.

Once the scent was memorized, the sculpture went back into a pocket for safe keeping. Dúl might kill me if I lost it.

Next, I closed my eyes and turned my attention to transforming the rest of my body. My skin tingled in the thousands of spots where fur sprouted. Bone and muscle drew inward, reshaping and reforming into a more compact body—a wolf's body.

In this new figure, I wriggled and stretched, settling in. Now to sniff out the queen.

She wouldn't cross the border, so I loped along and followed a snowy range that brought me what I guessed to be north. Directions were tough in the Dreaming.

Snow flurries fell, landing fat flakes on my nose and tongue. It was tempting to start frolicking—it would be a wolfy thing to do—but I restrained myself. No need to draw attention.

I was amazed at how much distance I covered with-out feeling the least bit tired. In a two-legged form, I would have needed to stop and walk a few times. The pads of my feet were getting a little cold and sore, but I still hadn't caught the queen's scent.

It made perfect sense that the castle wouldn't be too close to the border, but it sure was a hassle to me when I was so pressed for time.

Eventually, I found the woods that surrounded the castle and the paths Dúl and Rebus described.

From the cover of the trees, I glimpsed the Winter Castle, spires sparkling in the moonlight. It resembled a giant ice sculpture, and I couldn't imagine what kind of person—fey or otherwise—would live in such a cold place.

Like the miniature raven, it was enchanted not to melt. It made sense that I could see, through a ground-floor window, a fire burning in what appeared to be a sitting room. Why it was burning in an empty room, I didn't understand.

Relocating, I glimpsed the kitchen, bustling with cooks and servers. Moving around the perimeter a little more, I found a dining room.

A big fire blazed on one side of the room. In the center was a massive oval table, big enough to easily seat twenty. Only two diners ate tonight.

The Winter Queen sat at one end facing the forest. I slinked back afraid she might see me, even though I knew trees and darkness concealed me. I hesitated to pull the shadows around me in case she could sense the use of magic near her.

The queen's companion made my heart sink. I hadn't wanted to confirm bad news for Dúl and hoped there was a reasonable explanation for his suspicions. But the proof was right here. Serg Chevalier leaned back in a chair on the queen's left, too comfortable, as if being at court was a regular occurrence.

I needed to get closer. That meant breaking cover. Right now, my fur was black, to blend with the night. I would need to match the snow and ice if I were going to come out in the open.

I circled the perimeter more, to get out of the sight line of the dining room window. Then the color drained out of my fur and absorbed into my skin as I turned as pale gray as the ground beneath my feet.

Crouching low, I crept across the span between the tree line and the castle. Slowly, I reached the side of the building, and then worked my way back toward the dining room.

There was a small terrace about three feet off the ground with a tight crawl space beneath it. I used this to partially hide as I poked my head as much as I dared over the edge in the corner nearest the room.

Close up, I could now tell that the room was open— no walls or doors. That would explain why Chevalier and the queen both wore thick fur robes and why the fire blazed so high.

An internal alarm tweaked at my tail. What kind of place in a cold climate had open rooms? I retreated under the terrace and listened. The gentle wind whispered their voices out to me as my ears twitched and turned following the sounds.

They conversed, the queen with a haughty speech pattern that reminded me of Morgan, and Chevalier with his thick French accent.

"...losses were inconsequential. All of them were expendable. Ultimately unworthy of the spirit of the *Lemooria*. I mean," he huffed, "to be taken down by a bunch of stupid fey-bloods."

I couldn't see the queen's reaction to his insult, but he paused, and then followed up with, "All due respect, of course."

"Do you know why the shifter continues to thwart you, Monsieur Chevalier? With your experience and age, you should not have been out-strategized, yet your operation has been greatly set back. You, sir, are arrogant, and you underestimate your opponent. True, compared to us, this Merc is little more than a child, but a clever and precocious one." The queen sounded impressed.

A giggle, and the voice of a young child said, "She speaks truth, Chevalieeeeer. Bested by a babe!" The voice took up a chant and branched off into several singsong voices, all taunting him. "Bested by a babe! Bested by a babe!"

I didn't know what to feel—pride that the queen thought me a worthy adversary or anger that Psycho Kiddie was calling me a baby. I went with the first choice. It seemed more productive.

A glass shattered, and a growl arose. I had to look. I peeked from my hiding spot. Chevalier lurched to his feet, holding the sides of his head and grimacing. As suddenly as the childlike voices appeared, they stopped. When Chevalier finally opened his eyes, he glared at the queen.

"Did you enjoy that little show? I never thought to meet anyone who liked causing others pain more than I do." He actually grinned as if he were turned on by that. By her.

Ew.

I noticed then that the servers had left, and only Chevalier and Nemesis remained in the room. The queen stood, picked up a wine glass with pink liquid inside, and sipped. She stared into the night as she lifted the glass with her right hand.

Holy shit. Not Nemesis after all. Then who?

"While I don't particularly care one way or another about your sado-masochistic relationship with your parasitic passengers, I would venture to say that our guest found that display disturbing. Isn't that right, little shifter?"

How the hell? That just sucks.

No way was I revealing my location in this form, so I started my change back to a human shape, but not my usual one. I adopted pale, almost translucent skin and long, blond hair in two braids down my back.

As I was changing, Chevalier said, "Who are you talking to?" Footsteps moved toward the terrace.

"This is why your species is inferior. While that spirit toyed with you, your enemy was sneaking up, right under your nose." She approached the terrace now. "Come out, shifter. It makes no difference what you look like. I can *smell* you."

The way she said the word "smell" made me think she was smiling on the inside if not on the outside.

What a relief that this wasn't Dúl's sister. The holidays would have been brutal. "No, I won't come over for the Solstice. Why? Because your sister is creepy, and weird, and brags about smelling people."

Transformation done, I uncoiled myself from under the crawl space and retreated a few paces. Chevalier and pseudo-queen were at the threshold between the building and the terrace.

Chevalier glowered, which would have been more effective if he hadn't just allowed the queen to insult him with no response.

"How long have you known I was here?" I said, addressing the real threat.

"Oh, since you reached the tree line. Clever to change your appearance, but it won't help against my kind. I'd recognize your scent under any circumstance."

Her statement gave me chills, but I recovered quickly. "Something told me to shower before I left." Since she made no move to attack me, and since I was on lower ground, I climbed onto the terrace, leaving ample distance between us. "Obviously, you're not the real Winter Queen. Mind telling me who, or what, you are exactly?"

The pseudo-queen smiled, and I could see why Nemesis never did. That face just looked wrong, like a Halloween mask. I moved away a step.

"Oh, I'm not your enemy, child." She smiled again, but this one was softer, almost wistful. "Him, on the other hand... As for what I am, that question will be answered when the time is right. You see, unlike my partner, such that he is, I have planned for the long game. Good luck, little shifter."

Her form shimmered. Dark smoke seeped into her body from the bottom up, as if she were a vessel being filled. The smoke undulated in the air, and flew away, like an airborne snake.

I couldn't help being impressed at the exit.

Chevalier cut short my awe, reminding me that he was still there for me to deal with.

Chapter 16

"Your partner doesn't seem to respect you much." Now that I was alone with Chevalier, my hand went to the small of my back. I loosened my shadow dagger's sheath. "I wouldn't put up with that. So, what's the plan, anyway? What the hell does a vampire want in the Dreaming?"

He smiled broadly, and I noticed that he had a dimple in one cheek. The expression reminded me of the look on his face when he left me to kill Paris as I fought for my life. "I want nothing in the Dreaming. It is the Waking I'm after. Once we help our partners wrest control of the Dreaming from the last court, they will help us to subdue every living creature in the Waking."

As goals went, those were about the craziest I had ever heard. But it didn't matter because he wasn't leaving here alive. I owed him for what he did to Paris and to me.

The hilt of my dagger fit my hand perfectly as my fingers wrapped around it. It slid from its sheath as if gliding through butter. I met Chevalier's eyes. "What next? No one's here to fight your battles for you. You gonna run away again?"

Right on cue, Psycho Kiddie chimed in with a mocking giggle, although whether it was mocking him or me, I couldn't be sure. The *Lemooria*, as he had called the spirit, didn't seem to have any loyalty to anything but its own amusement. Suddenly, the vamp way of life made a lot more sense. If I had to spend the rest of eternity listening to that thing, I'd probably stay wasted too.

If my goading didn't work on Chevalier, the spirit's taunts had the desired effect. He snarled, baring sharp fangs behind red lips. Through the light brown lenses of his shades, his eyes began to glow. A growl rumbled up from his chest, turning into a roar as he charged. His fingers curled. His nails formed sharp talons. I braced myself.

Chevalier flung himself at me. I wasn't stupid enough to try to stop him. Ducking under his outstretched arms, I let him whiz by me and then kicked back, catching him behind the knee. He stumbled but didn't go down as I expected. He wheeled and backhanded me across the face. I went airborne.

The dagger flew out of my hand when I landed with a thud in the snow outside the terrace. My breath rushed out in a *whoof*.

Chevalier took two running steps and leapt over the icy railing with a roar. I rolled to the left as his feet planted where my ribs had been only a fraction of a second before. With perfect timing, my dagger found its way back to my hand. I sliced in a side arc and severed his Achilles tendon. He screamed French curses at me.

Hopping to my feet, I prepared to meet another charge, but faster than I could follow, he barreled into my middle, bowling me to the ground again. One hand grabbed my chin, forcing my head back to expose my throat. The other was raised to slash across my neck.

His knees pinned my arms. Curling my legs up and in, like I was heading into a backward roll, I hooked my calves around his torso and forced him off me. His head drove into the snow. His claws, punctured my leg instead of ripping my throat open. It stung, but I could live with that.

Chevalier rolled to all fours, sputtering, trying to clear his glowing eyes of snow. Before he could get the upper hand again, I leapt onto his back and positioned my dagger before his eyes.

Grabbing a handful of my jacket, he tossed me like a used tissue. The frozen railing along the terrace splintered as I crashed through it. As much as my ego wanted to keep this up, my body knew it couldn't go toe-to-toe with this seasoned vampire much longer.

On his feet, he crouched and turned to me with a sneer. I willed my throwing daggers into my hands, but I didn't move to get up. He stalked toward me.

"Arrogant little bitch. The dragons think you are so special, but you are nothing. And you have interfered with me for the last time." The *Lemooria* shrieked laughter.

Dragons? What was he talking about? He'd never explain, so I filed the information away for later. My daggers flew. One after the other, they lodged in his eye sockets. His mouth opened in surprise, or maybe he had meant to insult me some more.

Ichor oozed from his eyes and mouth. His body shriveled. The castle was still, and I was grateful that the stupid *Lemooria* had finally shut up for now.

I struggled my feet, bruised bones aching with every tiny movement. With a quick assessment, I released a relieved breath. Nothing was broken, and I wasn't bleeding enough to worry about immediately. Time to get out of here.

Slow clapping from somewhere above disrupted the peaceful moment.

On another balcony one floor up, Pseudo-Queen grinned and applauded. Had she watched the whole fight? Why didn't she help Chevalier?

"Bravo, young one. But you aren't finished yet."

Her smile disappeared, mercifully, and she shouted, "Guards! Intruder!"

Ugh, you bitch.

I reached into my left pant leg pocket and felt the portal rune inside. I pulled it out, tossed it, and prepared to dive through to home and safety. Dúl would be relieved to know that his sister was innocent, and then we could start tracking her down.

No portal.

The black stone lay in the snow like a lump of shit.

A magical item had never failed me. It wasn't like

these things were mass produced. They couldn't be bought at Rune Stone Mart. How was it possible that I got a dud?

"Oh, did I forget to mention? The castle grounds are warded. No portals in or out. You'll have to return the way you came, child." Giving me a queenly wave with her left hand, the Nemesis imposter turned. "We'll meet again, I am certain. Will you recognize me then?" She disappeared into the castle.

I hadn't learned everything I wanted to, but I acquired what I needed for now. No reason to hang around and get turned into a Merc-pop.

I ran.

Four Winter guards chased me. Their advantage of knowing the woods around the castle quickly whittled away at my lead as I stumbled over roots and took at least two wrong turns. All I had in my favor was that the snow muffled what otherwise would have been thundering footfalls.

They closed in. A blast of ice hit a tree only inches from my head.

My lungs burned, and my punctured leg ached. But as Rebus always said, "When you're being chased, you can rest when you're either dead or you escape." My legs pumped faster.

Directly ahead, a shadowy, cave-like spot sat in the middle of a clearing beyond the grounds—the Night Lanes.

Please don't follow me in here.

I crashed into the Lanes with a splash.

Water rushed in to fill my boots up to my thighs, slowing my steps. The stink slammed into my nostrils like a hammer.

This was a tunnel—a sewer tunnel almost identical to the one we had slogged through weeks ago under the vampire's lab.

It was odd because I hadn't been especially afraid in those sewers, and the Night Lanes played on the traveler's deepest fears.

Deepest, darkest fears...

A sensation washed over me that I had to push aside.

The Winter guard gave up their pursuit, so I stopped running. My heart was beating like a hummingbird's wings. I needed to calm myself and patted my pockets trying to remember where I had stashed a mini head-lamp. Forgetting where I stored my gear proved how tense I was.

Come on, focus.

My hearing took over in the darkness while I eased the lamp down over my forehead.

Occasional drips echoed through the passage. Far behind me, steady swishing, like running water, made a white noise that did nothing to make me feel any better.

That call had been too close.

Breathing deeply and ignoring the stench, I worked to relax. But my brain refused to settle. This was why I almost never traveled these Lanes alone.

If I couldn't stop the churning memories, I had to

move faster. I had been lucky earlier. Maybe the luck would hold.

With each step, suction pulled on the bottoms of my feet. Each foot lifted out of the muck below the water's surface with a sucking *ffloooop*.

Thoughts of all the different infections I could be getting in my leg tried to worm into my consciousness, but those weren't the worst ones to keep at bay.

My connection with Dúl niggled at me, like something was wrong with him. Not mortal danger, but he was definitely unsettled? Upset? I couldn't pinpoint it. Was that the effect of the Night Lanes, or had something really happened? *This* dug into my worst fear—losing those I loved. Losing Dúl literally would be like losing a piece of myself. But I had to ignore the sensation. I couldn't afford to think about him right now.

Losing Rebus or Nat... I had to stop. This was definitely the malevolent surroundings getting to me.

Thinking of them brought back another memory. I didn't fight this one. In the grand scheme of things, it might give the Lanes less to use against me.

A few years after Rebus and Nat took me in, they decided I should go to school. Prior to that, Nat had homeschooled me. All that meant was that I was learning about reading and math alongside sneaking, spying, and thieving.

They had faked all the necessary documents and registered me as "Mercy Gantry." I hadn't had much experience with human kids. Walking into a fourth grade class where all the students already knew each other was a nightmare. Of course, they picked on me, verbally more so than physically once they realized I could kick their little punk asses.

One day, a kid named Gabe came up to me and said he felt bad about how the others were treating me. Desperate for acceptance, I fell for it. Walking home after school, he told me a story about how his cousin's pet baby alligator had been flushed down the toilet and into the sewers. Every day for a week, he told me stories of encounters he had heard of with people being eaten by these giant sewer alligators.

By the end of the week, I was refusing to shower. When I started to smell bad, Gabe led some other boys up to me and shouted, "Mercy, you smell! What's the matter? Afraid the sewer alligators are gonna get you?"

I bloodied his nose, got suspended, and took a leave from public education until high school, when I was enrolled in private school.

Still, Gabe's damage had been done, and the idea of sewer alligators had always stayed in the back of my mind. Logically, there was nothing to fear, but the imagination isn't logical.

Maybe it was the recent pranks, or maybe the recent sewer experience had freed the idea from its little mental box. But now, I couldn't stop thinking that my next step would be on hard, spiky scales that would shift under my feet.

I started to sing to myself, but the echo of my voice

off the tunnel walls reminded me of the *Lemooria*, which creeped me out, so I stopped.

Something splashed in the water behind me. I froze.

Just your imagination.

Another sound like rusted metal yawning open.

Keep moving.

Yet my feet slowed. Afraid to attract the attention of what was back there. Afraid to find out what was ahead.

Something brushed my leg—something long and thick and rough. My hand flew to my dagger. I clamped my teeth together to keep from crying out. A clawed foot landed on mine before moving on. Maybe if I held still enough, it would just continue on its way.

I couldn't give "it" a name because that would make it more real. I suppressed a squeak at the back of my throat. I watched the surface of the water. There wasn't so much as a ripple. The beam of my lamp light bobbed and danced on top of the water as my body quivered.

One more clawed foot scraped my boot. This time it stopped.

Seconds later it moved.

A dark mass towered up at least seven feet. It slammed down on top of me. The impact knocked my dagger flying. I went under, barely catching a gulp of air before being submerged. The dim light of my lamp was useless, only illuminating a frenzy of bubbles churning around me in the murky liquid.

Dizzy and disoriented, I almost couldn't hold my

breath. With my heart speeding up even more, my body screamed for oxygen.

Something the size of a log crashed into me. I flew from the water, then splashed back down. The lamp was ripped from my head. The next thing I knew, a giant vise clamped down on my side, crushing my arms and chest. Ribs cracked. Any last bit of air in my lungs was squeezed out.

Holy shit... It's eating me!

My eyes bulged. I stared into a black void. The color of my death.

Now my body went cold. The pressure around me eased. I knew the alligator was still there, a sort of tickle told me it was still in the same place. But instead of clamping down, it was biting...through me. I reached down with both hands to push it away.

There was some resistance, but then *I* passed through *its* body, like a glob of viscous batter through a sieve. The gator's jaws snapped at nothing.

Did I understand what was happening? Nope. Only that I was in a lot of pain but also somehow free. I began to stagger forward. It was now easier to move through the sewage. My feet weren't sticking in the mud as before. I was gliding. Like a ghost.

"You are a ghost, love."

Damn, and I was doing relatively well. This was the anxiety I'd tamped down earlier. "I'm not and neither are you." I turned to face my fear.

A translucent gray Dúl, bloodied and broken, smiled through swollen lips. One eye, the size of a golf ball, was shut. My heart lurched seeing him that way. Could the vampires or fake Nemesis or even Orion have done something to him while I was off playing spy master? That niggling—did it mean he needed me and I wasn't there for him?

I steeled myself against the racing thoughts and clung to the fact that the Lanes routinely lied. "You are safe back in the Waking."

"Am I?" he singsonged. "I'm dead. You're dead. Your family is dead dead dead…"

I turned my back on him and walked away, now more angry than afraid. Dúl was fine, and I was going to prove it to myself. I needed to get out of here. Now. I wasn't a ghost and was very much alive, gasping for breath. My heartbeat still thundered in my ears. Not a ghost.

That still didn't explain what happened with the gator.

Fleeing Shadows

Dúl would never admit it to anyone, but Merc unintentionally shamed him into returning to the castle. Merc and the report that arrived just after they left. A wretched and battered sea eagle delivered the note. Dúl instructed his ravens to show the messenger proper hospitality before sending it to the aviary for a rest.

The Dawn Court had been firebombed with stolen weapons from the Summer Court.

Your highness,

Our king, your brother, has been abducted. Queen Melodia fights for her life. As the highest ranking guard, I have been chosen to lead our forces and civilians. Any aid you might be inclined to offer would be met with our deepest thanks.

The note was signed *Betania, Elite Guard of the Dawn King.*

Dúl fought against a twinge of annoyance. In all the years he had been fighting with Orion, he had never managed to capture him. It would have taken someone he knew and trusted to trick him into a vulnerable position. An inside job. But how?

A problem for later. Now, with the benefit of the advance warning, he needed to evacuate. Fortunately, he and Morgan had prepared for an attack on the Shadow Court ages ago, when the fight against his brother had started. In an odd way, it seemed he owed Orion a debt today.

Dúl's first task was to send out an alarm. He opened the door to the castle's main aviary. The round tower stretched up high above. Ravens black as tar covered every inch of stone and every perch. He called to them now.

"My messengers! The time has come. You know what to do. Sound the alarm. Get our people to safety. Fly!"

In unison, a single, croaking caw answered him. For a moment, chaos erupted. Hundreds of ravens streamed from the rooftop opening, spattering the sky with ink-black spots.

The organized exit as well as the evacuation drills were Morgan's brainchildren. He was glad they were on better terms now. She portaled to the Waking to organize the evacuees at RavCorp.

He marched back to the main public room of the castle where he typically saw to civilian business. The staff were already waiting, their families anticipating his instructions. He strode to the front of the room. A wave of his hand opened a portal through to the bunkers beneath the RavCorp building.

Any fullbloods on the outskirts of court might be able to teleport from their locations if they had the means. Otherwise... well, he never expected to be able to save everyone.

The staff members themselves would not leave until the last possible minute, so Dúl left them in charge and headed to his quarters to salvage a few important items he wouldn't want destroyed if it came to that.

The dagger his father had given him as a coming-of-age gift was now in safe keeping with Merc, providing they were safe, of course. He couldn't get a clear read on them as his own emotions were so scrambled.

He found his scrying glass, wiped any dust from the concave surface with his sleeve, and gazed into its shiny, black depths.

"Looking for me?" Her voice came from the front sitting room of his suite.

Dúl turned to see just the fey he had been looking for. Her image in the glass now showed her standing behind him.

"So, sister, you are behind this. I didn't want to believe it. Forgive me for saying so, but this seems beneath you."

"Hmm...no, I don't think I will forgive you, but I will explain later, if only to enjoy the look on your face. I see Umbra hasn't returned yet. Are you wondering if the vampire is feasting on her?"

Like a stab to the heart, the image stole his breath, but only for a moment. Dúl could not let this imposter shake his focus. And he did know, now, that this look-alike was not his sister.

"I understand now why you would not talk with me before. Who are you and where is my sister? All my siblings for that matter."

The little things gave this creature away as a fraud—the slightly wrong inflections in her speech, the missing tension at the corner of her mouth due to the pain she always felt in her right shoulder, the humor in her tone.

"Well done, Shadow King. It took you long enough. And while you were staying your hand with your sentimentality, I was breaking down you Azuath bit-by-bit."

Azuath? His family had not gone by that title for at least a generation. Not since his father's reign over all the Dreaming.

"Who are you?"

"Eager, aren't we? All in good time, young one. All in good time."

Moving faster than expected, the mysterious villain flicked her fingers in his direction. Eight black darts pricked Dúl in his neck, his face, and his hands when he put them up to protect himself. Immediately, the world went dark, yet he knew he was still standing.

Shadows. She had attacked and blinded him—the *lord* of the shadows—with his own weapon.

A thud sounded in his skull a moment before a starburst of pain lit the darkness behind his eyes.

Chapter 17

I guess I must have been thinking too much about home because I came out of the Night Lanes in the Fringe, on the train tracks near the bank of the Hudson, a few blocks from Rebus and Nat's place.

The sky was a wall of pale gray. Snow flurries cast a hush over the land.

Wet from my trek through the sewers, I jogged the whole way, as much to stay warm as to get to one of the few places in either world where I felt truly safe. The unease about Dúl had shifted. Before I had felt a low-level distress. Now there was blankness. A void. Yet I knew he was still on the other side of it.

Maybe I could talk it out with Nat and Rebus over some of her award-winning hot cocoa. That thought was like a warm hug I desperately needed.

From a block away, I could see The Bar. The lights were still on. What were they still doing up? It was a weeknight, or at least I thought it was. The days were starting to blend together.

Once I reached the sidewalk outside the building, I slowed to a walk. It was oddly quiet. Whenever my parents were in the bar, there was some kind of noise, even if it was just a radio or the television. With a frown, I started inside.

Focused on scanning the depth of the room, I nearly tripped over—*What the hell?* The two Shadows I assigned to The Bar sprawled across my path, unconscious.

"Merc! Run!" A strangled gasp cut off Nat's voice.

Rebus screamed before my brain processed the warning or the scene at the back of the taproom.

Some kind of black shell encased Rebus near one of the corner tables. The bald patch at the top of his head gleamed with sweat. His mouth was wide open, face red and contorted in a scream.

Next to him, in a similar casing was Nat. *Nat?* Her head lolled back at a weird angle, red hair cascading down the side of the black... *coffin.*

No. "Nat?" It came out of me on a whimper. Something here still eluded me. What was happening?

Then I saw him.

Stepping out of the corner shadows—no, that wasn't right. He didn't step. He *formed* out of the shadows.

A young man, around my age, stalked a few paces toward me and paused between my family and me. His skin was black as pitch, his eyes even darker. Straight hair poked up in a short, spiked mohawk. He was only a couple of inches taller than me and wiry.

I could kill him. Easily.

With a feral yell, I hurled myself toward him, not

thinking, just wanting to annihilate this piece of shit who had taken from me the only mom I knew. Nat, who kissed my boo-boos and made me hot cocoa and warned me of danger. Even if it meant sacrificing herself.

The distance between us closed, and then I was lost in darkness until I landed on the other side of the two black shells.

I whipped around. The guy was still there, turning slowly to face me. Somehow, I had gone through him.

He grinned, and then his face morphed. His skin lightened to tan, his hair lengthened into a flowing, red mass of curls. His face turned into—

"Son of a bitch!" In an instant, my shadow daggers appeared in my hands and flew toward his throat.

Again, it was like trying to hit a hologram. They went right through. I froze, stunned.

"I told this changeling to stay quiet. Then she went all mother-trying-to-protect-her-baby, right?" The guy shifted back to that dark, mohawked form. His eyes glowed yellow. "But she's not your mother, is she, princess?" His grin showed white teeth.

"Why...?" My voice sounded breathy and weak to my own ears. *She can't be gone.*

"Why? Because there are things you need to understand. You're fighting for the wrong side, and you don't even know it. These fey and their changeling bastards need to be eradicated."

I gritted my teeth, trying to control the rage swelling

inside me. "I will never be part of any side you're on. Not if my life depends on it."

"Ha! It might, princess. But please, refuse. I'd love the excuse to kill you slowly."

I shrieked again and took two running steps before lifting both feet from the ground in a flying kick. This time, he ghosted to the side, a trail of shadow behind him. I crashed to the ground flat on my back. The air left my lungs, and my ribs screamed at me where the alligator had crushed me.

The dude continued talking as if I had sat down and offered him a coffee. "We're off to a bad start, princess. Just wanted to tell you that the queen—the real one, not that wrinkly bitch you've been stressing over—the queen sends her regards, and she'll come for you soon. Until we meet again..."

He dissolved from black to gray, wafted up toward the ceiling, and was gone.

My thoughts churned and spun. None of this made sense. I was still in the Night Lanes. That was the only answer because this was impossible. I couldn't force myself to look in Nat's direction.

Rebus's shouts cut through the miasma in my brain.

"Merc! Get me out! Nat! Natalie!" In his make-shift prison, he was rocking side to side, bucking to break free.

I ran to him and pried at the top. Willing my shadow dagger into my hand, I intended to cut the pod open. As soon as the dagger point contacted the shell, the shell disappeared in a poof.

Neither of us stopped to ponder that. Together, we rushed to Nat. I freed her. Rebus caught her body before it hit the ground. He collapsed and rocked her, crying her name over and over. In a second, I was on my knees beside him, hugging him, and wishing her to open her eyes like I used to when I couldn't sleep and would wake her up to tuck me back into bed.

Gone? But why? Because she warned me? It was so pointless. With the two fey on the ground, I already knew something was wrong. As the guy admitted—he killed her for pleasure.

And who was this "queen" who was coming for me? Tears streamed down my cheeks. I didn't want to move or think, but the image of a hideous, mom-slaying hag put a fire under my feet.

"Reeb? Rebus, we have to call the police and get out of here. Whoever's doing this might be back." *And I can't lose you both.*

It took a few tries to get through to him, but finally, he shook off his stupor and answered. "No cops. We have to call her people. They'll know what to do for her. Before you showed up, Merc, he said some things. I don't know if they're true, but I think maybe they were."

A chill spread from my heart through every cell. "What things?" What could be shocking enough to pull Rebus's attention from the grief of losing Nat?

"For one, the entire Dreaming is under attack. After the Dawn Court was bombed, your king evacuated most of the Shadow Court to RavCorp holdings."

My mouth gaped. My brain was shutting down. I was incapable of processing more.

"Merc, we have to get down there. And whoever is doing this—" He gazed down at Nat with the most twisted, tortured expression I had ever seen. It broke my heart. "I'm going to rip their intestines out with my bare hands."

I was with him on that point.

We took Nat up to the apartment and laid her out in bed. Rebus placed a kiss on her mouth, and I kissed her forehead before we left. Her family would come for her and make sure to care for her remains according to their traditions.

Rebus and I went off to take our revenge.

~*~

Upset as he was, Rebus drove us south, navigating the New York City traffic like a professional cabbie. In other words, once we passed Riverdale in the Bronx, my eyes were squeezed shut most of the time.

Before we reached the building, I had to say something. "Rebus. I'm so sorry. This was all my fault."

"Stop. Stop right there. Don't you dare get caught up in that self-blame bullshit. Stay focused, kid. Mind on one task at a time. First, we fill the king in. Next, we find whoever is attacking the courts, and then we bring them down. When all that is done, we grieve. Properly. We owe that to her." The last word choked him. He took a deep breath and kept his eyes on the road.

He was right. Rebus was the most disciplined fey

I knew. The most disciplined *person* in the Waking or the Dreaming. I couldn't let him down by forgetting what he taught me. After being in the Winter Court, it was obvious where that control came from. And why Nemesis hadn't wanted to let him go.

I directed him to the underground garage. The gate was down. No one answered when I pressed the button several times.

"We'll have to go through the main entrance," I said, gathering my gear from the back.

We walked around the corner to the front of the building. Everything looked normal from the outside. It was a little after ten, so most people were settling into their offices. Plenty still rushed along the streets. Cars, bikes, and buses all rolled along, ignorant that anything was amiss in the world. New York City was oblivious to the Dreaming's problems.

I led the way through the revolving doors, and the scene inside stopped me cold.

Three portals on one side of the entrance hall glowed blue, green, and red. A steady stream of fey and changelings balanced every possession they could each carry. In the crowd, I picked out members of the Shadow Court—the building receptionist, some of my Shadows and seniors, and finally Morgan over near the information desk. They directed the crowd toward the elevator banks.

I gestured for Rebus to follow me toward Morgan.

I didn't like what I saw. From ten feet away, the clench of her teeth with each word made her tension clear. From five feet away, I noticed her that hands shook as she gesticulated and pointed while barking orders. In the weeks I had known her, I had never seen Morgan shaken. Not even when she was imprisoned in the sewer.

She finished with the fey she had been addressing. I finally caught her eye. "We need to talk. Nemesis is innocent, and—"

"Not here, Merc. Give me a moment, and you can fill me in upstairs. We have a situation here. The Dreaming is under siege. I've sent emissaries to offer sanctuary to any refugees from all courts. We reached nearly everyone in the Shadow Court. A fire alarm got our human clients out of the building. The fire department cleared us to let the staff back in now. By Najat's count we're sheltering about six hundred non-fighting women, children, elders, and infirm in the subterranean bunkers. Another four hundred fighters are spread throughout the building awaiting orders and weapons."

"Okay, that's great, and I'll help however I can, but I need to talk to you and the king. We have to go after the imposter, and there were others—"

"Not. Here."

Her tone chafed at me, but a steadying hand on my shoulder helped me to keep my mouth in check. "Fine."

Morgan worked her administrator magic and within seconds had freed up the Shadow operatives and herded us all to a conference room on the ground floor. When she saw Rebus trailing me, she gave me an arched look, her lips pressed into an almost non-existent line.

"He's with me, and he stays."

After a pause, she nodded and shut the door behind us. She strode to the front of the room.

I assumed all the dour expressions were a direct result of the refugee situation and the attacks. Many Shadow Court changelings had relatives in other courts. As one body, everyone sat around the long, rectangular table. Everyone except me. I was too wound up to sit and remained standing near an empty coffee service cart and a radiator. A vacant chair was directly in front of me.

"All right, Merc. Brief us, quickly."

I started to explain what had happened in the Winter Court, but then paused. "Shouldn't we wait for the king? He'd want to know about this too."

Morgan opened her mouth as if she were going to say something, but then she stopped, rubbed both hands over her face, and tightly wound her fingers together in front of her mouth. Her eyes didn't leave mine for long seconds. Sad eyes finally redirected to her right, toward Najat.

Tynan cleared his throat. "Chief...Merc, the king went to the Dreaming to oversee the evacuations."

"Oh-kay. That's good..."

"You don't understand. The king, like the other sovereigns, was taken. We have an idea—"

"What? What do you mean 'taken?'" I moved toward

the chair, gripping the back of it for support. "Did anyone check the castle? He has to be somewhere in the castle. Brooding or maybe he just wanted to be alone..."

I wasn't making a lick of sense, but nothing made sense. The last point of light in an otherwise dark sky had just blinked out, leaving me blind and lost.

Tynan continued in hushed, careful tones. "Merc, like the others, there was a message. They're all still alive, if the culprits are being truthful. We need to pull all the courts together to launch—"

"The courts?" My voice rose. "Fuck the courts! I don't care about attacks. I don't give two shits about anything except getting him back. Now!"

I ran out of the room, letting the door slam behind me.

Chapter 18

I took the stairs up to Dúl's office, to work off some stress before attempting... Attempting what? By the time I reached the top floor, I was winded but calmer. Enough to realize what an ass I'd made of myself and how stupid I was being. If the Shadows didn't hate me before, they sure would now.

As soon as I exited the stairwell, I had even more reason to kick myself. Morgan stood near the elevator bank, arms crossed, one foot tapping. Even during a crisis, she looked immaculate in jeans, a long-sleeved silk tee, and high heeled boots.

She didn't say anything. Didn't have to. The twist of her lips and arced eyebrow said it all.

"Okay, so that happened. I'm an asshole. Now everyone knows it. Let's move on. What new information do we have?"

Morgan nodded. "Glad to see you've regained your senses. I believe you will owe a few hundred apologies for that outburst, but for the moment...I am sorry about your adopted mother. Rebus explained what happened."

Sympathy was the last thing I expected, and it ripped the growing hole in my heart even wider. "Thanks, but I can't...I need to focus on what's going on here. I don't mean to be rude, it's just—"

"Understood." She started toward Dúl's office, and I followed. Weren't we in a similar position just a matter of weeks ago? But the world wasn't going to shit then.

"So," Morgan said, "Had you not engaged in your momentary lapse of judgment, we could have told you that you should see for yourself what was left at the scene. A raven came—"

I gasped.

"Not one of his two pets. They're safe in the aviary here."

It was such a small thing, but relief washed over me, and my muscles melted to jelly.

"One of the ravens in the Dreaming came to find me. It told me that The Winter Queen turned to black smoke and then took him away. Considering what you said earlier, there are clearly other shifters in play."

"Yeah, seems so. And they claim to know something about my past. The one who...attacked us said something about catching up. But I swear Morgan, I have no idea who or what they are."

Outside the office, she stopped and turned to me. "I know you don't, Umbra. I fear more *for* you than *of* you, child."

We entered the dark room, which appeared untouched. Inside, we stopped between the desk and the aviary. She held her hands out, and a black orb grew between them, enlarging until it engulfed us. A moment later, we were in Dúl's wing of the castle.

I started across the suite, my body threatening to eject its last meal. The bed was disheveled. The housekeeping staff must have been too busy running for their lives.

On the opposite side of the bed near the balcony from where I'd watched the sunset so many times, Dúl's scrying glass lay broken on the woven carpet.

"Morgan, over here." I pointed at the shiny shards of the tool. "He must have been trying to figure out what she was up to right until the last minute." I swallowed a sob.

"I believe he was also salvaging precious keepsakes. Who knew he had such a sentimental side?"

Among other things piled on the bed was the feather he used to share some of his shadow powers to me, binding us inextricably together. A tear fell from my eye.

I glanced down at the glass again. Careful not to move anything, I examined it more closely. In a large piece, about the size of my entire hand, it looked like an image was trapped within the dark reflection.

"Morgan, take a look at this." Without shifting the piece, I pointed to what I wanted her to see. "What do you think?"

She turned and tilted her head, inspecting from different angles. "It appears to be one image superimposed over another. One looks like the Winter Queen, and the other is just a dark, curvy shape."

"The same one I met at the Winter Court. So, she comes here as Nemesis and somehow subdues him. It's pretty clear she the one after the Dreaming. Where would she take the sovereigns if she wanted to use them as leverage?"

"Wait. There's more." She led me out to the balcony. At first, I didn't see it, facing away from the building. "Turn around and look up."

The words SINS OF THE FATHER, scrawled in black, spanned the width of the balcony.

"I remember seeing that." I thought back. "When Athena was taken. What does it mean though? What could their father have done to bring all this down on his children? It's been ages since his reign."

"Oh, he did many immoral things and made many enemies. The only way to know which one we are dealing with is to ask the closest living source to our former ruler."

I waited for her to clarify.

"The Queen Mother, Merc. You're going to meet the fey who will someday call one of us daughter-in-law. Preferably you."

"Let's get him back here before we worry about that."

~*~

What a way to meet my boyfriend's mom—*Oh, hi, Dúl's mom. I'm your son's significant other. Yes, I'm aware he's engaged. Anyway, we seem to have misplaced him, all your children, in fact. Could you maybe tell us which of the dozens of your late husband's enemies might have taken them and where they might be?*

During their rule, Dúl's father and the queen lived in a castle at the center of the Dreaming. This was before they split the lands into courts among their four offspring. Once borders were drawn, and the father died, Queen Sera wanted to avoid showing favoritism to any of her children. They all agreed to create a neutral zone, unaffiliated with any court.

This all sounded good in theory, but realistically, unless she found another dimension to live in, she had to physically be in *someone's* lands.

Or so I thought.

When the realm was divided, the siblings created a sort of pocket realm, outside the Dreaming, which was equally accessible from all the courts. The neutral territory, called Alanur, had representation of each court's element. Snowcapped mountains descended into a rainforest paradise. Every morning, a brilliant sunrise graced the skies. Each evening, an amazing sunset ushered in the night.

At least that was how Morgan described it as we climbed the stone stairs to the highest tower of the Shadow castle. A heavy thought hit me when we reached the top.

"Morgan, if this Alanur can be entered from any court, how do we know the Queen Mother hasn't been attacked too?"

"We don't. But unless her children sold her out, I believe she's safe."

Morgan lit a candle from a sconce outside the room and carried it inside. The round tower had a ten-foot diameter and no windows. The air was a bit stale, but not as much as I expected. Footprints in a thick layer of dust led across the stone floor. Someone had been here recently. Dúl hadn't mentioned anything to me about his mother being alive, let alone visiting her. While this was on brand for him, it was a habit he really needed to break. Of course, he had to survive this mess first.

The place was empty except for a single, oval mirror on a stand. Morgan straightened it, gazed into it, and said a brief chant in a language that sounded vaguely familiar, but that I didn't understand.

"*Eze nwanyị ne, nye anyị n'enweghị ihe ize ndụ gị n'ógbè.*" She turned to me, and my expression must have read as confused. "In the Ibo language, it means, 'Great queen mother, grant us safe passage to your realm'. That's the part of the Waking that corresponds to where she grew up in the Dreaming."

The gray stone bounced our voices back to us.

"Where's that?"

"Nigeria."

"So, the queen mother is...African?"

"She's fey." Morgan shook her head in exasperation. "Humans."

The mirror's surface rippled like water. Morgan

stepped into it, so I followed. The queen's realm was much more than Morgan described. It stole my breath.

It was like stepping into a landscape postcard. Clear blue skies merged with a calm aquamarine ocean. We stood at the top of a cliff looking down onto a horseshoe shaped beach and lagoon. Wood pylons supported a huge cabin with a wraparound porch and a grass thatched roof. Off the cabin's porch, a pier stretched out over the water with a massive ship moored to it. This wasn't a modern luxury yacht, but rather an old-fashioned, wooden ship with a second cabin on top. I questioned its seaworthiness but guessed it was probably enchanted not to sink.

And here I had expected her to be living out her life in a grand castle.

At the stern of the ship, in a brilliant green halter and wrap skirt combo, an ebony skinned woman with kinky curls almost to her waist grinned and waved. I could see now why Dúl liked my hair so much. One other thing I noticed about his mother at once was that she looked closer to Morgan's age, certainly way younger than Nemesis.

Dúl's resemblance to his mom's slender physique, dark eyes, and lush lips was evident. Athena had her complexion and curls while Orion shared her tanned skin and connection to the water. There were even hints of Nemesis's proud stature and long, crinkly hair. Now I was curious to see a picture of Dúl's father.

A steep stone staircase took us down to the beach. We trekked through the sand and climbed the steps up to the porch. When the queen approached, Morgan bowed at the waist, and I copied her, peeking up to see Queen Sera's reaction. She seemed to float down a gangplank with the help of a handsome, burly escort who kissed her hand when she stopped before he stepped back several paces to stand at attention.

"Please, rise. How lovely that I finally get to meet the keeper of my youngest son's heart. No offense, Morgan."

"None taken, your majesty."

I almost choked. It was unsettling enough to find out that Dúl's mother was alive, but to learn that she knew about me was enough to make my brain glitch for a good long while. My mouth hung open.

"My apologies, darling. My son has always kept his secrets, hasn't he? Where is Dúl? He left abruptly when he last visited and promised to return soon."

"Umm..." I began. So eloquent.

Morgan straightened. "Majesty, there's trouble in the Dreaming. I regret to report that your children are being held hostage by an unknown enemy. We hoped you could help us to identify the culprit."

The queen's breath hitched. Her gaze dropped to her hands, now tightly clasped together. Otherwise, she stood solid as an oak tree. When she looked up, her eyes were wide, but her voice was steady. "My children...Sit down and tell me what's happened. Of course, I will do anything in my power to help. Are you certain they're alive?"

Morgan hesitated, and I stepped in. "No, your

majesty. We're not sure of anything, but I can still sense Dúl. The connection is faint, but I believe if he weren't alive, I'd know. That gives me hope for the others. This person, creature, seems to be toying with them. Trying to send a message."

She directed us to a round table and chairs under the porch eave. Her attendant whispered something, received an order, and disappeared into the main house.

We explained the chain of events, starting with Morgan's abduction by the vampires. Every new twist in the tale paled the Queen Mother's face more. I had never in my life felt so awful delivering bad news.

When we finished, Queen Sera said, "And you say these creatures shifted forms similar to the way you do, Umbra?"

"Yes, your majesty, but—"

"And tell me again about your experience in the Night Lanes."

I repeated it.

She stared quietly toward the lagoon for several minutes.

How might these creatures be connected to me? Dread filled me with each breath I forced into my lungs. Finally, the queen looked each of us in the eye.

"I believe I know who is behind all this."

The Queen's Tale

"It was more than a generation ago." The Queen Mother sipped from an ornate crystal goblet, which her attendant brought along with water for Merc and Morgan. "You have to understand what it was like back then. My late husband, while able to unite the fey all over the Dreaming, was constantly at war with the other neighboring races."

During the reign of King Wymond of the Azuath Queen Sera stood next to her husband on the southern battlement of the castle tower and watched with growing unease. Airborne shapes, larger than birds of prey, but smaller than the massive gold and silver dragons that used to plague the realm, swooped through the sky. Their broad wings fluttered back into wisps of smoke, and standing, they towered over even the tallest fey.

"We must help, Wymond. Those villagers in the valley will be nearly powerless."

Her husband grunted undecipherable words and then said, "I've had enough of the shadow dragons.

These raids are slowly wearing down our forces. If we don't eliminate them soon, it will be the end of us. I've dispatched the fourth cavalry to aid the village."

"Why not negotiate?" Sera had made this plea to her husband for ages. "All they want is a small area of the Dreaming where they can exist in peace. We don't—"

He wheeled on her. "Silence! You are my consort, not a general."

"Your only mind these days is for conquest and greed. And it will be the undoing of all fey."

Wymond snarled and stalked away. What could she do? He had changed over the years since they were first joined in marriage. His intention had been to unite the entire realm, but little by little, he had seized more and more lands, running the non-fey races out of the Dreaming to make their own way in the Waking world.

The shadow dragons in the midlands and the giants in the north were the only ones left with any territory of value. Wymond's only interest, Sera was sure, was controlling the dragons' land and not in protecting the villagers from the rebellious raids and mayhem.

Sera was about to go check on the children, Orion and Nemesis. It should be time for their lessons. Dúl was toddling around the castle making mischief these days, while tiny Athena lay in her crib in the next room. As Sera turned, she caught sight of the king.

On the back of a silver steed, Wymond wore a full suit of armor. A long sword bounced at his hip as the horse carried him toward the village where the raid was still in full swing. Black smoke rose up from the homes and merchant shops.

What was he thinking? Granted he had heirs, but they were mere children, in no state to assume the duties of ruling should their father fall in battle. Sera, no stranger to the battlefield herself, rushed out of the room toward the armory.

Donning a custom suit of lightweight pixie mail that had been sent as tribute when they surrendered to Azuath control in the north, Sera topped it with her pale blue enchanted cloak. The hooded garment would deflect a strike from any weapon. With it streaming out behind her, she raced after him to the valley. No one would ever turn away her healing skills. Saving even one life would be worth Wymond's anger.

She knew why he was leaving the safety of the castle—his younger brother led the fourth cavalry. At times, Wymond still showed traces of the virtue that had made her fall in love with him long ago.

She traveled at top speed. The village was only two short miles away. Sera reached it within minutes.

Dark shadows crossed overhead each time one of the dragons arced in midair or swooped to send a black blast of energy at a target, causing the target's shadow to expand and engulf it, leaving behind a darkened spot like a burn.

Men shouted and hollered. Women shrieked and cried out. Weapons clanged. Dragons roared, as Sera circled the outskirts of the village trying to locate her husband. As she rounded a corner of a barn, a horrific cry followed by gurgling drew her attention.

Wymond's horse lay injured on its side, pinning the king beneath it. He shouted from the same direction. "No! Rafaon!"

Sera rushed to Rafaon's side—the one with the most critical injury. Blood spurted from a gash across his throat. His attempts to slow the bleeding were in vain. He dropped to his knees a moment later.

A few feet away, a male figure had darkened to black before sprouting wings, his face lengthening, teeth becoming jagged and sharp and sprouting an extra row.

It turned to Sera and chuckled. "Ah, the healer. I believe you are too late for that one. How fortunate that your king chose to send his brother to face me today. Now he can watch his kin die the way we have at the hands of you fey." The dragon spread his wings and reared up, eight feet tall from the base of his tail to the tip of his nose.

From behind her, Wymond screamed and spat. "You will pay dearly for this, Isquill! There will never be negotiations and no mercy! I will destroy you, your kin... everyone and everything you love! I will see your entire race annihilated!"

Finally freeing his leg, he scrambled to his feet, sword raised, and swung it in an arc at the dragon's neck. The weapon passed through cleanly. The dragon was unaffected. Wymond tried again, this time stabbing at where the dragon's heart had been when it took a fey form. He might as well have been slicing water.

The shadow dragon bounded up and circled overhead, laughing at his enemy's failure. His forces followed. "Leave us to our lands, Wymond, and we will leave you to yours!" In a tight formation, they flew up and around to the other side of the mountains.

When Sera next looked, her brother-in-law was dead, and all that remained was the pile of clothing and armor her husband cradled in his arms.

After the loss of his brother, Wymond's cruelty toward all non-fey races was unbridled. It became his mission to cleanse the Dreaming of all but the fey. When he succeeded, he relentlessly pursued the shadow dragons.

Systematically, he whittled down their numbers, razed their homes in the mountain caves, captured and tortured their warriors. During that time, every fey shaman, alchemist, and sorcerer was set to the task of finding ways to prevent the shadow dragons from transforming or becoming incorporeal. By the time Athena was walking, they succeeded.

The shadow dragons had been driven back to the base of the largest mountain range separating the northlands from the south. Wymond's forces were starving and dehydrated, so he called them back and sent a unit in on a suicide mission to capture the dragon leaders and use them to break the will of the remaining enemy.

They sustained heavy losses but succeeded in

capturing the dragon queen—Liffi—and her personal guard. A message was sent to Isquill—if he wanted her back alive, he would take his forces and leave the Dreaming forever.

~*~

"She was savagely beaten, paraded through the capital, and then drugged to keep her from shifting or escaping. I tried to stop Wymond, but he was too far gone. Insane. The remaining Shadow dragons came for her. When Isquill saw his mate...

"He didn't know the Dragon Queen carried un-spawned eggs. He released her as agreed. She couldn't shift. Her kin had to support her under the wings across the courtyard. Isquill stayed behind until she was safe, and then he gave Wymond a look filled with such loathing and anger, I thought he would attack right then."

~*~

Isquill carried himself with dignity as he retreated. He reached the gate and turned back for one last glare at his enemy. Wymond stood with one hand raised.

"Archers!"

Isquill's focus shot up to the battlements where twenty archers pointed poisoned arrows at him. "Faithless scum! We had an agreement!"

Wymond's arm came down. Arrows pierced Isquill's body before he could transform.

His mate, Liffi, let out an unearthly roar of despair and desperation. They shared a last glance, and then Isquill shut his eyes forever.

~*~

"After that, I couldn't share a bed with Wymond. I moved to another part of the castle. He died sometime later in a skirmish with the giants of the north. He never did manage to banish them."

"So, what happened to the Shadow Dragons? If they were banished, how did they work their way back into the Dreaming?" I was horrified knowing how cruel Dúl's father had been. Because of *land*.

"I don't know. There were patrols and wards in place, but if one wants something badly enough, they can make anything happen."

"And the eggs? I'm guessing you don't know what happened to them." I don't know why I asked, but it felt important.

"Actually... As I said, Wymond didn't know she was carrying eggs. I was horrified at her treatment. During her captivity, I visited her and tried to offer some small comfort to her.

"The poor thing was delirious when I first saw her. She kept repeating that it was almost time and the word 'Savatos,' which is a triplet of mountain ranges. At one time when she was clearheaded, I admitted to hearing her ramblings. She begged me to keep her secret because if she lived, she wouldn't have time or the strength to prepare a new nest farther away.

"After he murdered Isquill, Wymond was convinced that the dragons fled the realm. Eventually he turned his attention to other matters. I've kept her secret until now.

"As for the fate of the eggs, it would have taken take a great deal of damage to make them inviable. I believe if they survived and spawned, she would have hidden them in the Savatos Mountains. You think Isquill's offspring might be responsible for these attacks?"

"No idea. But we'll find out."

Morgan set her goblet down. "Thank you, my queen, for sharing this with us. I think the information will prove to be quite valuable."

"I hope it is. And I hope you will be able to find a more peaceful resolution against the shadow dragons this time. As much as I want the Dreaming to be safe, I understand their rage."

Unfortunately, so did I.

Chapter 19

When we headed back downstairs, I could feel eyes stealing glances at me and tongues wagging and lips whispering.

"Did you hear…"

"… doesn't care about…"

I held my head up, but it was a struggle. "I screwed up again. I tried to tell him before all this started—I'm no good with a team. I'm not a leader, and it showed again. They probably all hate me. Again."

Morgan's eyes flicked in my direction, but she never broke her stride. "You have very little faith in yourself or in your Shadows and their ability to see past a minor transgression like an emotional outburst."

"But all these people are talking…"

"It gives them something to focus on other than being displaced from their homes, Merc." She stopped walking for a moment and grasped my arms. "If I had been in your position—losing my mother and then finding Najat gone—I would have tried to burn both worlds to ash. The fact that you didn't and merely said some mildly insulting things, shows you are exactly the leader they need right now." She released me.

I was dumbstruck for a moment and had to jog to catch up. At the conference room, I took a deep breath before entering. My SO's were all still there, working. As if Morgan and I had just stepped out for a coffee break. When we entered, they shuffled around until they were all in their seats as before.

At the head of the table with Morgan to my right, I jammed my hands in my pants pockets. It occurred to me then that I had met Dúl's mother in dirty, sweaty, black fatigues. I coughed to clear my throat.

"Before I tell you what we found, I, um, would like to apologize. Things have been spiraling out of control, and when I learned that he—the king—is in danger, it was kind of the last straw. I do care what happens to the Dreaming and to the courts, this one especially. The Shadow Court is my home now, and—"

"Are you going to tell us something we don't know, Chief?" Tynan's sad smile conveyed his sympathy.

Cari rolled her eyes and chimed in. "I think what the idiot is trying to say is that we get it. You and Mr. Rebus..." She nodded toward him respectfully. "... have our condolences. We've all seen you put yourself on the line. No one here doubts you. Just tell us what to do and consider it done."

I had to swallow a few times. The lump in my throat was a big one. When I could finally speak, I said. "Um... Thank you. I don't know if the civilians will feel the same way, but that's a problem for later. Here's what we know so far."

I recounted the Queen Mother's story about the dragon wars.

The room went silent. Frowns, furrowed brows, and even teardrops marred every expression.

Someone said, "How do we even know the siblings are alive? The dragons might have slit all their throats by now."

"We don't know for sure, but it seems that these dragons want to make them suffer. I think they'll keep them alive to witness the destruction of their homes."

Tynan swiped his hands over his face and cleared his throat. "To sum up, these dragons want revenge for the near annihilation of their kind. Many weapons, especially the shadow ones, are useless against them, and they could be anywhere in either world because they're shapeshifters."

The word shapeshifters put into that context made me squirm. "Mostly right," I said. "I've been thinking, and I believe they're still in the Summerlands. The dragons' lands were originally in what used to be the midlands, which... Najat, map?"

She projected a map of the Dreaming onto the wall behind me.

I pointed to three mountain ranges in Columbia. "Here is where the Savatos Mountains would be in the Dreaming. I think the dragons are probably holed up somewhere around there now. I mean, if the eggs stayed hidden for fifty years, why couldn't a handful of shapeshifting dragons live there undetected?"

"But there were wards, protections. Wouldn't that have alerted someone if they tried to return to the Dreaming?" Riz squirmed, as if uncomfortable, in his seat.

"No one even seems to have given the dragons any thought after they were exiled. Wouldn't wards have to be maintained?" I looked to Rebus for the answer.

"They would. I was a kid when all that happened, and I can tell you that in the Winter Court, these dragons were never mentioned."

Tynan shrugged. "Makes sense. It was a shameful thing. Who would want to remember?"

There were mutters of agreement all around the table.

"I doubt Nemesis would see it as shameful." I said. "But right now, we've got two problems. The kings and queen are out of commission, and the courts are in chaos. If we can free the rulers, they can lead their forces in taking back the courts."

"You mean slaughter the dragons again and take back the lands we stole in the first place? Seems to me that's what got us into this mess."

Riz was right. "No, but we can't just keep all the fey here indefinitely either. Maybe the siblings will figure out a way to negotiate and end this peacefully. From what their mother said, this all happened when they were children. Hopefully, they'll do better."

"And if the dragons won't negotiate?" Cari said.

I sighed because I had no answers. "We let them make that call. One thing at a time." We had to focus on the problem we could solve, which was getting back Dúl and his family. "Look at the bright side—at least the vampires should be out of our hair. With Chevalier dead, I doubt they'll be able to organize enough to fight."

We spent the next few hours planning, sometimes arguing. Eventually, we came up with a viable scheme and a couple of off-the-wall contingencies. Then we decided to address the civilians. They couldn't be privy to everything, but they did deserve to know what was being done to return them safely to their homes.

Gathering all the refugees into the auditorium, which I swore seemed to have tripled inside, Morgan, Tania, Rebus, a fullblood representative of the Summer Court, and I all took to the stage. Morgan stood behind a podium and waited for the din to die down.

"Welcome, fey kin, to the Shadow Court. It is unfortunate that I am addressing you under these dire circumstances. We, the representatives of your courts, wish to assure you that all in our combined power is being done to rectify this situation and to get you back to your respective homes. And now, please give your attention to our Shadow Master who can fill you in on some of the details."

Morgan waved me over, and I crossed the stage as stiff as the Tin Man. "What are you doing?" I hissed, making sure I was away from any microphone or other amplification device.

"Say something comforting and inspirational."

"You couldn't do that?"

Morgan smirked. "I've never been known as inspiring, and I have a reputation to uphold." She sashayed over to where the others stood, intently watching me.

I caught Rebus's eye, and he nodded at me. I could do this. "Uh, hello everyone. I know you all must be exhausted and terrified. Our revered leaders have been taken from us, and I know for myself at least, it feels like being set adrift. You probably heard about my little meltdown earlier." There were a couple of chuckles.

"I'm probably not the only one who's lost it today. But here's the thing. Those leaders need *us* now. They need us to be strong and to pull together for them. They are each the heart of our respective courts, and our enemies know this. We can't let their absence break us. We must let it bring us together so we can fight for those we know would sacrifice their lives for ours without a moment's hesitation."

There was some rustling and stirring among the crowd, but they were listening.

"We have a plan to bring them home. All I ask of you is that you remain calm and stay strong. When we get the lords and queens back, they'll lead us to victory against our common enemy, and you'll be able to go home again."

Some murmurs, and it felt like a collective sigh went through the room.

"However, they may call on all of you to fight for your homes. Prepare yourselves. And I need to ask a favor as well. If any of you have talismans, potions—any enchanted items that can help us rescue the lords and queens, please see one of us on the podium as soon as possible.

"Thank you, and don't give up hope! We've only just started to fight." *Lame.*

The civilians applauded, but I felt like my pep talks were going to need a lot of work if I was going to be expected to do this after today.

Chapter 20

We reconvened in the conference room. "Okay, now considering I just lied my ass off to almost the whole population of the Dreaming, we need a plan."

The most obvious course of action would be to sneak into the Summer Court and save the siblings. It was exactly what everyone wanted to do.

"That's what they'll expect. These dragons have had years to watch how the courts operate and know how we will respond to anything they throw at us. We need to change the game."

There were skeptical expressions all around me, on every face except for Morgan's. I couldn't tell what she thought. "All right, what do you propose?"

"Negotiation. Have someone walk right in and talk to these dragons, and—"

"That's ridiculous!" Of course, Tania wouldn't want the option that didn't involve a fight. This was the first thing she'd said to me since that last meeting.

I held up my hands to show there was more. "Hang on. I'm not done. *They* would also think it's crazy for anyone to present themselves as a negotiator. We'd catch them off guard, and while they're distracted, someone else can sneak in to free the sovereigns."

Everyone went quiet as they digested my idea, more like tried to come up with reasons why it wouldn't work.

Only Rebus watched me shrewdly. "Say we go along with this, sweetheart. Which sacrificial lamb do you propose to hand over?"

"Well..." I braced myself for the arguments. "It would look odd for only one person to show up alone, so I propose three 'diplomats' and another team for the extraction."

"Who, Merc? Don't bullshit me."

I couldn't even bring myself to glare at him because I knew where his objection was coming from. This was so unfair to do to him, but it was necessary. "Fine. I'll go in to talk with them. Ty and Renea can back me up. Riz and Tania will lead the other group along with Cari." As one of Athena's personal guards, Renea knew all the secret entrances into the Summer Court and would give the others specific directions. "It'll be fine. I can't exactly explain why, but I feel like the dragons aren't interested in hurting me. They've had two opportunities already—"

"And instead, they took your mother." Rebus looked like he wanted to spit nails at me. "I'm not about to lose you too in some suicide mission. If you plan to go, so am I."

"Absolutely not," Morgan said in the bossy tone that shut down argument. "What part of diplomacy do you not understand? You have my sympathy, Rebus. But if you go there ready to tear heads off, you'll destroy any hope Merc has of holding their attention long enough to get the others out. Frankly, you shouldn't be allowed anywhere near the Summer Court in the emotional state you're in."

Rebus slammed his fists on the table and jumped to his feet. Knocking his chair to the floor, he stormed out of the room and slammed the door behind him.

Even though it broke my heart to continue without him, I laid out my idea. While we prepared, Morgan offered to go after him and make sure he was all right. I needed to stay on task if I was going to get everyone out of the Dreaming alive.

~*~

Our typical arsenal at RavCorp was useless against the shadow dragons, so we had to rely on other items, donated or otherwise "acquired."

Fortunately, I still had my duplication cuff.

Since the point was getting in and out without a battle, we agreed that only five court members would make up the extraction team after Tynan, Renea, and I waved the white flags.

Najat would stay in remote communication with everyone, and Morgan coordinated backup squads to help if either group ran into trouble. With the way things had been going lately, problems were almost guaranteed.

After gearing up, we took a portal to an unoccupied border between the Dawn and Summer Courts. Now in the Dreaming, I noticed that I felt different here. I had been spending a lot of time in the realm but had been distracted by any number of other things, mainly Dúl.

But for some reason, stepping into the Summerlands this time, I sensed its magic tingling around and coursing through me. Colors always seemed more vivid to me in the Dreaming, like a super-HD version of the Waking. Now it was more than that. My vision was sharper. I could see farther and clearer than ever.

As opposed to despair and sadness weighing me down, my body was energized, my focus like a laser.

We crossed into the Summer Court in the Amazon. Renea explained that Athena liked to spend time all around her court instead of one main castle. There were three villas, which in the Waking coincided with the Amazon rainforest, Kenya and Malaysia.

Meshua, the former capital of the Dreamlands had been much farther north, around Mexico, while the lands the dragons claimed sat near the Magdalena Valley in Columbia. Even though Athena had been abducted from the Malaysian locale, we reasoned that the captives were probably being held at the capitol of the Summer Court in Brazil.

We had abandoned all our winter gear in favor of lightweight, long-sleeved shirts to protect from the intense sun, camos, and boots. We left behind the Kevlar because it would only add heat and weight without offering any protection from the dragons' shadow magic.

Almost immediately, the humidity started sweat pouring out of me like I stepped into the shower. I stripped off my long sleeve down to my black tank. Then I altered my skin to green and scouted ahead. Renea, petite and agile, took to the trees and surveyed from above.

I looked around in all directions giving Najat a visual of where we were thanks to special enchanted contact lenses from the Dawn Court that allowed me to see as if it were daytime. The Dawn soldiers often used these lenses for underwater recon. They would dissolve in my eyes in a couple of hours but until then would transmit images back to Najat. I could have commented about the spy-like gear, but I chose not to antagonize Tania.

The Summer Court had the same vividness and sparkle that I remembered during the short time I spent there as a child. Waterfalls rushed over high cliffs in the distance. Animals I had never seen or heard of flitted, buzzed, chirped, and cawed. I ducked as one insect, with a proboscis as long as my hand and a body bigger than my head, whizzed by. It would suck to be that thing's next meal.

As we approached the villa, a tower rose high above the trees.

"They could be up there," I said so Najat could hear me through our earbuds. "I'll request the dragons give me some proof of life. That should give us some clues as to what type of space they're being held in. Then you can send in team two."

Renea descended from the branches. "There's good news and bad news. The vampires apparently didn't get the message that their leader is dead, so they're still serving the dragons."

"Is that the good news or bad?"

"That's the bad. Good is that there's a patrol we can turn ourselves over to about three hundred paces away." She pointed out the direction we needed to go.

We had brought white handkerchiefs with us and tied one now to a fallen tree branch. The vampires lived in the Waking, so we knew they would recognize the symbol.

On silent feet, we jogged among palm trees and over ancient immense roots. We came to a small clearing and waited.

We heard the vamps before we saw them. Instead of startling them, I called out. "Hello! My name is Merc! I'm an emissary of the Shadow Court. We want to negotiate."

The footsteps stopped, and voices seemed to be debating whether or not to kill us on sight. I waved the white flag ahead of me and walked toward them.

"We're unarmed. Just here to talk. No one else needs to get hurt. Please just take us to whoever is in charge."

There were only two of them, but being that it was night, that would likely be enough to damage us more than we could afford. The *Lemooria* began its giggling, faint and far off. However, it wasn't talking directly to the vampires, who didn't seem to notice the spirit's amusement. I guessed that they were relatively new.

One of the vampires stepped forward, a young, slender guy with spiky hair. He reminded me of Paris. Regret stabbed into my heart. "How'd you get here? This whole place is warded." He held a machete that glowed red while his partner pointed a crossbow at us that glowed orange.

I held my hands out so they could see there were no weapons in them. They didn't need to know that my shadow dagger was just a thought away, and they weren't immune. "We walked. From the Dawn court. Figured if we crossed any closer to the villa, we'd be shot on sight."

He grunted and glanced over at his partner who shrugged. "Whatever. Since we're under orders to bring any stray fey to the castle, we won't rip you to shreds. Down on the ground, hands behind your heads."

Their Waking upbringings were obvious when they patted us down. They had obviously watched too many crime dramas, but they hadn't paid close enough attention. They were more interested in free gropes on Renea and me, and whacking Tynan in the balls, to actually look for weapons. So, they missed the blade in Ty's boot and the bola Renea had wrapped around her waist like a belt and tucked into her waistband.

My weapons wouldn't have been detected by Batman.

Satisfied that we were telling the truth, they led us to the villa to meet the dragons.

~*~

The outside of Athena's rainforest villa looked like a hotel with dozens of rooms, balconies that wrapped all around the second floor, and tan walls with white accents. A long palm-lined pathway led to immense red doors. The vamps ushered us straight to a throne room done up with red tapestries. Behind two thrones, one slightly smaller than the other, a colorful mural of a bird of paradise with spread wings covered an entire wall.

Sitting upright in front of the thrones were two black dragons unlike anything I imagined. For one thing, they were pony sized. Their wings folded along their backs, and their tails wrapped around their bodies, catlike. When we were brought in, they turned. The one on my right seemed to melt, first into a black blob, but then into a bipedal frame. It reminded me of homicide outlines—two arms, two legs, but no hair, no face, no definition.

The darkness near the top opened to reveal a kind of mouth so it could speak to us. "I see your curiosity did get the better of you, shifter." This was the same soft voice that had addressed me in the Winter Court.

"Is this what you really look like?" I mentally kicked myself for sounding so impressed and for opening with such a stupid question instead of something more important.

The shape laughed. Something prickled at the back of my mind, but I couldn't sort it from everything else swirling through my consciousness. "I won't answer that. How stupid do you think I am?"

"Not stupid at all... How should I address you?"

"I am a queen among my kind. Your majesty will do. This was quite foolish, you know—coming here your-self instead of sending your underlings. I'm somewhat disappointed."

I couldn't let myself be goaded into saying any other dumb thing, so I stuck to the script. "We've come to negotiate the release of the fey court rulers. Clearly, from the messages you've left, you've been wronged in some way. But it also seems that this was done when your captives were children. I'm sure a peaceful solution can be reached if they are freed."

She laughed at me. I thought she might, but then she turned to the vampires who had bagged us. "Bring the captives to the banquet hall and take these two there now. Give me a moment with Umbra."

Hearing my birth name from her again made my heart stutter.

The other dragon and the vamps steered Ty and Renea out to clear the room. They shot me confused looks, and I nodded that it was okay. They followed the enemies out. Our situation might not have been okay, but pretending it was seemed to be the safest move.

When we were alone, the dragon queen slithered into the larger of the two thrones. "So, young one, what makes you think I won't strike you and the scum you serve down where you stand? Give me one good reason why I should release my enemies. And not that nonsense about a peaceful solution. The truth."

This was better than I had expected—I had her talking, and Najat was on the other end listening for my signal. "I think you could have killed me more than once, so if you wanted me dead, I wouldn't be standing here. You want something else, so what is it? I know about what happened to your kind under the old king's rule, and it was awful, but it's no better to make innocents pay for his crimes. They were mere children at the time."

She studied me for a moment, at least I think that's what she was doing. Her shape leaned in my direction, but with no eyes, she could have been napping for all I knew.

"Why do you defend them? Serve them? You are neither fey nor changeling. Do you not see how they exploit you? Even your lover lied and manipulated you, and then engaged you to work in his service before bedding you. Don't you think you deserve better?"

Ouch. *She's just trying to get in your head. Ignore it.* "My relationship is my private business. As for not being one of them, I don't remember much of who or what I am. But I do know that when I was a starving and terrified child, a group of changelings helped me reach safety. A fey tried to help me before I ran away from her. Then a fey and changeling couple raised me as their own. One of whom—" I had to swallow to keep my voice from cracking. "One of whom your partner killed with no provocation while she was bound and helpless."

She sighed. "Yet you still hope for peace? The changeling's death was regrettable and not what I ordered. I'm afraid that peace is impossible at this point."

She was right. The moment I got the chance, I would want revenge on that other dragon for Nat's death. But I had to keep trying for now. "This isn't about me or my personal pain. I don't want any more collateral deaths."

"Hmm..." Another lull. "And what would you offer in exchange for the release of the so-called rulers?"

"Umm..." I was caught off guard. "Y-you mean like a trade? I—"

"Come, young one. We shall see. These fey are so important to you, I wonder how much you mean to them."

She rose and started for the door. When she passed me, her form was over a foot taller than my 5'8". Her legs mimicked walking, but it was she more like she glided across the floor.

Wondering what I was in for next, I trailed her across the corridor into the banquet room.

~*~

The decor in the large hall was more subdued with pale walls and smaller tapestries. Ferns and miniature palm trees grew in pots in the two far corners behind a grand table. Seated around the table with their hands bound were the four siblings and my two companions.

On instinct, I bolted toward Dúl.

"Merc, no." He winced as the dragon from the other room cuffed him in the side of the head and then put a claw to his throat. I froze, stifling a whimper, and hoped my gaze could communicate everything I was feeling.

I could see in the lines around his lips regret and sadness that I had come. Yet he had to know I would never leave him to whatever fate these dragons had in store.

As the last taken, he appeared to be in the best shape, so there was one small relief.

Nemesis looked the worst of the four, by far. Her hair hung in limp strings around her smudged face. Her fingers, twisted and skeletal, rested on the table. Red welts where restraints had been digging into her skin were clearly visible, even from several feet away.

Athena huddled close to her big sister, who didn't reject the attention, and stroked her hair, whispering to and fussing over the former enemy. Maybe something good would come of this mess after all.

I turned to the silhouette of a person beside me. "Okay, we're all here. What is it that you want? You suggested a trade."

"Patience, young one. Besides, now that your rulers are here, shouldn't they be the ones to negotiate?"

A growl erupted from Orion. "Why would we deal with kidnappers and murderers?"

Dúl awkwardly reached over and put his hands over

Orion's. Orion turned, they exchanged a glance, and then he quieted.

"We're listening." Dúl sat back. This was his kingly side—cool and self-possessed even under the worst circumstances.

Pride welled up in me, and at that moment, inspired me to sacrifice anything to get them out of here.

The dragon queen approached the seat at the head of the table. Gentle pressure at my back guided me toward the one to its right. A few chairs separated Ty and me. I trusted that Najat was still listening in.

"Now then, I understand you've developed some sort of democratic system among yourselves. You will each get a vote. Not the underlings, of course. However, if all goes well here, you will be released, unharmed."

Was this some kind of show of goodwill? What was her game?

"Let's start with the eldest, shall we? By the way, our thanks for the generous use of your lands and your form. A bit cold for our tastes, but very well equipped. Here is our offer. We will release you in exchange for the shifter."

All heads turned toward the shadow. Dúl lunged forward. "No!" The dragon restrained him.

Nemesis lifted her head slowly, as if it pained her to do so. "Why? What do you want with them?"

"Does that matter? You wanted them yourself, did you not? You recognized their talent and value years ago, swooping in to woo them to your court before the others learned of their location."

"Yes, and they rejected my liaison's offer." Nemesis peered at me through tired eyes, apparently with no hard feelings. "Do you intend to harm or to exploit them?"

"I would not harm Umbra, and I would utilize their abilities no more or less than you."

"No matter, I would not be the one to hand the child over. They should be the one to decide."

The Dragon Queen turned to Athena next. "And you? Will you agree to a peaceful exchange?"

Athena glared. "No. You steal my home and use my own weapons to burn my brother's land? I do not agree to an exchange. I would not trust you to honor an agreement for dinner, let alone a hostage. My vote is no."

"Ah, and is this because of concern over the shifter's welfare or because you wish to spare your brother's feelings?"

I wished she'd stop referring to me as 'the shifter,' highlighting my difference from the changeling and fey around the table. Like I was some alien creature that they had no allegiance to. Although... wasn't that the truth?

Athena's mouth opened and closed. She shifted in her seat, glanced at Dúl. "It is for both."

The shadow leaned toward me. "She lies. To the summer brat you are little more than an accessory for her dear brother. This is who you would sacrifice yourself for?" To Orion she said, "And what of you, Dawn King? The animosity between you and your brother is well known. By removing his shifter, you'd weaken him while freeing the rest of you. You could resume your petty fighting. What say you?"

"If you think I would be so dishonorable—"

"You imprisoned Umbra yourself not long ago, did you not?"

"That was before I knew who she was...uh, who they were. I agree with Nemesis. If Merc is to be unharmed, I would leave the choice to them. However, if they choose to stay, I insist that negotiations continue and that they be treated well, not as a prisoner."

Dúl huffed and peered sideways at his brother. I couldn't imagine what was going through his head about Orion, but I knew what his response was going to be to the shadow.

I tried to head him off. "Dúl, *amor*, your court needs its king a lot more than it needs me. They won't hurt me."

"No, love. Don't ask me to leave you here. Please."

The last thing I wanted was for him to look weak in front of these creatures, and it broke my heart to hear him beg. I also knew that if I agreed to stay no force in the Dreaming or Waking would keep him from coming after me.

As much as it killed me, I broke eye contact with him to face our enemy. "I want other concessions."

The mouth on the otherwise featureless face curved up to one side. "That may change the agreement."

"In addition to releasing all four of the realm's leaders, I want the vampires out of the realm and the civilians allowed to return to their homes."

Now she laughed at me. "So, they can rise up and attack us the moment they have their arsenals and weapons restored to them? Four sovereigns and two whelps for you. That is the offer. Take it or leave it. If it eases your mind, don't think for a moment that they won't try to attack and retrieve you anyway. The Dawn King's method of 'negotiation' has always been and will always be war. Just like his father."

If she knew they'd come back to fight her anyway, then what did she hope to gain by keeping me? "Then why bother? If you think you'll turn me against them, against *him*, you greatly underestimate me."

"We shall see."

"Merc..."

I didn't want to see the pain in his eyes, but I had to have one last look. "All right. I'll stay. Will you at least allow me a moment to say goodbye?"

"Go right ahead." She drawled out the words, not about to give us any privacy. The bitch.

I glanced at Tynan, and he gave me a tiny nod. This hadn't been anywhere close to the plan, but it was working out in a way that we could manage. The second team didn't need to do a retrieval. They could start organizing a strike force. Slowly, I got to my feet and walked over to Dúl. The dragon finally released him but stayed close.

I leaned down and kissed him, long and deeply.

When our lips parted, I took his face in both my hands and looked him square in the eyes before whispering in his ear, pretending to nuzzle his cheek. "I'll only be here for a short while. Don't be angry. I always have a backup plan. Take care of Rebus for me. He's going to need all the support he can get." I kissed him again and hoped that this gamble didn't end up biting me in the ass. "I love you."

His face pinched, but he nodded, showing that he trusted me. Najat, if she was still listening, would get the message for Morgan to get every able body armed and ready. The lords and ladies would be coming home to lead them into battle.

Whether or not I could escape before then was another matter altogether.

The queen escorted me to a room on the second floor that appeared to be some kind of servant quarters—small and plain but clean. When there were only the two of us in there, with her back to me, she said in a drawl, "You don't really think I intend to wait around for them to regroup, do you? I kept you here for your own safety. We will soon attack the Shadow headquarters in the Waking, where they have stored all their civilians. They will watch as their people are cut down before their eyes, just as we did."

The door shut with a quiet click behind her. The lock turned in the tumbler. While I was shut up in this room, the RavCorp building was about to fall under siege.

Dragon Spawn

Only a handful of them remained now. Liffi's brother and one cousin; Isquill's two siblings and one of their mates. Most had already fled to the mountain range in the Waking—the Andes they were called. But Liffi was in no condition to travel. She needed to heal. And to secure the eggs, her first hatchlings, and probably the only ones she would ever have now that Isquill was gone.

Deep in the caves of the Savatos, she slept and mourned in alternating cycles. Her external wounds closed, broken bones knitted together. She drank and fished from the waters of the small underground river running beneath the hills.

And she plotted. The fey and their greed would pay dearly for all they had stolen—her home, her mate... Isquill would have settled for a small territory and lived in peace with the fey. But no, Wymond demanded it all.

He would have nothing when Liffi was done. Isquill had traveled far north to ally with the giants, the only other race that had stood against the fey. When she healed, she would be certain to keep that pact alive.

The fire of her rage warmed her during the cool nights until the first twinge tightened her belly. Alone, she pushed out the first egg, cleaned it, and buried it in her nest. Perfectly oval shaped and black as obsidian, her egg, the size of one of her enemy's infants, pulsed with the rhythm of life like music to its mother.

The second egg did not come so easily.

Liffi had heard of such situations, when the egg became stuck within the tract. She traveled to a warm spring. Hours and days, she soaked and pushed, straining, laboring. She felt every tear and rupture inside her but could not roar out her agony. She could not risk discovery.

Eventually, she transformed only her claws into fey-shaped hands. Delicately, wincing with every inch of progress, she reached in and eased the egg the rest of the way out. A tiny rupture at the top of the shell.

Silent tears flowed from Liffi's eyes as she picked up her damaged egg and struggled to her feet. She would not abandon it. There was hope for its survival if only the outer shell had been cracked and the inner was still watertight.

She brought it back to her den and buried it next to its sibling before resting. She'd chosen this place for its privacy and temperature. Her eggs would be warm enough, and even during the rainy season, they would stay dry and secure. By the time they were ready to hatch, ten cycles—fifty of the humans' years, she calculated—the defeat of the dragons would be a memory to her enemies.

But Liffi would never forget. And she would never forgive.

~*~

The time of hatching approached. Liffi had stayed in the warm lands of the Waking for all these years, biding her time. She maintained communication with the giants, making the arduous journey to their lands once, twenty-five human years ago.

Since the time of their near-extermination, the dragons had recovered. Two of their number aside from Liffi also carried eggs at the time of the exile, but they had more time to prepare to birth their young in the Waking.

The eggs hatched faster in the Waking, but the hatchlings seemed to have diminished abilities without the magic of the Dreaming infusing their bodies. Liffi wondered if the hatchlings would regain their power with regular exposure to the Dreaming's magic. The dragons needed to reclaim the Dreamlands, or eventually, they'd be as good as extinct.

But now, she had urgent matters to see to.

Guaro, Isquill's brother who lost his mate during the war and was now raising their young, came to her.

"Liffi, I insist you let us go with you. What if you are wrong and you can't pass through giant country? What if there are different wards? Renewed wards? What if—"

She placed her palms against his human visage. "Guaro, you have become a treasured companion. And Panaqual has become like my own son. But you are needed here, and I must do this alone. I will return, fate willing, with both of my young. All will be well."

He pulled her to him and kissed her fiercely. She would never experience quite the same affection or passion she had felt for Isquill, but somewhere along the path, she and Guaro came to rely on each other, and then to mean more than simple confidantes.

Liffi pulled away, took a last long look. Pan, hidden behind a tree, glared. Her explanation and reassurance the previous night did nothing to quell the little one's tears as he pummeled her with tiny fists and begged her to stay. "Give Pan my love. I will return."

Transforming into a large, bronze-skinned man in a linen shirt and khaki shorts, Liffi lifted a pack in each hand and headed west toward the ocean.

She boarded a freighter sailing north. The oceans no longer held the fascination for her that they did in the early days. She had worked on crews over the past years, preparing for this journey. Temperatures changed from sweltering to cold, but still, she had not reached her destination. When the ships took Liffi as far as they could.

In the beginning of the winter season, long nights would make it easier to fly unseen. She trekked into the forest at the southern Greenland coast, changed into her natural form, and leapt into the sky. It had been so long since she stretched her wings. Flying by night, and shifting into a wolf by day, it took months of near constant motion until she finally reached the pass into the giant's Dreaming territory.

Liffi rested for a few days to get her strength back, and then crossed the shimmering magical barrier. She would have to remain in her wolf form from now until she reached her destination. Hopefully, no fey would hunt her.

Time grew short.

A great change had come over the Dreaming. Liffi gleaned that the king perished, and his heirs split the realm among themselves. They were said to spend their days squabbling among themselves. Of course they did. Some of them were still children. And after their father purged other races from the realm, who else was left for them to fight?

This development could work in her favor.

A fey queen had taken control of this region—a harsh one but nevertheless revered by her subjects.

The giant settlements Liffi passed were quieter. Peaceful. Their numbers had decreased since her last visit—many had gone into the Waking and farther north. Still, those who remained honored the former alliance and allowed her safe passage as far as they were able.

A Shadow Court had been created. Interesting. Had old Wymond somehow stolen power from Isquill's dying body? Power that was somehow bequeathed to the prince? However this court came about, the young shadow lord despised his elder brother, and that could benefit Liffi someday.

Traveling south, she noticed the changes in the atmosphere and climate that signaled she was nearing her destination. Even after all this time, the floral and loamy scents, the spark of magic, and the welcoming warmth of this temperate region transported her back to happier times. At first the nostalgia was more sweet than bitter. Yet the closer Liffi came to the former fey capital, the thicker the air became and the tighter her skin felt against her bones.

She didn't intend to tempt fate by coming so close. Her feet seemed to carry her along of their own will. Before her brain could reason, her body remembered where she'd arrived, and it revolted. Suddenly the light blinded her. Phantom versions of herself, half dead, and of her beloved Isquill full of poisoned arrows haunted her. Liffi's lungs seized, and she fell to her knees. This place was too hot, too heavy.

Was the very air poisoned? Perhaps Isquill's spirit cursed these trees and cliffs. Or maybe he blamed her for his death. Her weakness. Had she not allowed herself to be captured, he might have evaded the fey king. Defeated the despot.

What right did she have now to hope that her eggs would have been safe all this time? Liffi lay on her side, lightheaded from the lack of air. She fought to push the memories away, but the barrage went on. It was only when she felt her body begin to shift that she found the slightest bit of strength. She could not give in. Even if the chance of her eggs surviving was miniscule, if they survived, they would need her. She couldn't risk being discovered—captured—again.

Taking slow, shallow breaths, Liffi gained control of her body and silenced her thoughts. Staying in one spot made her anxious, but she had to wait, to pull herself together before she could continue. Once she was moving again, each step was like dragging weights by her paws. But finally, she was away from that wretched location and crossed the border into the youngest fey princess's lands.

The child was rumored to be a spoiled nuisance. The regent of her court succumbed to her every whim. Liffi realized that these new fey leaders may prove to be weak, but she hoped that the Dreaming would survive. She wanted the satisfaction of being the one to destroy all of Wymond's progeny.

Weeks into her journey, as she hunted in the lands of her stolen home, she smelled the warm soil and relished the humid air against her wolf fur. Some days in the Waking it had seemed she would never see her homeland again.

Stepping a paw down, she heard a snap only a hair of a second before pain ripped through her ankle. Liffi howled in agony, a long, keening sound that erupted from the deepest part of her soul. To be so close only to misstep on a branch into a foxhole.

Her ankle bent in an unnatural direction, and her other three legs twisted awkwardly. There was no way to free herself from the hole in this form.

Listening for any threats, Liffi ensured that it was safe enough to risk a shift. Swallowing her pain, she set it aside and focused on the transformation. When she morphed to a fey body, the paw changed to a wrist and reset itself in the socket. She pushed up to a standing position, cradling her arm against her body. The different shape made it easier to extract herself from the hole, but now her wrist was swelling rapidly.

Using two sticks and some vine, Liffi splinted the wrist and continued on in the fey shape. She had been right—the wards were faded. No alarms or reactions to a shadow dragon reentering the realm after all this time.

She reached the Savatos range and followed its base until she reached her destination. There they were—the nest coverings around her eggs, soon to be her hatchlings. Very soon. She did not disturb them and instead went to the warm springs to wash.

Her wrist had already started to heal, her powers accelerated in the Dreaming where she belonged. She envisioned the day when she would call this place home again.

A pulse, like electricity, rippled through her. It was time.

She assumed her natural form and hurried back to the nest where her eggs had hidden for so long. Unlike the hatchlings forced to gestate in the Waking, Liffi's offspring benefitted from the Dreaming's magic. They would be powerful and would play vital roles in the reclaiming of the Dragonlands.

Rustling ahead sped her steps. She reached the nest to find the first egg rocking back and forth. A faint *tap tap tap* came from within.

"I'm here, little one," she told it with her mind. *"Come. Join me."* Her hatchling proved strong when the egg cracked a moment later, a dark head poking through and mewling like a kitten. Liffi was ready with freshly caught fish that she chewed and regurgitated into the young's mouth.

The second egg had yet to move.

When the first hatchling was sated and resting, Liffi crept over to the nest. With her claws, she gently pulled the coverings away.

The second egg was cold, gray and petrified. It had not survived after all.

One more crime to avenge with fey blood.

She returned to her sleeping young and curled her body around the little female. They would have to wait a few days before trying to rejoin the dragons back in the Waking. Even without the benefits of growing up in the Dreaming as she should, Liffi sensed this strong hatchling would be special. This little dragon might even be the key to bringing down the fey once and for all.

Siege

The vampire guards escorted Dúl, his siblings, and the two Shadows through a portal to the Shadow Court, and then ordered them out of the realm. He could see how much it strained Orion and Athena to not fight, but they had to keep up the pretense of following the agreement. Regroup and make sure the civilians were being looked after.

Then he would go back for Merc, with or without his siblings.

The group arrived in Dúl's office. Feathers of all colors floated behind the glass of the aviary from the tropical and sea birds taking refuge there. Morgan perched against the desk, a pad in her hand, while Najat sat behind it clacking away at her keyboard.

"Sire, are you all right?" Morgan met his gaze. Was that sympathy in her eyes?

"No. Far from it."

Najat started to gather up her laptop, but Dúl waved her back down. "Sisters, please sit. Orion—" He pushed one of the guest chairs toward his brother while Athena and Morgan helped Nemesis to the couch.

"Tynan, gather the rest of your unit along with the other lieutenants and bring them and Rebus to the interior conference room. We'll join you there shortly. Morgan, what's happening here, and please tell me you've found places for the displaced fey."

"We heard everything that happened. The most pressing thing is that the dragons know we've brought the refugees here from the other courts. They plan to attack imminently."

"Faithless bastards!" Orion shot to his feet.

"Sit down, Orion." A loud cough wracked Nemesis. "Of course, they were going to attack while we are still in chaos. It's what I would have done. The question is, can we defend?"

"Yes. The building has state-of-the-art security. Najat?" Dúl turned to her.

"All clear for five blocks in every direction, Sire."

"Good. Lock down the building. Morgan, where are the refugees?"

"Spread between the lobby and second floors. We expanded the space as much as we could, but..."

"You did well. Once the building is secure, a call will go out reporting a fake bomb threat, and a team of changelings will be dispatched disguised as police. That should keep humans away from the scene. The outside will be masked to look like everything is normal inside. Short of an actual explosion, they should remain ignorant."

Dúl noticed Orion watching him with a strange expression. "What?"

"Nothing. I'm usually the one giving orders. Feels odd."

Was that meant as a compliment or a barb? Dúl didn't have time to unpack the statement. "Let's get to the conference room."

~*~

Fifteen bodies squeezed into the windowless space. Morgan claimed the far end of a long, rectangular table. Orion and Dúl's sisters took seats to her right. Rebus, Tania, and Merc's squad sat opposite the three sovereigns. A few other high-ranking court agents stood behind them. Dúl breathed in before taking the last seat at the head of the table.

Rebus had not stood up when his former queen entered, yet his scowl softened as he took in her slight limp and bedraggled appearance.

"Spare me your pity, Rebus," she said without seeming to look his way. "I haven't had a chance to freshen up after weeks of imprisonment and torture. Here, does this make you feel better?" Nemesis waved her hand, whisking away the layers of dirt and grime. Her hair, skin, and robe all sparkled white. "I'd have thought it would have given you some satisfaction to see me brought down a notch, however temporarily."

"I honestly don't care what happened to you, but your appearance coupled with my child's noticeable absence are concerning." He focused his gaze on Dúl.

"Where is Merc?" His hands balled into fists that couldn't contain the worry and rage coming off him.

Dúl hadn't had the opportunity to get to know this fey well, but Rebus was the most important person in Merc's life, and the idea of becoming the target of his wrath was as unappealing as it was unavoidable.

The responsibilities of being a king really sucked at times. "Merc made a deal with the enemy—a prisoner exchange as it were. However, I have no intention of leaving—"

Rebus deflated and scrubbed his hands over his face. "I knew they'd do something like this. I can't lose Merc too. Not after Nat."

Dúl shot a questioning glance at Morgan. Her frown told him all he needed to know— the dragons somehow killed the only mother Merc knew. The suicidal mission made even more sense now. Yet they wouldn't intentionally bring Rebus additional pain. Dúl had to trust that Merc had the situation in hand.

The fey had bigger problems right now and needed their leaders. His first duty was to the subjects who needed him.

"I'm sorry for your loss, Rebus. I would never have agreed to leave Merc unless I thought they'd be safe for the time being. The dragons seem to not want them harmed. Once we secure the—"

A metallic shriek tore into Dúl's mind. He clasped his head and was aware of the others around the table doing the same. An external intrusion, then. He stumbled out to the balcony looking down to the ground-floor atrium. He saw nothing.

"Azuath!" The voice came from above. A blue-haired being in jeans and no shirt hovered near the ceiling. "I bring warm regards from the Dragon Queen!" He raised his hands. A black disc appeared before him. "Warm—who am I kidding?" The creature grinned. "I'm about to rain hell down on you!"

The disc stretched and grew, quickly expanding to the size of the ceiling before the sides began to drip down. Teeth formed around the perimeter of the opening. It was becoming a creature swallowing everyone in the area. Inside the mouth, storm clouds threatened in the distance over a wasteland of gray rubble and debris.

"The Night Lanes." Dúl realized after a beat that he'd whispered the words out loud.

"Yes," Orion said. "And a Djanin controlling them."

They were supposed to be extinct. Then again, Dúl had never heard anything of shadow dragons either. What other ancient enemies had the Dragon Queen rallied to her cause? "Down to the atrium. Now."

That was the extent of conversation they could manage before the first giant serpent slithered down toward the civilians. Dúl tapped the screen of his watch. The numbers on the face swirled and a graphic of a raven filled the display. From the upper floors, huge birds representing each court streamed in from the aviary.

Oedipus, attack! Dúl mentally commanded. The owl

screeched, adding to a din of raven caws and other bird cries. Dozens of eagles, birds of paradise, and ravens converged on the djanin.

He blinked out of existence. An illusion. But he must be somewhere close. Still, the priority was the protection of all civilians, who were scrambling in every direction. Their screams and shouts raised the level of pandemonium. They were trapped now that he'd ordered the building sealed. Damn that Dragon Queen. She'd played them. Worse, Dúl had been so distracted, he hadn't seen the trick coming.

Fireballs and stone projectiles rained down on the scattering crowd. Alien looking creatures and small monsters materialized from the walls and floor. The atrium was bedlam.

Most of the civilian fey and changelings panicked, but some turned to fight. The Shadows stood back-to-back with Winter soldiers, blinding creatures and blasting through illusions. Summer and Dawn soldiers swung swords and fists against crawling, flying, and oozing monstrosities.

Two of the birds broke off and flew towards Athena and Orion. They leapt over the railing onto the birds' backs who transported them to the ground floor and headed back up to the battle. The birds were now keeping a second giant serpent occupied.

Dúl turned to Nemesis. She whispered something to a tiny creature in her hand. It ballooned into a spider the size of a car. It scooped her into its forelegs and climbed over the side, lowering her to the atrium with the others.

He took one last moment to send a mental message to his ravens—*Hunt the creature doing this*—before he dissolved into shadow and sailed down to join the fight.

Reforming on the ground about thirty feet from Athena, Dúl cursed his miscalculation. A mass of writhing vines wrapped around her. Her blade sliced through them. Some of the vines formed legs that transitioned into a humanoid torso and birdlike talons for arms. The head was an eyeless mass of vines with an open maw of sharpened sticks for teeth.

Before he could shout Athena's name, the giant beast turned white with frost. Nemesis stood behind it, arms outstretched, freezing it from the bottom up. She retracted her arms and then thrust them forward. The creature exploded into a hail of shattering ice. Athena was freed. Nemesis swayed on her feet.

She doesn't have the strength for this yet.

"Look out!" Athena cried. Sword in hand, she leapt into the air and brought her sword down in an arc. It ignited in flames and sliced through a boulder headed straight at Nemesis. The elder barely seemed to notice and swayed on her feet as they both resumed fighting stances.

A cloud of screeching bats assaulting his head brought Dúl back to his own situation. He swatted at them as a female Dawn soldier he recognized faced off against a wolf with the grinning head of a dreadlocked male. He also seemed familiar to Dúl, but just then the ground around him shook. A ten-foot-tall suit of black armor approached Orion a few feet away. It pointed a deadly lance at the fey leader. Challenging. No, taunting.

Baring his teeth in a sneer, Orion gripped a glowing blue broadsword in both hands and ground his feet to charge the giant knight. It lifted its visor.

Orion froze.

The bleeding face and vacant stare inside the helm belonged to Melodia. Had she been killed in the attack on the Dawn Court? It didn't matter right now. Orion's sword and body both sagged. The fey needed him—their leader for better or worse—to stand and fight.

"Curse this madness!" Dúl summoned a shadow from the far corner of the room. It wrapped around the tip of the lance and yanked it upward, away from Orion's chest.

That seemed to revive him. With a feral yell, Orion charged. He cleaved the armor in half. It burst into dust.

"Thanks, brother."

"Don't thank me yet. This doesn't end until we locate that Djanin and bring him down!"

Chapter 21

When I first took on my position as Shadow Master, the building's defenses were all explained to me, in great—and very boring—detail. Now I was glad for that orientation because I could assume that once I got out of here, I'd have only one means of getting in—through the aviary—bird shit and feather heaven itself. I tried not to worry about how I would get up to the roof. Unless I escaped here, it wouldn't matter.

I took a better look at what I had to work with in my mini-jail. The room was ten by ten, no windows and no visible lock on the door. Unless Athena was super paranoid about her people stealing sheets and towels, there shouldn't be any kind of magical lock either. That meant a guard or multiple guards outside.

When I had memorized the layout of the villa, I had also committed to memory the little rooms like this in case I needed to hide. Now I had a strong idea of where I was and where the exits were. This was all working out well so far.

Assuming most of the dragons and vamps would be engaged in the fighting, there couldn't be too many here to stop me. On the downside, I had no real knowledge how these creatures operated, although the sense of familiarity stuck with me like an itch deep under your skin that you can't quite reach. Fighting that one guy hadn't gone in my favor. Being made of shadows, my weapons were useless for now. But they must be vulnerable to something.

I leaned my cheek against the door. There were no sounds on the opposite side of it that I could hear with my naked ear. Wound into my hair, I had hidden a threadlike wire. After retrieving it, I slid one end under the door while holding the other to my ear.

The wire picked up a slight rustle that reminded me of soft-soled moccasins pacing back and forth in the hall. Once I retracted and stowed the line, I lightly touched the door handle to make sure it wouldn't zap me. It didn't.

As silent as a ghost, I eased the door open a crack expecting to see a two-legged guard. But a dragon, slightly larger than the others I had seen, patrolled the hall where I was being held. Well, if I had to learn how to fight these dragons, might as well be a big one.

Unlike the Shadow Castle or anywhere in the Shadow Court, this place was all light and brightness. It sucked for sneaking. Sometimes life just makes choices for you.

When the dragon's back was turned, I ran. Diagonal from my room and down a ways, the hall ended in a T shape. On tiptoes, I shot toward it and was almost there when a laugh froze me.

It wasn't the Lemooria. This deep chuckle told me I was busted and that my escape wouldn't be so easy. Damn.

The dragon stalked toward me. "By all means, run. It will make things so much better."

That voice. My teeth gnashed together as I snarled and crouched into an aggressive stance. "You." I would never forget the voice of the dragon who killed Nat. Fury licked through me, the thought of ripping this piece of shit limb from limb cycloning through my mind. But I controlled the urge. I had to be smart. I had to get out.

"Princess." The word dripped from his snout as if a trickle of rotten fish was falling from his mouth. Whoever this entity was, his hatred of me went beyond my connection to the fey. This was personal. Anger rolled off him in waves. Good. We were even.

If I charged him, he'd only dissolve into shadow. What if I did the same? Only one way to find out. I rushed at him. He ducked down and braced to meet me head on. At the last second, wisps of smoky shadow signaled that he was going incorporeal.

Faster than I had ever shifted, I willed my own body to become smoke, while also envisioning my hands as claws raking their way through my enemy. We passed through each other, but there was something more.

The moment I was inside him, I *felt* more than heard a scream of pain come from him. My mind caught a glimpse of his—flashes of what I figured to be memories. A little boy with a mohawk laughing with a younger girl... the female black dragon bellowing a grief-stricken roar and shifting between dragon and woman... the woman's face... I shook off the images.

Rattled, I resolidified and spun to meet another attack.

Several slashes split the skin of the dragon's chest. He growled. "Interesting, Princess. You've learned some tricks from your fey lover. They won't be enough to save you, even if the queen has commanded that you remain unharmed for now."

"Pretty sure I figured that move out on my own, asshole. And I'll deal with your queen later. Right now, this is about you taking my mom from me."

He shifted into the form he wore when he killed Nat—ebony skin, mohawk hairstyle, jeans, moccasins, and a gray tee. "Imbecile. That was not your mother." Now he ran at me, fists balled as if he actually planned to fight me.

I widened my stance and prepared to block the hit. His punch flew at me from the side. I ducked and caught him in his injured midsection with an upper-cut. His grunt brought a satisfied smile to my lips. "She raised me. She *was* my mother, and you're gonna pay."

He hooked a strong hand behind my knee. It buckled, dropping me onto my back. I kicked up with the other foot and reveled in the crunch of his jaw. He stumbled like a drunken boxer. With a sneer, he wiped black blood from his mouth. I scrambled to my feet, but he just stood there.

The hairs on the back of my neck twitched. I turned to the side, able to watch him but also checking behind me. The hall ended about thirty feet down. No other corridors branched off, yet I sensed something—*someone*—there.

Big bubbles moved under the wall's surface. A peach-colored mass formed out of it, darkening to black and then reshaping into the blob woman who the dragons called their queen. "That's enough, Panaqual. Leave us."

"Mother—"

"Now. I will deal with our guest."

With a scowl, he dissolved and floated down the corridor I had been aiming for.

"Will you fight *me* now, child?" Why did her voice hold a hint of sadness?

"If that's what it takes."

"Fair warning, I'm not as easy an opponent as my son."

"I would have thought he was still attached to you by some umbilical or whatever you... things use to connect to your offspring." I crouched, watching the dark form for any hint that she was about to spring or dissolve. Her calmness threatened to unnerve me. I needed some way to disable her and make a quick break for it. Something in my gut told me I was outmatched against her, at least until I figured out her weakness.

"No, although we've bonded as if he were my own, he is actually my stepson. I can only claim one hatchling as my natural born. There were two, but one twin was destroyed by the fey you love so much." A snarl slipped in when she mentioned the fey.

"Not them. Their father. Never met the guy. Should I blame *you* for your stepson killing my mom?"

"That changeling did not birth you." A faint growl, then a pause. "However, Panaqual's orders were to delay you from reaching RavCorp, not to harm your caregivers."

"Still, by your own logic, you are responsible for his actions."

"Why do you persist in defending them?" she hissed. "They massacred my family. Robbed me of my mate. Murdered my unborn young. I will not allow them to steal you too... *Umbra*."

"No... There is no way in hell." My insides churned. As pieces began to click together, my brain rejected her meaning and smashed the puzzle apart. It could only process one thing. I had to get away—now—and she needed to shut up.

I sprinted forward and then leapt into her, fading to a shadow like I did with Panaqual. This time I visualized punching and kicking at vital organs until I passed all the way through. Not hesitating, I whirled and came back at her in my solid form, fists flailing. A rage unlike any I had ever experienced consumed me. It strengthened each blow.

She didn't dissolve but blocked every hit. Toying with me. Finally, she laughed. "You've learned much, my child. And you know I speak the truth."

This was pointless. I was only wearing myself out. Venting my fury. My skin tightened, and my bones softened. A shift was coming on—against my will—and something told me that would only make her happier. Time to end this while I still had control.

I couldn't use my shadow weapons, and she was too strong to beat down. But that didn't mean she was immune to other forms of magic. And unfortunately for the queen, her vamp lackeys hadn't searched us thoroughly when they brought us in.

My duplication cuff circled my wrist in plain sight. They never blinked at it. Because who wouldn't wear accessories to a hostage negotiation?

"Screw you, whatever or whoever you are. *Dekrar*!"

Five more Mercs surrounded me. In a V formation, we all charged at the queen, jumped, and piled on. Well, they piled on. I raced down the corridor and broke for the nearest window. I had a loose plan with zero idea if it would work or not.

It took two seconds for the queen to dispel my clones. But it was enough. With a roar, she trailed me. "Umbra! You cannot escape the fact that you belong with us!"

I refused to accept that.

Crashing through the window, I glanced over my shoulder to see her at the far end of the hall. Even as she barreled toward me, she shifted from her murder-victim-outline into a winged dragon. But I was too far ahead.

The shift that had been trying to take over now

exploded out of me. In a blink, wings sprouted from my back, scales covered my body, my limbs shrank, and my body lengthened. Squeezing my eyes shut, I fell and spread my wings. I prayed she wouldn't follow me.

Gliding was one thing, but evasive maneuvers were something else entirely.

As my wings beat the air and my altitude increased, I opened my eyes. This flying thing was much easier than I imagined. Risking a glimpse behind me, I saw the dragon queen shift to her earlier form as she watched me disappear from her place at the window, not even trying to subdue me. That couldn't be good. What was worse—her laughter did reach me, making my skin crawl and my gut clench.

Thoughts of what she said fought their way to the front of my mind, but I had to wrench them back or I would screw up. My biggest concern had to be getting to the aviary in the Waking, without being seen, before there was no more Shadow Court.

~*~

I crossed the border into the Dawn lands, which wasn't any safer than the Summer Court. Who knew how many allies the dragons had recruited? How many displaced races from the time of Wymond's reign wanted revenge? A question to worry about later.

For now, I needed a portal. Tucked into a tiny pocket in my waistband, I hid a rune stone. I couldn't get to RavCorp, but it would get me as far as the shadow castle. I thought about using the Night Lanes, but my mind was so scattered from my encounter with the queen, I'd get myself killed for sure. The long way it was.

I appeared outside the castle's massive front gate, and my breath caught. The scene before me was something out of a World War II movie. Only half a castle lingered, rubble and debris everywhere. Towers lay demolished on the ground. Scorch marks stained the remaining stone. An apocalypse had hit the Shadow court, and I had to wonder what the Dawn castle looked like.

My fists clenched, and my nails dug painfully into my palms. This place was becoming home to me. If the dragon queen told the truth and was my mother, did she think destroying everything I loved would bring me to her side? That I'd abandon my chosen life for a blood tie I didn't even remember? If that was her plan, she was a moron.

At least I knew Dúl had gotten most of the fey to safety, and now that I had a quiet moment, I sensed that he was okay. Stressed, but alive. That got me moving. I stepped over hunks of stone and waded through ankle-deep ash until I reached the building. The front doors had been smashed in. Part of one hung by a stubborn upper hinge. Was the portal in my suite intact?

Carefully, I climbed the precarious stairs up to the second floor, occasionally skirting around holes or hugging the wall where the outer railing was gone.

By some miracle, my mirror survived. Without

wasting another moment, I took a deep breath to steady my nerves and stepped through, into my Yorktown apartment. It was closer to the city than Rebus's place. Plus, I couldn't deal with going there and facing the temptation to check and see if Nat's family had come for her body. The replay of Panaqual's attack would surely crush me the minute I entered their bedroom.

I ordered a car and then geared up while I waited. A human driver showed up within a few minutes and shot down the Henry Hudson Parkway at record speed. A folded hundred dollar bill waved between the front seats might have enhanced the driver's skills. I spared a moment to remember the time—the very recent time—when I couldn't have flashed as much as a twenty. Memories.

The car dropped me two blocks from RavCorp. Who knew if there might be enemies camped out around the perimeter watching to make sure no one escaped? To humans, the building would appear to be business as usual. During the evacuation, Morgan would have sent our team of four psionic fey and changelings—those who could use psychic abilities to project illusions—to glamour the entire block to hide anything magical happening inside.

I stood outside a fancy McDonald's in a generic high-rise office. A second door led from the fast-food place out to the sidewalk. Perfect. I slipped inside, nonchalantly entered a bathroom stall, and shifted into a middle-aged mail carrier—brown uniform, stocky male frame, balding at the top of a pale skull. Some of my gear became a stack of parcels. Exiting into the office's interior, I took the elevator to the topmost floor and searched for a stairway that would take me to the roof.

The wind swept the dusting of snow across the top of the building. I used a pair of high powered, miniature binoculars to scan RavCorp's surroundings. As expected, the psychic squad was camouflaged and in position, locked in deep concentration. My entry point was also visible—a small, curved vent that fed into the aviary. Now that I knew I could shift into a dragon and fly successfully, getting over there would be simple. Getting there without being seen...

The sky had darkened to steel gray. I memorized the subtle variations in its tones and the shapes of the clouds. With them in mind, my body reverted to its dragon form in the mottled colors of the sky. Hoping for the best, I leapt up and climbed, the muscles in my back bunching as my wings carried me higher. Then I glided across to RavCorp's roof. If anyone saw me, maybe they'd think I was just a big bird. Or a drone. Hopefully none of the ground team would mistake me for the enemy.

Shifting back to my previous size allowed me to fit into the inverted L-shaped vent after hooking a rope to the edge of the opening that would bypass the penthouse and a few of the upper floors. About five stories down, the pathway would have a magical block on it that I would need to get through. I clicked on a head lamp, clipped the rope to a climbing harness, and began to rappel down. The shaft was about five feet in diameter, tight but manageable.

Even this high up, things sounded much different inside than they had from the outside. Muffled booms and crashing echoed up the shaft. Occasionally, the walls shook like an earthquake hit. It was hard not to think the worst, not to worry about the fey and changelings fighting down there, some of whom had started to feel like a new family.

Hell, Rebus, the last remaining member of my *actual* family was down there too. Was he driven to recklessness from grieving his murdered wife? Was Dúl distracted by concern over me? I couldn't join the battle fast enough.

When my feet touched a magical barrier, I shrank down more so that I could jackknife my body until I was upside-down. With my bare palm over the barrier, I spoke the passphrase Dúl had given me weeks ago, "The Shadow King is the hottest fey in the Dreaming." A smile spread from cheek to cheek as I recalled how serious he tried to be when he told it to me.

The obstacle dissipated with a gentle hiss. Echoes of the fight amplified as I righted myself and went down a few more levels. At the twenty-fifth floor, I found the outline of the square hatch I needed. It was loosely fit into an opening about a yard around. I pried the it open with my fingers and kicked my feet through the hole.

Dúl's office held a small section of the aviary, but

the main part was fifteen stories higher and spanned the entire floor of the building. This was where I now found myself. As much as I loved the ravens, way too much bird shit and far too many feathers littered the space for me to pay any future visits by choice. But at least I was in the building and could do some real work.

Chapter 22

One would think that in a place where magic is the norm, there'd be some magical means of cleaning up bird shit. Nope. Lucky for me. Running into a cleaning person after going to such lengths to sneak in would have been humiliating. I left the aviary toward a stairwell that would take me to the main action.

The hall was dark, only lit by emergency lights. At one end, daylight illuminated a small ring around a gaping hole in the wall. Testing the floor beneath the hole, the telltale crunch of debris told me something shot through this space. What could have fit? My shoe nudged something, and I bent to pick it up. A runestone. Someone shot it in and created a portal.

I moved over to the stairs, cracked the door, and eased it open. Unnatural silence and intense darkness greeted me.

There were no emergency lights here. The dark wrapped tighter around me than the shafts I was in earlier. I removed my headlamp from my forehead and wrapped the strap around my wrist to keep the light low as I tiptoed through the claustrophobic atmosphere. Each step's echo seemed to boom. Time dragged as I descended, listening at each landing until I reached floor ten—where my office and Dúl's were.

It would have been wonderful to find him sitting there with his feet up waiting for me. But fantasies wouldn't save us from this mess.

I made a beeline to my office and my stash of weapons hidden in the wall safe. Would the dragons have checked each room?

Apparently not. Everything was exactly where I left it, and I exhaled my first relieved sigh in hours. Shadow daggers were nice, but cold iron and flames were more up to this task. I double-timed it down the stairs again, less concerned now about being spotted.

Around the seventh floor, the air changed. The hairs on my arms stood on end. When I stepped, my foot landed on something slimy. Outside the stairwell door, shouts and explosions whispered, distant again despite me being closer.

I peeked out. The landscape deflated my heart. I tried to deny what I knew I was seeing, but my gut scolded me to accept the facts and deal with them.

Snowcapped mountains spit out crimson lava. My gut said that was the core of the bedlam. A sickly green sky blanketed the ground around the mountains made of gray ash and bubbling green swamps. Sulfur and rot permeated the air. From my right, a streak of lightning whizzed by me toward a fey hiding behind a stone boulder about a hundred yards away.

Somehow, the dragons or their allies figured out

how to pull seven whole floors of the RavCorp building into the Night Lanes. This was someone's idea of the ultimate nightmare. Or, I reasoned, if the fey and changelings had been pulled in, maybe it was one, big collective nightmare generated by everyone fighting in here. Either way, all the levels of hell converged where I usually sipped a morning cocoa.

My first instinct was to find Dúl. But I sensed he didn't need me at the moment. A sort of euphoria was running through him. Not exactly bloodlust, but he might be enjoying a good fight against someone other than his brother for a change.

Next task—find whoever was trapping us in the Night Lanes and take them out. I retreated into my hiding spot, let the door close, and slid my back down the wall to rest for a second.

This won't be at all like trying to find a needle in a stack of needles. Who or what was I even looking for?

"Think, Merc," Rebus's instructor voice commanded from my memory bank for the first time in ages.

All right, Rebus. And you better not be getting yourself killed.

Whoever had control of the Night Lanes would most likely be somewhere near the volcano, between the fourth and third floors, centrally positioned. I seemed to be above where most of the horrors were manifesting.

Who had that kind of power? The changelings and fey wouldn't do this to themselves. The dragon queen and her stepson had been busy with me—did the dragons' magic even work this way? That didn't seem right. Dragons, vampires... I had heard the word giants recently—these were all races that had been persecuted by Wymond. There had to be one or more other races in play, teamed up with the dragons and seeking revenge.

No way to puzzle it out now, but at least I knew to guard my mind. The bigger problem now was moving between floors when there were no elevator shafts. An idea formed as I sneaked to the fourth floor and stepped into the horror show.

The landscape was similar, but I was farther from the frozen volcano, almost as if I had moved sideways instead of vertically. The Night Lanes were distorting the rules of direction and space. How was I supposed to reach the center now? Maybe I could move straight ahead—toward the middle of the building—using a point overhead to as a guide. It made as much sense as anything else under these circumstances.

I'd have to navigate the battle raging ahead, but at least I found the fey.

Magic of every kind and element imaginable streaked in all directions. Fey hurled fireballs, ice arrows, water cyclones, and lightning from the ground. Dragons exploited shadows from above. Nameless monsters appeared randomly to attack fey—their nightmares coming to life. As much as I wanted to help, I needed the distraction of the battle as cover.

I shifted into a shadow dragon, which was starting to feel a little too comfortable for my liking. Shoving the thought aside before it could come back to haunt me, I opened the door wider and leapt into the green sky. Its thick stench clogged my lungs. Climbing high, I soared above the fray and prayed my own people wouldn't take me down before I reached my goal.

It looked like it offered protection and what seemed to be a crevice. I reached it and scanned around the base of the mountain, which shrank the closer I got. Sure enough, it was now the size of an igloo. I had found what I was looking for.

A trail of lava forked above a small opening.

I glided toward it. Pain suddenly sliced across my back. I glanced over my wing. Above me, a soldier with a water whip dove at me on one of their giant eagles. A Dawn soldier I recognized. She looped around to take another pass, a grimace of pure fury contorting her face.

I plunged for the entrance, had to outrun her, trying not to freak out about the memory of the poison they used in their weapons. I told myself that my dragon scales would protect me—anything to keep the fear at bay before the Lanes used it against me.

The moment my talons touched down, I shifted back to the form she knew. "Tania, stop!" I ducked under the tip of the whip as it buzzed past my cheek.

"Shit! Merc!" The eagle swooped close. She jumped from its back. "I thought—" She hesitated. "Why would you look like..." Her eyes narrowed. "Prove it's you."

"What?"

"Tell me the last thing my brother said to both of us." Tania's whip was ready to strike if I said the wrong thing.

Now I understood. She wanted to make sure I wasn't a shadow dragon shapeshifting into an imposter of me. "He told us to finish the mission."

She paused, but then slowly lowered her whip to her side. "Are you trying to get yourself killed posing as the enemy?"

"Long story. How is everyone? Rebus? My king?" As short as time was, I had to know.

"All holding their own last I saw. Rebus was alongside Morgan. And the rulers... they were amazing—all in a circle, fighting back-to-back. Almost as if they never hated each other." Half of a wistful smile told me she didn't expect that bond to hold once their common enemies were defeated. Finally, she held out a hand for me to shake. "It's good to see you unharmed."

Maybe it was too much to expect that we would be friends after I got her brother killed. I smacked my palm into hers and squeezed. "Comrades" was a good enough place to start. "What are you doing here?"

"The kings think that the culprit keeping us in these Night Lanes is hiding here. But you figured that out on your own." As she whispered, we moved into the mouth of the ice dwelling, out of sight.

"Do they have any theories on who or what has the power to do this?"

"They believe it may be a member of one of the

vanquished races—the Djanin. I can give you a full history later, but if this creature thinks it can't win, it will make a bargain. Guard your mind."

"Okay. Subdue, don't kill. Got it. Shall we?" For a change, having backup was comforting instead of stressful. We entered the igloo together and found that it led into a deep cave.

Several feet inside the opening, huge stalactites hung from the ceiling like bars and embedded into the ground, preventing any further progress into the space. Not suspicious at all. Some mini firebombs should do the trick. I attached a half dozen of them on three of the icicles before pulling Tania back a few feet.

"There's a word... I didn't really have time to master any of these weapons. Kuckoma... Kuchima... Ugh!" Frustration was causing my brain to blank out. "Wait, it's *Kuchoma! Kuchoma!*"

With six tiny pops like firecrackers, the bombs blazed into blue-hot flames. They hissed. Steam rose from where they burned through the bars. Within a few seconds, three segments fell to the ground. We pulled the bottom pieces out of our way.

With lava coming out of the top of the dome, the cave should have been hot, but the temperature was mild—neither hot nor cold. We brandished weapons —Tania her whip, two shadow daggers for me—then moved forward, each scanning the area for trouble. At a junction where the cave bent, light glowed from around the corner.

"That must be our Janie or whatever you called it."

"Djanin." Tania nodded and tightened her grip.

I signaled her to hang back while I merged with the shadows along the cave walls. This tunnel opened into a clearing about fifty yards down. A rectangular platform generated the light we had seen. The Djanin levitated in the air, arms and legs spread wide as if it—he—was suspended by invisible chains from the ceiling. Skin the color of amber stretched across bare, rippling muscles, and his eyes were empty black pits that stared straight up. Curly, electric blue hair topped his head while tight jeans showed every contour of his lower half. He appeared to be in a deep trance.

The dragon queen should have spared an extra body to give this guy some backup.

I waved Tania forward so she could look for herself. She charged, swinging the whip in a blinding arc. It snapped around the Djanin's legs, and she yanked him down to the ground. Before he could recover, I summoned shadow restraints and bound his hands.

He didn't wake up even after all that. Any hope of making him release RavCorp from the Night Lanes depended on forcing him out of his stupor. I kicked him in the kidney.

Suddenly, his eyes turned the same electric blue as his hair and laser-focused on me. He sprang to his feet, arms freed, and swept me into an incredible, toe-curling kiss. One hand palmed my ass while the other squeezed my breast. Out of my control, my legs went around his waist as I grinded against him, intense waves of pleasure licking through my core—

"Merc!" Tania gave my arm a rough shake. "Your eyes changed. Like his. And you were moaning." A smile twitched at one corner of her mouth as she tried to keep a straight face.

The Djanin was still restrained, and his eyes were two lumps of coal again. I was on my knees beside him.

"Son of a bitch." My voice sounded like I had just run a sprint. "That was so real, and it hit me so fast..." So real, that I felt both violated and guilty. "Son of a *bitch!*" I slapped him once front-hand, then back-handed him for good measure. The eyes flickered to blue, but he didn't wake.

Tania snickered, almost as if she had seen what I had. "Told you, guard your mind. I forgot to mention, my lord said that the few remaining Djanin living in the Waking are 'dirty little shits.' One of them owns the largest porn site on the internet."

"Shut up and go get me one of those icicles."

That made her laugh for real. "What did you—"

"Not for me, stupid!" Deep embarrassment joined my current collection of emotions.

She went to do as I asked, but her laughter stayed to keep me company. I made sure to avoid looking at our captive until she returned.

When she did, I called up a shadow dagger and sliced off the tip of the stalactite. I unbuttoned the perv's jeans and huffed in irritation. Commando in jeans? Just my luck. I averted my eyes, dropped the ice down the front of his pants, and rebuttoned them. A moment later, his eyes bulged, and those blue orbs turned on Tania this time.

I immediately saw what she meant about my eyes changing. Hers went empty and black in an instant. I used his attention on her to our advantage, and kicked him, savagely, in the nuts.

He squealed, writhing on his back as he realized he was tied up. "Aagh!" His garbled scream lasted only a moment. The cave shook, pieces of rock and ice raining down over us. Then it abruptly stopped. He retreated into his trance.

Now Tania was panting. "He got me, didn't he?"

I nodded. "Not a great feeling, is it? Do you need a cold drink? A cigarette?" I smiled innocently.

"Ha ha. The problem is whoever is watching him will get caught up in his illusion, and we don't know which one of us he will target."

I saw her point. "Okay. I think I have an idea that should work." I explained it. "Question is, which one of us is going to volunteer to be the bait?"

"I will!"

My eyebrows arched at her eagerness.

"What? I'm single. A smutty illusion with a hot guy won't hurt me. You're the one in love with a king." The playful lilt in her accented voice made me want to hug her. "Just plug your ears."

We both laughed and prepared to execute my plan.

First, we moved the body to prop him between two

rocks and stabilized his head so he could only look in one direction. Tania stood back and slashed her whip across his chest. When he only jerked slightly, she hit him again. He gasped and blue eyes bugged out of his head, latching onto hers. From behind him, I shouted in his ear, "That whip was poisoned. You either stay awake and tell us what we want to know, or we let you die. Either way, in thirty seconds, you will release the Shadow Court from whatever you're doing."

The poison would take longer to kick in, as I well remembered, but he didn't need to know that. His lids fluttered. He strained against the restraints. Tania shook off the illusion and nodded. We had his attention.

"First things first. Release the building from the Night Lanes."

The cave shuddered again, and everything went black. Air whooshed around us as if a sudden tornado struck. Light returned, and we were in some kind of empty storage closet. A three-wick candle burned inside a hurricane glass. Tania turned her back to the prisoner before he could trap her again.

I had expected to end up in an elevator shaft. This was an improvement. "Excellent. Next, how many more of you are there, and what are the numbers attacking the court?"

"Jeez, kitten, give a guy a minute to wake up." He closed his eyes and groaned.

"I would, but neither of us have much time. You

got a name?" If we were only going to subdue the guy, might as well be decent about it.

"Nettle. Cash Nettle."

I wouldn't comment on how his first name sounded very porn-starish. "Okay, Cash. You're running out of time. By now, you should start to feel numbness in your chest and limbs. If you cooperate, we have an antidote."

He hesitated for only two blinks of my eyes. "It's just me. The dragons and vamps were spread thin from attacking on the other courts, and this wasn't their endgame. They just wanted the Dreaming cleared out so they could walk in and occupy it. Worked like a charm. Good? How 'bout that antidote?"

"Wait, what? Are you saying you're the only one here and that there's no big fight happening on the lower floors? That this whole thing was orchestrated to get the siblings to evacuate the courts?"

Cash grinned.

"And what's in it for you?"

"Well, they pay me, don't they? To be perfectly honest, I'm not so interested in the big vendetta the dragons and vampires and giants have against the fey. There were never many of us Djanin to begin with, and we never claimed any territory as our own. Still, inconveniencing the offspring of that jackhole, Wymond... couldn't pass up the chance for a tiny bit of payback. Now, about that cure you promised? I'd be happy to tell you anything else I know about their operation for a fair price, but we had a deal."

"Yes. We did." I reached around and covered his eyes with my hands. "T, go ahead."

She pulled a tiny vial from her boot, uncapped it, and jabbed it into his neck.

"Ah, thank y..."

Together, Tania and I carried his unconscious body down to where I hoped to find my people unharmed. I promised he would live; I never said we'd let him walk away so he could come back and harm us again.

The Dragon Queen wasn't done with us. This had been a trick, which meant she had to have something worse than an all-out attack up her sleeve. Whatever it was, we would have to be ready.

And if what she said was true, I would have to be prepared to fight my birth mother.

Damage Control

Dúl approached the "fishing shack" on the water-front of Baltimore Harbor on foot. The stinging cold felt good against his cheeks, and the dusting of snow beneath his boots made a satisfying crunch. In the blue light before dawn, silhouetted fishers with hushed tones prepared to head out for the day.

When he entered the neutral meeting room, he hid his surprise that Orion was already sitting at the picnic table. It was bare except for two large paper cups. The scent of strong coffee wafted toward the open door. On the other side of the room, a small fire glowed, warming the small space.

Dúl sat across from his brother and accepted the extended beverage with a muffled, "Thanks."

Orion had seen better days. At least today his hair was combed. There were no red streaks giving away his lack of sleep. Normally, Dúl would have preferred to see Orion weakened, but his perspective had shifted recently.

"How is Melodia faring? Any change?" Dúl sipped his coffee.

"Still in the infirmary, but she was able to walk yesterday." Orion's voice was hoarse. "I still marvel at what she accomplished—getting so many to safety before she succumbed to her injuries."

"I would expect no less than capability and strength from your consort. I'm pleased that she is recovering well."

Orion nodded his appreciation of the comment before going quieter than was his usual. There would never be small talk between the brothers, even now. The siblings were all well aware of where things stood for them.

Someone leaked to the news outlets that RavCorp had suffered a terrorist attack. While the company's stocks steadily dropped, Dúl spent exhausting hours doing damage control. This included appearances on business shows and podcasts to assure the public that of course, he hadn't been taken hostage and was perfectly fine.

Delays and slowdowns suddenly plagued Orion's shipping company. The staff at Athena's hotels were trying to unionize. The dragons had somehow created enough chaos for the siblings in the Waking to keep them from mobilizing their forces in the Dreaming.

"Is our sister also healing well?" Orion said.

"She is still convalescing at Rebus's home. I believe having someone to care for distracts him from his grief. He's been helpful, hiring some of the displaced fey to temporarily cover The Bar and to watch over Nemesis when he and Merc go south."

"It was kind of his wife's family to delay her funeral rites to wait for them." Orion sipped his drink and paused to stare at it, clutching the white cup with both hands. Hesitation was not his style, and it made Dúl uneasy.

"Speaking of Merc, brother..." Orion continued. He shifted in his seat. "I asked you here to discuss your request."

"I'm listening." It was a struggle for Dúl to keep his tone even, but he couldn't antagonize Orion.

The silence stretched between them before Orion finally gathered his thoughts and proceeded. "I agree that Morgan has earned the right to openly continue her relationship."

"I sense a 'but' coming."

"Dúl," Orion finally met his younger brother's eyes. "Have you considered the implications of recent events? What is your end game here?"

Dúl's eyes narrowed. "I believe I was clear about that."

"Yes, you want to be free to marry Merc, and I will grant that they have been our steadfast ally thus far."

"If you're implying that Merc is anything less than loyal—"

"Peace, brother." Orion put up a placating hand. "That isn't what I mean, and I don't want to fight." He paused. "I owe you a debt of gratitude. You protected the civilians of the Dawn Court. To be frank, I was surprised."

Dúl smirked. "As was I. In fact, it had been my

intention to let you put your forces on the front line against the dragons."

"I sense a 'but' coming," Orion said with a small smile.

"But... when the moment came to act, it occurred to me that they were non-combatants, and in the end, we are all fey. I suppose Merc has affected my conscience."

Orion grunted. "Blood ties aren't inconsequential. For all our personal discord, we've stopped short at outright killing each other."

Dúl frowned, sensing that the conversation had taken a turn he wasn't going to like. When had Orion learned to manipulate? It seemed Dúl wasn't the only one who had been changed lately.

"Dúl, you acted as a king, in the interest of our subjects' wellbeing. Do you honestly see a way where we can protect our people without the annihilation of the shadow dragons?"

Dúl's shot to his feet, glowering.

"I don't mean Merc!" He waited for his brother to be seated again. "But how can you expect them to be indifferent to the eradication of their entire race? To the family they just rediscovered? Not only the principal actors in this attack, but *all* of the dragons? Because that's what it will take to keep our people safe. Are you prepared to do that to Merc?"

Dúl opened his mouth to speak, but stopped himself as Orion's words sank in. Merc had been working to recover the memories of their family, and it seemed their birth mother had been nothing but loving. However, with these attacks on the fey, especially with Natalie's murder, they might see justice in eliminating the Dragon Queen.

Innocent bystanders were another story.

Protecting the weak and innocent was a way of life for Merc.

Damned Orion.

There had to be a way out of this. A way to protect the fey without scarring his beloved. He just had to find it. "Merc and I will work it out," he finally said.

Orion nodded solemnly. "Then you are free of your betrothal and to marry whomever you choose." He stood to leave, headed toward the door, and then backed up. He placed a hand on Dúl's shoulder. "If anyone can create a solution, brother, it's you, and I sincerely wish you luck."

Tommy

Tommy rolled his SUV to a stop in front of a blue house. It was one of the few on the block that didn't have boards in the windows or a lopsided gate with a broken latch. He could have stayed a little farther from The Cache, his late cousin's bar and center of operations, but he preferred to be in the thick of things rather than at some quaint, manicured spot. Out of touch. In his opinion, the niceties had made Donny weak over the years. He'd never been too smart to begin with.

The wife had been sent to the family in Jersey. She'd be taken care of. But the businesses needed to be sorted out, especially now that the vampires seemed to be leaderless after losing the French guy. It was a perfect time to take advantage of the power vacuum in the Fringe and prove his worth to his uncle. He'd get the money flowing again and take revenge on that shifter on behalf of the family. Donny might not have been popular, but he was still blood.

Tommy got out of the car, took a large duffel from the front seat and started up the walkway. No need to lock the car. If anyone messed with it, they'd face swift consequences. He almost hoped someone would. Speed up the process of making his presence felt here.

His phone vibrated in his pocket, and he stopped at the bottom step to answer. "Yeah, just got here... How was my trip? I just came from Jersey, for fuck's sake. Not Siberia." Tommy ran his hand over his face. "Whatever. Listen. Gather up the boys and meet me at The Cache in an hour. I want full reports on every-thing that's been going on since Donny bit it." He ended the call without waiting for a response.

How was your trip? What kind of yahoos was he dealing with? With a shake of his head, Tommy went up the stairs and into the house. Forget unpacking. A cruise around the territory suddenly seemed like a better idea. Dropping the duffel, he went back out. He had a big job ahead. The sooner he got started, the better.

Epilogue

It was a few days before Dúl and I were able to talk at length about everything that had happened. The day before my flight to Texas, I stood with my back to him, his arms wrapped around me, watching the ravens in the aviary.

"How are you holding up after all the bombshells that were dropped on you?" He knew all about what the dragon queen had told me.

"Okay, I guess. It's a lot to take in and really hard to believe because not only don't I want to, but also because I still don't remember anything like what she said." The new rages, abilities, and ease with which I could use the shadows made a lot more sense now. "What about the civilians?"

The scouts had said the courts were all in ruins. "Obviously, no one can return to their homes in the Dreaming until the threat is completely neutralized, but even after that, it will take time to rebuild." The sovereigns all agreed to find temporary safe spaces for the fey within the Waking. Athena opened up long-term blocks in some of her hotels, and Orion booked several residences midway between their courts. Dúl and Nemesis made similar arrangements up north.

"There's something else I wanted to fill you in on. I went to see my mother a while ago to ask if there was any precedent for ending my engagement."

"Did you?"

He nodded. "I didn't tell you beforehand in case the news was not what I hoped for. At any rate, I've spoken with my brother—"

"And you're both still in one piece. Progress."

"Under the circumstances, he's agreed to grant it. I know this isn't the right time to discuss our future together, but I want you to know that I'm working to make certain that nothing will stand in our way should we decide to take the next step. Also, I think you would agree that Morgan and Najat deserve to be together without having to hide it."

"Definitely. But what about this claim that the Dragon Queen is my mother? That may complicate things."

"It will, but we'll deal with whatever comes."

I turned to look up at him. I sensed something behind his words—determination mixed with mild dread. As much as I wanted to press him to talk, I knew he would share his concerns when he was ready. For some reason, I also had the feeling that I might not want to know exactly what weighed on his mind. "No matter what she is, you and Rebus and the Shadow Court are my family."

His features relaxed as we held each other and

watched Oedipus with a mouse he'd captured in his talons. I wondered what the Dragon Queen's next move would be.

~*~

Rebus and I would have been content to board a commercial flight to San Antonio, but Dúl and his older sister would hear nothing of it. We took the company jet south. We drew the line at having a limo pick us up from the airport. It seemed disrespectful to Nat's family to flaunt that kind of wealth, so Dúl reserved us a more modest ride for the week. I didn't realize until it was too late that the car was a super fancy electric SUV.

When I scolded him about it, he said, "It's good for the environment and the company's PR. We need as much good press as we can get right now."

How could I argue against that?

The city was greener than I expected, and much more diverse too. The trip to the McFayden household took under thirty minutes. It felt like a month. Even with the AC blasting, the air in the back seat was stuffy. Rebus stared out his window and I stared out mine.

The neighborhood we came to reminded me a little of the Fringe back home, except flatter. Most of the homes we passed were single story dwellings, and they definitely looked "lived-in." One family had tables and, clothing racks, and assorted larger items —bikes and kid furniture—out on the sidewalk for a yard sale. This only seemed odd to me because it was a Thursday afternoon, yet a slow, steady trickle of customers stopped by.

Nat's family had two homes on the same street as the yard sellers. My adopted grandparents parents lived toward the beginning of the street, and two great aunts had homes across the street from each other farther down the block.

I broke the long silence that had grown between Rebus and me. "Um, I know this is a weird time to ask, but they know about me, right?" I'd never actually met any of Nat's family although I had heard plenty about them. Yet she had never visited them in all the years I'd been with her and Rebus. It only occurred to me to wonder why as we pulled into a driveway under the flimsy carport awning. There was space for two cars, but only one sat under the canopy.

"Of course." He answered but wasn't really with me. "She sent them pictures and holiday cards all the time." The landscape wasn't the only flat thing around us. When he wasn't running the bar and putting on a brave front for everyone, Rebus sounded as lifeless as Nat now was.

I let the conversation drop, sure I was about to get answers inside to questions I didn't even think of yet.

The middle of my stomach cramped when we reached the chain-link fence around the yard. It was well tended with an amazing garden of wildflowers in front of the house, which had a pale yellow paint-job that was neither brand new nor peeling. The windows were darkened, and no cars were in the driveway. Rebus marched up and rang the bell anyway.

"Reeb, maybe no one—" I started. It was like talking to a ghost.

Then the doorway was framing a large man with a bald head and cropped white beard. He had to be in his eighties, but he looked very fit for someone that age. And he wasn't even a changeling.

"Tim." Rebus held out his hand.

The man—Grandpa? Mr. McFayden?—nodded and stood to one side, but didn't shake. Rebus caught the closing door and followed him in. I hurried to catch up.

The only lights inside were small candles glowing around a large clay jar with colorful geometric designs painted on it. Flowers and a feast of different fruits and cured foods surrounded the jar, which I guessed was an urn with Nat's ashes in it.

A woman with flowing white curls kneeled before it. She stood and turned. From her resemblance to Nat, I caught a glimpse of the striking figure this fey would have made a couple of decades ago—a bit bohemian, voluptuous, and beautiful. Even with lines etched around her eyes, cheeks, and mouth, she was still gorgeous. The biggest difference from Nat was the lack of spark in her eyes. But who could blame her for that?

She rose, ushered us to the kitchen, slid the door shut behind us, and sat at the table. Natural light streamed in through sheer curtains, but the overhead lights were off. She studied me for a long moment with her head cocked to one side.

"Natalie always gushed about how you were so lovely, no matter what face you wore. I see what she meant now, Umbra. Or do you prefer Merc? Sit, please." She spoke in a whisper.

I had been leaning more into a more androgynous appearance lately, but today I felt more like being in the feminine expression I had worn for so long.

Somehow, it brought Nat closer.

I joined her mom across the table. Rebus stood behind me while Nat's dad stood at his wife's back. "I prefer Merc, but I'll answer to either. How should I address you?" I wiped my palms on my pants.

Her eyebrows lifted. "Oh. I hadn't thought of that." After a pause, she said, "Why don't you call us Raya and Tim for now."

As if an invisible layer of frost over us all had thawed, everyone's posture loosened slightly.

"Tim, Rebus, stop standing like sentinels. Rebus, have a seat. Tim, love, would you mind bringing some drinks?"

With a curt nod, he walked out a back door into a garage where the back of a pickup peeked into view.

While Tim was gone, Raya explained the reason for the lights being off, and what her traditions demanded for the next three days. Flora and Luz, Nat's fey aunts, would join us shortly for the silent vigil. They had brought Nat's body into a small corner of the now desolate Summer Court. They found it unguarded. I filed that information away for later.

Tim returned with his arms full of wine, water, and soda bottles. Rebus hopped up to relieve him and they set the bottles on the table. Tim then brought some glasses to the table along with bottle openers and a corkscrew.

The plan was to return Nat's ashes to the Dreaming after three days were up.

"Under the circumstances," Raya said. "It would be understandable, perhaps advisable, if you chose not to accompany us."

"She was my wife." Rebus's voice cracked as his conviction warred with his attempt to keep his volume in check.

I could see Raya's point and had to think about it. The dragon queen might have surveillance on me. But would the Dreaming be any more dangerous for Rebus and me than the Waking? If she wanted to attack us, she could do it in either place.

"We'd like to be there. I can't really explain it, but I don't think the dragon queen will disturb us, if she's aware of our movements at all. I think we'll be safe from her. For now."

"Hmph." Tim grunted. It was the first actual sound to come out of him since our arrival.

"Tim…" Raya said in an even softer, warning tone.

"No, Raya. He didn't keep our baby safe like he promised. And this one—" He gestured at me. "—it was *her* enemy that killed Natalie. I told Nat marrying you would lead to no good. And I was right." Tim's voice broke. He fell into his chair and buried his face in his hands.

No one touched their drinks. Sweat trickled down the sides of the bottles.

The aunts came in a few minutes later. They merely nodded when Raya introduced me. Flora, who walked with more of a shuffle, had a stooped posture. She passed Rebus with a pat to his back.

Luz wore her hair in short curls and was clearly the most active and youngest of the sisters. She hugged Rebus hard and whispered condolences to him. Then, before she entered the living room, doubled back to embrace me. "I know your loss is every bit as great as ours."

Finally, we all entered the consecrated vigil space. If we needed to speak or use the bathroom, we had to leave the room. The only thing we could do aside from quiet contemplation was to eat. Before anyone bit into their fruit or dried meat, they set a piece onto a dish closest to the urn.

I noticed two other things about the dimly lit area. First, there were no signs of any kind of insects— no mosquitoes or flies trying to get at the food. The other sign that we were in a fey household was that even once it was dark outside, the room remained at a constant level of illumination.

For three days, we watched over Nat's remains and shed tears without embarrassment or drama. In my mind, I had conversations with Nat. First apologizing for causing her death, for which she scolded me. Then they became more about what to do next, how to carry on, and how to help Rebus move forward. I'd doubted this practice, but by Sunday morning, I felt like Nat was right there with us, at peace and watching our backs from some other realm.

And why couldn't there be some other plane of existence if there was a Dreaming and Waking world?

Sunday afternoon, Raya finally stood and said, "Our vigil is now ended. Upon reflection, Natalie would want you, Rebus and Merc, to accompany us to her final resting place if you so wish."

We did.

They had planned to pile into Tim's car for a fifteen-hour drive to Mexico City. When I told Dúl, he insisted on flying us all. Tim resisted at first, but whatever Dúl said convinced him to accept the gift. Maybe it was the drastically reduced travel time, hence less time in our presence.

Rebus and I planned to find a motel until the next morning, but Raya kindly offered us their guest room. We all crashed after not really sleeping during the vigil, and by five AM, we were en route to the airport.

Leaning back in the spacious seat of the RavCorp jet, Tim bit into a breakfast burrito big enough to be worthy of the native Texan. "It must be nice having a fey king wrapped around your finger."

Since I didn't know if he was insulting me, I chose not to respond and watched the plane's nose angle up as we took off.

Behind me, Rebus was already snoring lightly. I recognized how much of a toll being around Nat's family, her dad in particular, was draining Rebus. We hadn't had any privacy to really talk about it, but I hoped he'd confide in me once we did. For now, I sat with my memories of Nat.

Of the times I was such a beast as a kid—sometimes literally—and she never raised her voice, much less a hand. Even that one time when she got hurt on a job because I didn't listen, she brought me cocoa and a hug while I hid out in my room, too ashamed and guilty to face her. She had been a better mother than I deserved. She'd been there for me while the dragon queen chose to seek revenge rather than claim her child. As far as I could see right now, I only had one true mother, and she was gone.

Throat clearing next to me brought me out of my wallowing.

Raya pointed to the adjacent seat and sat when I shrugged. "You must be exhausted."

"I could say the same for you. I thought you'd be sleeping like the others."

She smiled. "Perhaps you'll learn one day for yourself, but mothers don't really sleep."

I grunted.

"I hope you won't think too harshly about your grandfather."

At that, my head whipped toward her.

"Don't be so surprised. Parents aren't perfect people, Merc. We make mistakes, and sometimes live to regret them. I've decided not to continue making the same ones. Tim will come around. He's not really angry at you."

"No, he just hates my dad."

The plane shook, and the pilot instructed the flight crew to buckle in until the turbulence passed.

"Mmm... he doesn't hate Rebus. My husband simply never got over the fact that some other man replaced him in our daughter's life. He's a bit stubborn."

"That goes for both of them." I laughed. After a pause, I said quietly. "He'd be in his rights to be mad at me. It's my fault Nat is dead."

"That seems like fuzzy math to me. Wasn't it a shadow dragon who...murdered my daughter?"

"Yes, because she warned *me*. And if they're telling the truth, the dragon queen gave birth to me. I'm one of *them*." My voice shook, and I hoped the rattling of the plane covered for me.

Raya tsked. "Blood alone doesn't make a family, but I think you know that." She reached over and hugged me.

Back during my school days, kids always used to talk about how amazing their grandparents were. At the time, I assumed it was because their grandparents provided a steady supply of sugary treats, under-the-table cash, and access to any other taboos the parents set. Basking in Raya's warmth, I experienced a hint of what those kids really meant.

The sun was bright in the sky when we touched down in Mexico. A car picked us up from the tarmac and drove us an hour to *Parque Nacional Cumbres del Ajusco.* We had the clay urn and a couple of backpacks filled with candles, food, water, and some of the flowers from Raya's garden.

We started on a marked trail, but after about twenty minutes of climbing hills, we veered off it into the wilderness. A small rock formation, like some kind of animal den, cropped up in our path. Before I could fit my mouth around the words, "No way are we fitting in there," the shimmer around the entrance caught my eye. It seemed to grow as Raya strode in without the slightest hesitation. Her sisters followed, then me, with Rebus behind carrying Nat's ashes and Tim bringing up the rear.

A lush, verdant forest waited on the other side. It was like being in a 4k surround screen theater—brilliant colors, powerful perfumes, and all types of disembodied animal calls from every direction.

From head to toe, my skin buzzed. If I touched anyone, I'd deliver a static shock for sure. This was the too-muchness that I remembered from being in the Summerlands as a child, amplified by being away from the court. Nothing but the pure magic of the Dreaming. But now that I was an adult, rather than overwhelming me, a surge of power coursed through me. I could take on an entire dragon army alone.

"Heady, isn't it?" Tim said. That was quite an understatement. He skirted around me to help Raya and her sisters unpack near a tall pine tree, which seemed to stretch to the end of the sky's confines.

They waved Rebus and me over.

We each took a turn spreading Nat's ashes around the base of the tree, and then we placed candles in jars around it, making a bigger circle. Raya kneeled and began to hum a sad tune in a low contralto tone. She plunged her fingers into the ashes and earth. She coaxed flowers of all kinds from the soil. I recognized lilies, irises, and snapdragons, mainly because Nat loved them. My breath stopped.

Soon, the ring within the candles was one big garden. My skin prickled, and the tears flowed. Mine weren't the only ones.

We held hands outside the candle ring, allowing the pent-up sadness to pour out of us. Each of us took a turn to speak. The aunts promised Nat to take care of her parents for as long as they could.

Raya, on my left, squeezed my hand. "*Mija*, I'm sorry we wasted so much time, and I promise to watch over your husband and child as part of our family."

Rebus was to my right. "Nat," he croaked out. "I swear to find the guy who took you from us too soon, and I *will* avenge you."

My turn came next. Where could I start? There seemed to be so many things to apologize for and to vow. But everything that came to mind seemed either obvious or trite. Finally, I said, "Nat... Mom... I won't blame myself for what happened to you because I know you wouldn't want that. And I will do everything I can to be the person you've tried to teach me to be since the day you took me in." As I broke down, Rebus folded me into his arms.

Lastly, Tim's deep voice sounded like he was lifting a heavy weight. "Baby girl, I'm so sorry I let my pride and stubbornness keep us apart for so long. And I swear to—" He didn't finish. Instead, I felt another set of big arms engulfing me and Rebus. I could guess at his oath to his daughter.

A commotion erupted all around us. Both Rebus and I jumped into fighting stances, seeking vampires or shadow dragons that might have been trailing us.

An incredible array of colors surrounded us as different tropical birds all took to the sky, swooping and calling to each other.

We all looked at each other and laughed until we were crying again.

"Goodbye, Nat," I said in my mind. "And thanks for everything."

Rebus and I spent two more days with my grandparents—it was still weird to process that word—before we returned to New York. They said they'd visit. Tim was quite fond of RavCorp's food service. And we all had multiple ways to contact each other now.

As much as I missed Dúl, I didn't look forward to facing the situation with the dragon queen and the chaos back home. But whatever came next, I had so many allies and so much support behind me, it was like my own personal army.

I'd need it if I was going to take down my mother.

Andrea Stanet's fiction has appeared in several anthologies, an online literary magazine, the *Nightlight Horror Podcast.* She released her first independent novella, *Spirit of the Wolf* on Amazon in fall of 2022 followed by *Umbra* in spring 2023, the debut novel in her Fey and Fate series. In September of 2023, Andrea and her husband, Michael, developed the first role-playing game module, *Flight of the Dark Child*, set in the Fey and Fate world using a modified version of the Fate Accelerated game system. Most recently, the founder of Dragonlight Press released her multi-genre anthology *Anti-Villains.* While she doesn't shy away from any genre, her passion is writing speculative fiction for various age groups.

Andrea spent thirteen years tutoring English and Essay Writing online. Her hobbies include photography, studying languages, reading, gaming, and walking in the woods near her home in New York.

Website: http://andreastanet.com

Facebook: https://www.facebook.com/AndreaStanetauthor/

Twitter: https://twitter.com/AndreaStanet

Instagram: https://www.instagram.com/astanetauthor/

Goodreads: https://www.goodreads.com/author/dashboard

Other Works by Andrea Stanet

Umbra: Fey & Fate Trilogy book 1
Anti-Villains
Spirit of the Wolf
Flight of the Dark Child